I hurried after him. 'So, erm, are y[...]

He turned to me. 'No, Kelly [...] your boyfriend.'

'But why not? You said you liked me. It's because I'm not blonde, isn't it?'

'No, it's not that.'

'Too skinny?'

'Nah, it's just, well, um, no offence but, you know, I want a girlfriend and you're just, well, not sort of girly enough. More like a boy really.'

'Oh.'

'You're not upset? I mean, I never promised to go out with you. Today was just a sort of trial. It's not like I'm dumping you or anything.'

I flushed. Bloody hell, he wasn't feeling sorry for me, was he? I put on a totally unconcerned, happy voice. 'God, no, it's cool. No worries.'

Praise for *My Desperate Love Diary*:

'Heartfelt but at the same time fantastically funny, this is a must read' MIZZ

'A feel-good summer read' SUN

'Very funny ... the reader is drawn directly into Kelly Ann's world' WRITERS' NEWS

www.kidsatrandomhouse.co.uk

Also by Liz Rettig:

My Desperate Love Diary
My Now or Never Diary
Jumping to Confusions

MY dating DISASTERS DIARY

by kelly Ann

LIZ RETTIG

CORGI BOOKS

MY DATING DISASTERS DIARY
A CORGI BOOK 978 0 552 55758 0

Published in Great Britain by Corgi Books,
an imprint of Random House Children's Books
A Random House Group Company

This edition published 2009

1 3 5 7 9 10 8 6 4 2

The Random House Group Limited supports the Forest Stewardship Council
(FSC), the leading international forest certification organization. All our titles
that are printed on Greenpeace-approved FSC-certified paper carry the
FSC logo. Our paper procurement policy can be found
at www.rbooks.co.uk/environment.

Set in 11/16pt Palatino by
Falcon Oast Graphic Art Ltd.

Corgi Books are published by Random House Children's Books,
61–63 Uxbridge Road, London W5 5SA

www.kidsatrandomhouse.co.uk
www.rbooks.co.uk

Addresses for companies within The Random House Group Limited can be
found at: www.randomhouse.co.uk/offices.htm

THE RANDOM HOUSE GROUP Limited Reg. No. 954009

A CIP catalogue record for this book is available from the British Library.

Printed and bound in Great Britain by
CPI Bookmarque, Croydon, CR0 4TD

This book is dedicated to my son Chris
and my daughter Carol

With special thanks to Guy Rose, Kelly Hurst,
and my long-suffering husband Paul

I'm also grateful to Prince Charles and
Professor Richard Dawkins for
inspiring (unknowingly) some of the
fun in this book

And last, but by no means least, a huge thank you to all
my Kelly Ann fans around the world

FRIDAY JANUARY 1ST

I never have and I never will fancy any of the stupid boys at my school but I'm going to have to pretend I do or people will start thinking I'm weird. Honestly, just because I like football and can't be bothered with make-up, that doesn't make me a freak. Or a lesbian, as some people have suggested.

My best friend Liz, who's really into psychology, has tried to explain my tomboyish tendencies by saying that I'm suffering from a severe case of penis envy. She told me that a man called Freud, who was the most famous and brilliant psychologist in the world ever, has said that all girls are jealous of boys because they've got penises and we haven't. Most girls sort of get over it but obviously I'm still eaten up with jealousy, which is why I try to be like boys.

Told Liz that this was rubbish. This Freud person might have been really brilliant but he must have been totally mental too. And he obviously never played football either. There's no way I'd want to have a penis, etc. Especially when I see boys doubled up in agony after they've been hit with a football in the groin. It's just that I like to do lots of stuff that boys enjoy. What's wrong with that?

My parents aren't much help either, and Mum especially is always on at me these days.

You'd think they'd be happy I'm not interested in chasing boys so there's no chance of me getting pregnant and becoming a gymslip mum like the newspapers are always on about, but no.

When I pointed this out to them today, Mum said, 'You a mum? Don't make me laugh. Remember the doll we bought you for your seventh birthday? The one whose head you tore off and used for a football?'

This wasn't true actually. It was Chris's friend Gary who decapitated the doll when we couldn't find a ball to play with. But, OK, I didn't stop him, and since it was done anyway, there was no point in refusing to join in the game. Didn't mention any of this to Mum – even though it all happened seven years ago, it would only set her off again about how much the doll cost (it cried 'real tears' and wet itself!) – so she droned on.

'And the pram that you tied ropes to and used as a go-kart?'

This *was* true, I suppose, although of course I could only go downhill, and steering was a problem so I ended up knocking out my front tooth on a lamppost but it had been wobbly (the tooth, not the lamppost, of course) and due to come out anyway. Despite this my parents refused to fork out the usual one pound Tooth Fairy money, which I thought was a bit mean.

My dad's attitude doesn't help much either. When I mentioned the gymslip mum stuff to him he just glanced up from his paper and said, 'Do girls wear gymslips these days? I never see you in anything but scruffy jeans with holes in the arse and knees.'

So much for parental support. Wish everyone would just leave me alone. Still, I suppose I'll have to try and be a bit more feminine this year, if only to shut annoying people up, so I've added some girl stuff to my New Year resolutions:

My New Year Resolutions:

1. Never to argue with English teachers

If I'm tempted, I only have to remember what happened when I complained about being cast as the greedy, grumpy mum in *Jack and the Beanstalk* at Christmas. Mrs Conner changed my part to the back end of the cow Jack sold for magic beans at the market. Wouldn't have minded so much but the front half was Terry Docherty, who has personal hygiene problems – and excessive flatulence. I nearly passed out several times trying to hold my breath so as not to inhale the fumes.

2. *To play for the school football team.*

Though how I'm going to persuade our totally sexist PE teacher to let me join I don't know. Why can't he see that I'm just as good as any boy at football? Also I can swear and foul people better than most.

3. *To grow proper breasts.*

Not that I really want them as I'm sure they will slow me down at sports and encourage idiot boys to try and look down my front like they are always trying to do with Liz, who is a double D already. Still, I don't want to be a freak and I'm getting totally fed up with being called stupid names like Goose Bumps and Ikea Girl (flat-packed, ha ha).

My Aunt Kate has given me a leaflet with illustrated chest exercises to do. She says they helped her when she was my age but I'm *not* going to do them while chanting, *I must, I must, I must improve my bust!* as she suggested. I mean, it's not voodoo or anything so results can't depend on reciting a stupid mantra.

Mum doesn't think the exercises will work as she says they are really to develop supporting muscles for boobs and 'Ha ha, you don't really have anything *to* support yet, Kelly Ann.' Thanks, Mum. But I'll give the exercises a try anyway. Failing that I'll just have to save up for implants.

4. Never, ever to make a total idiot of myself by falling for any stupid boy.

Nearly all my friends have done this now – even Liz, who wore perfume that smelled like cat pee for a whole week because a boy she fancied said he liked it (until he told her he'd been joking and it smelled like cat pee). Still, that isn't as bad as some people like Fiona McNulty, who still keeps a Kleenex her boyfriend borrowed to blow his nose on their first date. I just can't understand it. Now don't get me wrong, I've got nothing against boys. In fact one of my best friends, Chris, is a boy, and he's great. Also boys are generally better at football, PlayStation games and climbing billboards – all stuff I really like – so they can actually be more fun than girls sometimes. But, honestly, fancy (never mind fall in love with) any of them? I mean, most of them are total idiots (except for people like Chris, who I must admit is really super smart and wants to be a doctor), and not many of them look like film stars exactly.

5. To snog at least one boy this year.

Yeah, I know this doesn't seem to gel with what I've just said but the fact is, my arch enemy Shelly is spreading rumours at school that I'm a lesbian. Just because I don't snog boys. Not that there's anything wrong with being gay of course, if you are gay, but I'm not and I definitely don't fancy girls. I guess the easiest way to stop Shelly is to get spotted tonguing some boy but I'm not sure who or how. Also it has occurred to me that maybe I'm not all that snoggable. I'm not blonde or busty like Liz, which is what most guys seem to like (though Liz says not). She is slightly plump, which really annoys her so she's always on some stupid diet or other. She says that guys actually like skinny girls like me but that, yeah, developing boobs might help.

Maybe I could bribe some boy to snog me? I bet Gary, Chris's best friend, would snog me if I lent him my PlayStation game *Demon Assassins*. He loves that game but can't find it anywhere now. But what if he told people about it afterwards? Could I trust Gary, or any boy really, to keep his mouth shut? If word got round that I'd practically paid someone to snog me it would be just too humiliating. No, it's too risky. I'll just have to try and attract one of them, though God knows how I'm supposed to do that.

SATURDAY JANUARY 2ND

Chris was a bit weird today. He came round to my house in the afternoon but when I opened the door to him, instead of walking in like normal he just stood there and gawped at me. Then he said, 'You look nice, Kelly Ann.'

I stared back at him, surprised. 'What?'

Then he seemed to realize how odd he'd sounded as he reddened and explained, 'I mean the skirt. Your skirt is nice. A Christmas present?'

I looked down at the short pink skirt Aunt Kate had bought me and frowned. Hated the stupid thing. I mean, did she have to buy pink? Anyway, I hate wearing skirts and much prefer jeans or combats but Mum has made me wear it. She says I'm too old to be a tomboy now and everyone will think I'm a dyke if I carry on like this.

Told Mum she can't call people that now, it's not right, and she has to say female gay person. Mum said, female gay person her arse, she hadn't got time for long-winded talk like that, but anyway I'd wear the skirt Aunt Kate bought for me or else. And while she was at it, the day I've got the money to fork out on my own clothes will be the day I tell her what to say or not to say in her own house, but she wouldn't advise it even then if I wanted to avoid a black eye and that's if I was lucky.

Charming.

I was still thinking about my argument with Mum when she came up behind me, smoking a fag as usual.

'Are you two going to stay there all day with the door wide open letting the cold in? It's Baltic out there, for God's sake. Well seen you lot don't pay the gas bill.'

Chris came in, closed the door behind him and said, 'Happy New Year, Mrs—'

Still annoyed with Mum, I interrupted, 'You can't let cold in, you can only let heat out.' I looked at Chris now. 'Isn't that right, Chris?'

I wasn't good at science the way Chris was, but I remember some teacher talking about this last year. I was sure Chris would back me up, but he wimped out.

He said, 'Er, erm, it depends on how you look at it, I suppose.'

My dad joined us in the hall then. 'There speaks a diplomat.' He shook Chris's hand. 'Happy New Year, son. Come on in and have a drink.'

We all piled into the living room, where my big sister Angela was sitting amusing herself by picking bits of pink fluff off a black jacket. She's done this every day since Christmas, when her boyfriend bought her an angora scarf which moults onto everything it touches. I'd have got rid of them (scarf and stupid boyfriend) but my sister is the sort of sad person who probably finds purpose in this pointless, neverending activity.

Since it was the first time Chris has been here since the New Year, Dad offered him a 'Lite' beer, which he usually keeps for adults who are driving and don't want to go over the limit. Don't know how anyone can drink beer. Even the smell of it is awful. Must say I'm glad I'm not a boy and so won't have to spend a lifetime drinking such vile stuff, although Chris seemed happy enough to accept it.

Mum and Dad used this lame excuse to start drinking

more alcohol too ('hair of the dog', Dad called it) but I just had Irn Bru. We toasted the New Year yet again, then Chris was made to kiss Mum and Angela. He must have thought he'd have to kiss me too as he leaned over towards me, but I saved him from this embarrassment by pulling away and high-fiving him.

Dad made the usual idiotic conversation with Chris that adults all seem to think is expected. 'Christ, son, you haven't half grown. You can't be far off six feet. Must be nearly as tall as your dad now and he's no midget.'

Chris muttered some polite reply.

I said, 'You only saw Chris a week ago, Dad. He can't have grown that much since then. He's not a mushroom.' I turned to Chris. 'C'mon, let's go upstairs. We can have a go on the new game I got for Christmas. Bring your beer with you.'

I made for the door and Chris got up to follow me but then Angela butted in with, 'Mum, you're not going to let her take a boy to her bedroom, are you? She's fourteen. Much too old for that now. You never let me take boyfriends to my bedroom, do you?'

Mum said, 'Oh for God's sake, Angela, it's only Chris.'

Dad backed her up. 'Don't be daft, Angela. They've known each other since they were not long out of nappies. Chris is just a pal.'

'Still, it's not fair,' Angela huffed. She looked at Mum. 'Aren't you going to stop her then?'

'Like your father said, she's known him since she gave

up nappies.' Mum looked at me and laughed. 'That will be nearly three years then.'

I sighed. 'Yeah, right, very funny, Mum.'

'Well, you did take a bloody long time to potty train. I'd visions of having to buy you Pampers for a wedding present.'

Why do all adults want to embarrass teenagers? Even people like your parents who are supposed to care about you. Come to think of it, *especially* people like your parents. Mind you, I think I must have the most embarrassing parents in the entire world. Even when, unlike Mum just now, they're not deliberately trying to be.

I said, 'Look, Chris, why don't we just go to your house? I could do with getting out of here for a while.'

Chris agreed so he quickly gulped down the rest of his beer and followed me into the hall. I put on my jacket then sat down on the stairs to pull on my trainers. Angela came out at this point. She said, 'What do you think you're doing?'

I tucked my laces into the sides of the trainers and stood up. 'What does it look like I'm doing? Duh!'

'You can't wear those with a skirt.'

'Can.'

'Can't.'

'Can, can, can.'

'Can't, can't— Oh, this is childish.' She opened the living-room door and screeched, 'Mum, look what she's wearing!'

Mum came out, still smoking her fag. Or probably another fag. 'Oh, for Christ's sake, what is it now?' She looked down at my feet and laughed. 'Bloody hell. It's Florence.'

'Florence Nightingale?' I said, puzzled. Couldn't see how I looked like a Victorian nurse.

'Florence from *The Magic Roundabout*, you eejit. Now go put on the shoes I bought you for Christmas. You asked for them, after all. They cost forty pounds and I'll be buggered if they're going to waste.'

'I asked for new trainers, not stupid high heels I can't walk in.'

But it was no use. Mum made me put them on. I'm sure Angela is to blame for this. She's probably told Mum I'm getting slagged off at school for being too boyish. Mum never used to notice or care what I wore before.

I put them on and teetered outside with Chris. It was cold but at least it had stopped raining – though the pavement was still soaking wet so there was no way I could take off the four-inch heels and walk in just thick black tights. Had to hold onto Chris's arm for support, which annoyed me but Chris didn't seem bothered and later put his arm around my waist to steady me further. I was almost starting to get the hang of balancing in the things with his help when we arrived at the bottom of the road, only to find it flooded right across from a blocked drain. Damn. Why hadn't Chris mentioned this to me?

'It's not deep, Kelly Ann. Just an inch or two at most on this side.'

I looked down at my feet in the stupid heels. It might have been OK if Mum had bought me wedges. Glanced over at Chris's footwear. Sturdy thick-soled leather boots. All right for some.

Chris glanced at my feet too, then back at me. 'No problem, Kelly Ann. I'll carry you.'

Considered this. Chris *had* got a lot taller, as Dad had said. It's odd to think that just two years ago we were around the same height but now he's nearly six inches taller even in heels – well, with me in heels, I mean. Unlike other boys in my year who'd grown suddenly, he wasn't spindly and was quite sturdily built, maybe because of all the football training he does. Since I'm skinny he could probably manage to carry me quite easily without dropping me but I decided against it. Seemed too pathetically girly. Besides, the narrowest bit of water was less than two metres across. I was sure I could clear it easily.

I said, 'No, it's fine. I can jump it.'

'Kelly Ann, I really don't think that's a good idea.'

'Rubbish! I came second in the long jump in the whole of our year last summer. Honestly, this will be easy.'

I squirmed free of Chris and took a few steps back to get a bit of a run at it.

Chris tried to stop me. 'No, Kelly Ann, don't! You weren't wearing heels when you—'

Too late. I'd tried to launch myself across but tripped and ended up face down in the cold, dirty water. At least it wasn't sewage water – or I hoped not anyway.

'– came second in the long jump,' Chris finished.

He helped me up and handed me my right shoe, which had come off. I squelched miserably back home with Chris in tow. Of course Mum got on at me for 'ruining' my outfit. I think she suspected I'd done it on purpose or something.

Changed into my comfy jeans in my room, then put on my new PlayStation game and shouted downstairs to Chris to come up and join me. A few moments later he knocked on my door then came in. I patted the space on my bed beside me and continued with my game but he didn't join me right away. Instead he stood by the door and said, 'Are you sure you're OK with me being here, Kelly Ann? Maybe you'd be more comfortable if we went downstairs.'

'Don't be stupid. Why would I feel uncomfortable? I never have before. Don't let that idiot sister of mine bother you. It's not like you're a normal boy to me, anyway. More like a brother.'

'Yeah.' Chris smiled, relieved. 'We're just good friends, right?'

'Course, I said, handing him his controller. 'The best. But I'm still gonna enjoy ripping you apart.'

'You wish! Prepare to die at the hands of Hawkeye.'

Although Chris had never played this particular game

before he still beat me, which was annoying but he *is* probably one of the best in our school at this kind of stuff.

Still, I'm no newbie and got pretty close. Took out three of his men in a single grenade attack and success-fully carjacked another. But when I hurtled down the hill in my jeep to splatter Chris, he killed me with a single sniper shot to the head. He's ace at these – that's why he's called Hawkeye. I was down to my last life and couldn't respawn, so that was that.

'Never mind, Kelly Ann. What about a game of Monopoly? You always win at that. Only because you cheat, of course.'

I kicked him playfully on the shin and got out the Monopoly board. We played for hours but eventually I bankrupted him and it was time for him to go home. God, how I loved Chris being around. Just hoped he would never change.

Before he left I said, 'We'll always be friends, Chris, won't we?'

'Sure. Why? What's the matter?'

'Nothing . . . It's just that, well, everyone seems to be changing this year. Practically all my friends have got obsessed with make-up and boys now.'

Chris smiled. 'Not likely to happen to me.'

'Suppose.' I smiled back. 'But you seemed a bit weird earlier. Different.'

Chris shrugged. 'I was just surprised at the skirt. Don't think I've ever seen you in a skirt. You looked, well' – he paused, then put on a stupid high-pitched Pinocchio voice – *'like a real girl.'*

'Idiot,' I laughed. But I repeated my question seriously, just to be sure. 'So we'll always be friends then?'

'Yeah, definitely. Always.'

MONDAY JANUARY 4TH

At last Liz called me. She'd been up in Aberdeen with her mum and dad visiting relatives all over Christmas and New Year and I hadn't seen her for nearly two weeks. I'd been looking forward to catching up on all the gossip so I was shocked when she interrupted my 'Hi, how are you I've been just so unbelievably bored' with: 'Kelly Ann, we've been burgled! Come on over, quick. Mum and Dad are going mental and the police are here. The young one's quite nice.'

Was going to go on my new skateboard but it didn't seem respectful in the circumstances so I grabbed a box of Celebrations instead (in case the burglars had stolen all the food) and just ran over.

It wasn't until I got to the door that it occurred to me the name of the chocolates wasn't too tactful. Liz didn't seem to mind though: she took the box from me and ushered me inside.

'Let's take these up to my room,' she whispered. 'The police are checking the upstairs now with Dad so we

1 5

might catch a glimpse of the young one on the way. He's got nice blue eyes and he's really tall.'

Just as we were about to go into Liz's room, her dad and two policemen came out of her parents' bedroom. Liz's dad looked grim, the policemen bored but trying to hide it. The older one spoke to Liz. 'Anything taken from your room, love?'

'Erm, I'm not sure actually.'

'Haven't you checked yet? Let's go in and have a look now.'

Liz opened her door and we all went in. Or tried to anyway. The door wouldn't open completely, but finally we all managed to squeeze inside. The policemen looked at the scene of devastation and shook their heads in disgust.

Every drawer of Liz's chest was open and the contents (T-shirts, bras, knickers and Kotex ultra-thin sanitary pads with wings) lay scattered around it. Her wardrobe was wide open but contained only hangers: jeans, skirts and tops were strewn all over the floor, bed and bedside table, along with piles of magazines, books, make-up and shoes.

The older policeman spoke first. 'Makes me sick. The dirty buggers have made a right mess in here. There's no need for it. It's one thing thieving but this is uncalled for. Just sheer bloody badness.' He paused for a moment then, looking at Liz, who was trying to unobtrusively kick her knickers under the bed while stuffing the Kotex in her pocket, he continued thoughtfully, 'This seems to be the only room in the house they've trashed though. Is there anyone you know who's got a grudge against you? Have you had a falling out with someone recently? Maybe some dodgy boyfriend?'

Liz's dad, who was now picking up the stuff that had been blocking the door, answered for her. 'No, Sergeant. Her room's always like this. In fact' – he stood up and scanned it briefly – 'yes, I'd say definitely a bit tidier than usual. Maybe the burglars straightened the place up a bit while they were looking for something to lift. Mind you, they'd be lucky to find anything they were looking for in my daughter's room. No one else has managed it.'

The policeman laughed, then turned to Liz again. 'So anything missing then?'

Liz reddened. 'Erm, I'm not quite sure . . . Oh yeah, maybe my radio alarm clock.'

Her dad picked up a bundle of clothes from Liz's bedside table to reveal the radio alarm clock underneath. 'This it by any chance?'

Liz flushed again. 'Yeah, erm, good, but I don't see my jewellery box.'

I said, 'It was under your bed last time I saw it, Liz, but your jewellery is in the pocket of your dressing gown, I think. That's where you usually keep it anyway.'

A quick check proved me correct on both counts. In fact it turned out that nothing was missing at all. Maybe, like her dad said, the burglars couldn't find anything in Liz's room.

We all went down to the kitchen, where Liz's mum was sitting miserably. She looked up as we came in and I could see that her eyes were red. 'They've taken everything. The TV, video, microwave. Everything. I'd offer you a cup of tea but they've even made off with the sodding kettle.'

The young policeman nodded sympathetically. 'Yes, they've really cleaned you out. You'll be able to claim on insurance though. And there's one piece of good news. Nothing's been taken from your daughter's room.'

Liz's mum stared at Liz in horror. 'You didn't let the policemen see your room, did you? You didn't let strangers see the pigsty you live in? Oh God, have you no shame!'

'Now, now, missus, don't upset yourself,' the older policeman soothed. 'In this business you see it all. Nothing could shock or surprise us.' He turned to his younger colleague. 'Isn't that right? There's no need for embarrassment.'

'Too right, Sarge. Those crack dens we raided last year were pretty nasty.'

'Aye, you're right. They were in a state. Nearly as bad as the room upstairs.'

The sergeant laughed at his own joke before asking Liz's mum and dad a few more questions then heading off to the station.

After they'd gone Liz and I made tea for the four of us by heating water in a pan on the cooker, which fortunately the burglars hadn't managed or bothered to make off with. As we sipped the tea Liz said solemnly to her parents, 'Of course we will all have to have extensive psychological counselling to help us cope with this awful trauma because, you know, in a sense we've been violated.'

Her dad looked at her. 'That's not how I see it. I think, actually, *in a sense* we've been burgled. The only thing that's been violated is my hard-earned bloody cash if I can't persuade the sods at the insurance company to pay up.'

'I was only trying to help,' Liz huffed. 'But OK, fine, if you want us all to suffer post-traumatic stress disorder with nightmares and flashbacks for years to come, then go ahead and ignore me. See if I care.'

'I'll post-traumatic stress you. Now why don't you go and tidy that shit heap you call a bedroom? Mind and unpack your suitcase while you're at it.'

Liz and I made ourselves scarce. As I was helping her lug her suitcase up the stairs Liz asked me, 'So what do you think?'

I said, 'It's awful, Liz. I mean, strangers breaking into your house, rummaging through all your personal things and stealing anything they can find. It's gross. No wonder your dad is mad.'

'Oh yeah, you're right, but, erm, what I meant was . . .

the young policeman? He was quite hot, don't you think? Nice eyes.' Without giving me a chance to reply she continued thoughtfully, 'Or maybe it's just the uniform and I'm displaying the classic female attraction to male authority figures. Do you think I'd still have fancied him if he'd turned up without his uniform?'

I giggled. 'Starkers, you mean? Well, maybe, but I think your mum and dad might have been a bit annoyed.'

Liz unpacked by emptying the contents of her suitcase onto the floor then scooping armfuls of clothes into a large laundry basket in the hall.

I removed her toilet bag, shoes, two paperbacks and a half-eaten Twix from the basket while Liz, declaring herself too traumatized for more tidying up, cleared a space on her bed for us to sit down and opened the chocolates I'd brought. As we munched our way through the box Liz confided that she'd intended to start her watercress-soup-and-grapefruit-juice-only-super-low-calorie-fat-burner New Year diet today, but of course, given the emotional upset, it would be psychologically unwise to deprive herself of comfort foods just yet.

I nodded sympathetically but knew that Liz had never kept to a diet for an entire day in her life. Don't know why she bothered to diet anyway: most people think she looks nice, particularly boys. I sighed. If I had Liz's bust I could play football and wear jeans all the time and still no one would think I was too boyish.

We'd finished off all our favourite Celebrations and were making our way through a box of Quality Street, which Liz produced from her underwear drawer, when her parents checked in on us. Seeing the state of the room, made worse by Liz having dropped the chocolate wrappers on the floor beside her bed, they weren't too pleased and suggested that I go home while Liz cleaned up.

They looked pretty mad so I quickly got up to go. Before I left, however, I offered them a Celebration and said, 'Erm, almost forgot, Happy New Year.'

Liz's parents just *looked* at me.

Hmm, yeah, definitely time to go.

TUESDAY JANUARY 5TH

Liz started her watercress-soup-and-grapefruit-juice-only super-low-calorie-fat-burner New Year diet this morning but had abandoned it by lunch time. She told me she'd just read that very low-calorie diets can actually make you fat. This is because they panic your body into thinking it's being starved so your body responds with trying to make the most of every calorie and laying down fat tissue for future emergencies.

This didn't seem very likely to me – after all, pictures of famine victims don't show enormously overweight people waddling about with fat wobbling everywhere –

but I didn't say anything as Liz can be quite touchy about stuff like that.

SATURDAY JANUARY 9TH

Went over to Liz's around lunch time to find her miserably eating plain boiled rice and skinned chicken so I guessed she was on another diet.

She left most of her lunch uneaten on the plate; opening a carton of natural yoghurt, she confided to me that she was on a 'white' diet. This meant that she could eat anything she liked, and as much as she liked, so long as it was white. That morning she'd had boiled eggs (yolks removed) with white bread (minus the crusts) and a glass of milk. Tonight she was going to have cod without batter, boiled, bleached potatoes and a skinned apple.

I thought this diet might actually work as it sounded boring enough to put you off food altogether but then Liz produced two Milky Bars and an enormous bag of white chocolate buttons and I decided that, then again, maybe not.

MONDAY JANUARY 11TH

First day back at school. Of course I don't walk to school with Angela, who says she wouldn't be seen dead anywhere around school with me 'cos I'm a complete embarrassment.

Well, the feeling is totally mutual. I'm sorry to say it but my sister is a very sad person. She wears her school blouse buttoned up to the neck and – get this – tucks it into her skirt. I kid you not. Also she carries a leather satchel rather than a rucksack, which she keeps polished. No, really, I've seen her do it. Of course her shoes gleam like mirrors and the pleats on her skirt are always ironed so sharp you could practically cut yourself on them. (She irons her knickers and tights too, but since no one can see this is just pointless rather than embarrassing.)

Naturally she wears the school tie and blazer, which might be OK if she wasn't also the only person in the entire school with the regulation striped scarf. Even Mr Smith, our assistant head teacher, was surprised when he saw it and told her he didn't know we *had* a school scarf. It's so humiliating. If she ever wears the school beret (I've seen it in old pictures of school pupils in the 1950s) I'll have to run away from home with the shame of it.

Angela went off to school first to ensure she kept her record for perfect time-keeping and attendance. Never mind that she has two free periods first thing, which I pointed out to her. She told me they were not free periods but study periods. Yeah, she's a swot too. Might be understandable if she was super smart but she's not. Despite all the studying, she's a straight-C pupil, except in Office

Studies, where she gets Bs and so will go to secretarial college next year. Can't wait.

After she left I had a good fifteen minutes before I needed to go, and as both my parents had already gone off to work I switched on my PlayStation. I would be able to play it loud for once without the usual 'Turn that thing down/off for God's sake before I throw it out the window.'

Unfortunately I lost track of time a bit so was late on my first day of term. Not a good start, particularly as Mr Smith has said he will lock the gates at five past nine and latecomers will have to wait outside until twenty past, when he will personally issue everyone with a punishment exercise and detention.

Got there at ten past to find I wasn't the only latecomer: there was a small crowd of pupils plus two embarrassed and annoyed-looking teachers waiting outside the locked gates.

Well, there was no way I was going to hang around in the freezing cold just because of a psycho assistant head teacher and locked school gates that were only about three metres high with plenty of footholds on the way up.

First I threw my rucksack over, then quickly climbed up the gates. Getting down the other side was a little more difficult but I managed it without too much bother, dropping down the last bit and landing on my rucksack. I stood up and bowed to the small crowd on the other side, who applauded me admiringly – even the teachers – then went to sit in the toilets until registration was over. Our regy teacher is getting on a bit and retires next year so I'll just tell the office he made a mistake not marking me present and they'll put it down to senility. Sorted. Maybe the year wasn't starting off too badly after all.

Spoke too soon. At lunch break today spotted Shelly and her fan club outside the hall. Shelly is blonde and good-looking (although I think she has a mean little mouth) and is usually surrounded by a group of admiring boys too stupid to see what nasty people she and her so-called friends (i.e. two scavenger girls who hope to pick up some of the boys Shelly rejects) really are.

My sister was patrolling the corridors as she is a prefect and of course, unlike most normal prefects who were probably down the pub with their fake IDs, she takes her duties seriously. Angela told us all we weren't allowed in this corridor now because of the prelim exams in the hall and shooed us out. Shelly argued that the prelims don't actually start for another two days so it didn't matter but Angela told her 'rules are rules' and insisted we leave.

Typical Angela. Still, there was no use arguing with her so we all reluctantly shuffled off. When we got out Liz begged me to exchange her natural yoghurt for the tube of wine gums I'd brought as she was sick of white food. I reluctantly agreed. We'd just swapped and I was opening my yoghurt without much enthusiasm when Shelly and her two scavengers came up to us.

Shelly said, 'Why don't you tell your sad sister to get a life?'

Shelly had some nerve, she really did, slagging off my sister. Angela may be a bit of a pain, but I wasn't going to let anyone else say so. Certainly not Shelly. Besides, it's not like Shelly's sister couldn't be embarrassing. 'Why don't *you* tell *your* slapper sister not to flash her boobs at the sixth-year Christmas parties.'

Shelly flushed then looked at my chest and said, 'At least she's got some.'

Liz cut in, 'Yeah, well, *everybody* knows that now.'

Shelly sneered at Liz. 'You talking to me, fat girl?'

That was it. She'd insulted my sister, me and my best friend within the space of less than a minute. Before Liz could reply I raised my arm over Shelly's head, then slowly and deliberately poured the yoghurt over her. Idiot was so gobsmacked she just stood there staring at me like she couldn't believe what was happening. Her friends just gawped at me.

'Oh look,' I said. 'An enormous pigeon has just done a giant crap on your head.'

Her 'friends' tittered nervously. Shelly's face flushed scarlet with rage and she tried to lunge at me but I was too fast for her and backed away. The yoghurt had now started to trickle down her forehead and into her eyes. She tried to wipe it away with her sleeve, which just smeared it all over her face and made her look even funnier.

Loads of people started gathering round to see what the fuss was about. When they laughed at her, Shelly, practically crying with humiliation and fury, shouted, 'I'll get you for this, Kelly Ann.' Then she ran off to the toilet to clean herself up.

God, that was so much fun, but unfortunately the incident was witnessed by Angela, who'd come out after us to make sure we were following her instructions. She reported me to Mr Smith because 'rules were rules' and she mustn't show any favouritism just because I was her sister. Yeah, right. Mustn't show any loyalty either.

So now I'm suspended for two days for 'bullying'. Honestly, it was just a tub of yoghurt. Can't people take a joke? It didn't do her any harm; in fact yoghurt is probably good for hair. Nourishing. In a sense I was kind of doing her a favour.

Put these arguments to Mr Smith (except for the doing-her-a-favour bit) but he wouldn't listen. Suspended on my first day back at school. This wasn't a good start.

TUESDAY JANUARY 12TH

Had to tell my parents about the suspension last night. They weren't too pleased. Dad asked why I'd done it. Didn't want to go into the boobs stuff so I just said she'd insulted my sister by calling her boring, which I thought would make my parents take my side.

They just looked at me for a moment, saying nothing at first but not appearing too outraged at the insult to their first-born daughter. Dad was the first to speak. 'Well, er, she's not exactly what you'd call a live wire, love, is she?'

Mum was blunter. 'I'd have a more interesting conversation with a flamin' speaking clock.'

Charming. Looks like I'm the only one in this house to understand the meaning of family loyalty.

Anyway, Dad said I'm grounded for the week and I'd better not get into any more trouble at school.

Mum said she'd dock my pocket money and I'd better not do anything with yoghurt except eat it. Then she laughed. 'Or use it to treat thrush – but we'll not go into that with your father here.'

Yeah, right, very funny, Mum.

Grounded and impoverished, all over a stupid yoghurt. Sometimes I think my parents are really Dementors in disguise. Their sole purpose seems to be to suck the joy out of my life.

Liz rang after school today and asked how I was. Stupidly told her I was depressed. She asked eagerly, 'Depressed? Tell me, do you have feelings of worthlessness, hopelessness and frequent suicidal thoughts?'

'Of course not.'

'You don't?' Liz sounded disappointed. 'Oh well, maybe it's just mild depression then, perhaps due to Seasonal Affective Disorder. Very common at this time of year. You're sure you're not having suicidal thoughts?'

'No, not suicidal. Homicidal maybe if you don't stop all this psychology rubbish with me. I've been grounded and my pocket money's been docked.'

Liz was nice then and promised to treat me to a pizza and a DVD over at her place when my grounding was finished, but of course had to backtrack on the DVD offer when I reminded her that the stolen DVD player and TV hadn't been replaced yet because, just like her dad had predicted, their insurers found some reason in the 'soddin' small print' not to pay up.

Yeah, not the best start to the year for either of us. Still, things can only get better.

WEDNESDAY JANUARY 13TH

Angela has said she's inviting her new boyfriend over to watch a movie tonight. This will be the first time any of us get to see him as he isn't at our school, and though she's been going out with him for a while now, she's never invited him round before.

Hope he isn't as bad as her first one, who always wore bright turquoise socks with too short trousers and whose hobbies were Scottish country dancing and making Eiffel

Tower models from matchsticks. God, it was so embarrassing.

Or the last one, who turned up at our house wearing tight, straight orange trousers and a yellow shirt. Mum nearly wet herself laughing afterwards and always referred to him as Big Bird. God, yeah, surely this one had to be better than that.

Aunt Kate came round for a nosy, as did two of Mum's workmates, the women next door and even Great-aunt Winnie.

Angela was furious. She cornered Mum in the kitchen. 'What's going on? I thought you and Dad were going out tonight. Are you selling tickets or something?'

I stared at her. Bloody hell – that was almost a joke!

Mum said, 'Keep your hair on. We're going soon enough. I just wanted to see your latest boyfriend in the hope he might be normal and not look as though he's about to lay a bloody great egg on my carpet.'

I don't usually get on with Angela but I did feel sorry for her tonight. I mean, adults are just so nosy about stuff like that. I went up to my room, and turning off the light (so I couldn't be seen from outside), I peered through a gap in my curtains to see if I could get a look at him before he got here. It was dark but the streetlights were on and I had a good view of our street in either direction. Only problem was, of course, I couldn't be sure who it was until he actually turned into our garden but I reckoned I could guess. The nerdiest teenager I saw was likely to be the one.

I didn't have long to wait. He was wearing corduroy trousers, an anorak and woollen gloves, all a dingy shade of light beige, something like the colour of elephant dung. He had tidy brown hair, a pale, anxious face, and sensible shoes. Still, at least his trousers brushed the tops of his shoes and he didn't have chicken legs. Maybe he'd be OK.

Or maybe not. When he got in he took off his anorak to reveal a chunky knit Arran cardigan with pockets and leather buttons. Now OK, I know Beckham looks totally cool in a cardigan but no other male in the entire galaxy can pull it off. Also he'd 'brightened up' the outfit with a lime-green tie. I really, really have nothing to add to this statement other than to say: how can anyone with normal vision have so little taste? I'm talking about Angela as much as her sad boyfriend.

Having said all this, I did feel sorry for him when he was invited to sit on one of the hard low chairs in the living room, then immediately interrogated by all the adults. Well, not all the adults. Dad just said, 'Hello, son,' then went back to reading his paper, only glancing up now and then to throw him a sympathetic look along with a *but-what-can-I-do?* shrug.

All the female adults surrounded Graham like piranhas and quickly stripped him of every bit of information about his life. From his job (assistant trainee manager of a small supermarket about four miles away) to the burial place of his great-granny (two plots down from Great-aunt Winnie's second cousin's final resting place).

Fortunately for him, none of the information was remotely interesting so people soon got fed up and left. Within half an hour I was the only person left in the house, not counting Angela and her dull new boyfriend. Yeah, somehow my sister has managed to do the impossible and find a boyfriend who's even more boring than her. Honestly, he's about as exciting as a boiled rice sandwich and I was dreading a night spent with the pair of them.

They had settled down on the living-room sofa and had put on some insufferably tedious film when Chris called me to say Rangers were playing Hearts tonight and did I want to come over. Was reluctantly telling Chris I couldn't as I'd been grounded when Angela interrupted me: 'Oh, just go on over, Kelly Ann – there's no point in you staying here tonight.'

I gawped at her. 'But I'm grounded.'

She flushed. 'Yes, well, erm, who's to know? I won't tell. Rules are, well, erm, made to be broken sometimes. Occasionally, anyway. Just this once.'

Graham handed me a fiver. 'Here. Treat yourself to a DVD or something.'

I grabbed the money and left. Who said miracles never happen?

Back at school and actually quite pleased. It's pretty boring during the day without your friends, and anyway, Mum made me do all the housework.

Told Liz about Angela and Graham's weirdly nice behaviour last night, saying I couldn't understand what had come over them – Angela bending rules and some guy I'd never met before giving me a fiver.

Liz said, 'Well, maybe they needed some privacy. You know, for, erm, sex. They've been going out for a while already.'

'Don't be stupid. Angela would never have sex with anyone. She's too neat and tidy. And someone like Graham wouldn't want to do it either. He's just so nerdish.'

'Hmm, I don't know,' Liz continued. 'The sex drive is very powerful, you know. It can make people do stuff they usually wouldn't.'

'Like what?'

'Well, like taking off their clothes in front of other people for a start. Or normally super-tidy people like your sister doing things that might make a mess. Or her boyfriend giving you a fiver even though he doesn't know you.'

I was sceptical. 'No, nothing is that powerful.'

But Liz was adamant. 'Did you know that when a male praying mantis has sex, the female sometimes bites off his head and eats it? And, get this, he just goes right on doing it.'

'Jesus, without a head?'

'Yeah,' Liz said. She dropped her voice to a whisper. 'He goes right on shagging. Headless.'

'Bloody hell, that's keen.'

Thought about it. If what Liz says is true and the sex drive is *that* powerful, it might explain their weird behaviour last night, I suppose. Maybe Angela and Graham are having sex. Gross.

FRIDAY JANUARY 15TH

Mr Smith has told me I've got detention for latecoming. Apparently someone (and I can guess who) informed him that I was not present at registration on Monday.

Told him that I couldn't go to detention as I was grounded but he wouldn't listen. Just said I'd to be there or else.

I suppose it hardly matters anyway whether I'm imprisoned at school or under house arrest at home. And this is supposed to be a free country. Yeah, right.

Saw Shelly and her scavengers smirking as I made for the detention room at four o'clock. Not that I let this bother me in the slightest, so standing on her foot as I passed was completely accidental and my apology totally sincere. Naturally.

MONDAY JANUARY 25TH

Was gobsmacked to see Diane buy a Tampax from the machine in the girls' toilets today.

Her nickname is Dopey Di because she is so un-coordinated she still has to wear Velcro trainers as she can't tie her laces yet. Also her mum has to write L and R in large felt-tip on the back of each hand every morning so she knows left from right. One day her mum just put the R on one hand, hoping that Diane would be able to work things out, but she got lost on her way to school. Yet she can obviously manage tampons.

Right, if Dopey Di can do it, so can I. It will be so much better for sports than wearing sanitary towels – and probably better for the environment since they are smaller. I draw the line at recycling sanitary towels.

TUESDAY JANUARY 26TH

'Borrowed' a Tampax from Angela's underwear drawer and went off to the toilet.

After trying several contorted squatting positions and becoming more familiar with certain bits of me than I ever wanted to be, I eventually managed to be kind of half successful (don't ask) with inserting the thing. Dad chose this moment to start hammering on the bathroom door for the third time.

'For Christ's sake, Kelly Ann, what are you doing in there? You've been at least half an hour. Open the bloody door. I need in. Now.'

I mean, what was I supposed to say? There should be a law against asking what anyone is doing in a toilet. Decided to give up on tampons. Especially as Liz says Dopey Di is just pretending to use them and she's seen her secretly dispose of used towels in the waste bin.

WEDNESDAY JANUARY 27TH

Went to the toilets at lunch time today. Shelly and her coven were looking at something on the wall behind the sink and cackling. When I came over to wash my hands they pushed off pretty sharpish, still sniggering nastily.

Someone, and I know who, had scrawled KELLY ANN IS GAY in red ink over the middle sink.

So totally childish. There was no way I was going to let Shelly's stupid actions bother me. Definitely not.

THURSDAY JANUARY 28TH

Georgiana, otherwise known as George, who is an incredibly butch built-like-a-tank lesbian, has invited me back to her place to try out her new PlayStation game. Love the game, but remembering that her console is in her bed-room I politely declined.

That's it. I'll have to get a boyfriend quick. Don't care what he looks like as long as he's not female.

MONDAY FEBRUARY 1 ST

There was a disgusting smell in the corridor today, and
not just the bit outside the boys' toilets. Suspected it was
the work of that moron Terry Docherty, the carrot-haired
first year with sticky-out ears and buck teeth who was the
front half of my pantomime cow at Christmas. Nearly
every other week he lets off stink bombs somewhere
around the school, which he seems to find hilarious.

Sure enough, spotted him giggling like a demented
hyena with his pals at the bottom of the stairs. Ignored
them, but one of his friends came up to me and said,
'Haw, Kelly Ann, ma pal Terry pure fancies ye, so he
does.'

At the same time Terry looked over at me and grinned
like a corpse's skull.

OK, last week when I said *any* boyfriend, I didn't
actually mean any boyfriend. Thinking about it, if there
was a nuclear holocaust and I had a choice between a

relationship with that obnoxious little gnome Terry or Georgiana, then it would have to be Georgiana. Even if the human race had to die out.

TUESDAY FEBRUARY 2ND

Was relieved that the cleaners have managed to get rid of the graffiti on the toilet walls, including the bit about me being a lesbian, but the rumour that I'm gay still hasn't died away and quite a few people have asked me to my face if it's true. Even people I know quite well.

That's it. I really will have to get a boyfriend.

Liz said she'd help and invited me over to her place after school to 'discuss tactics'.

Had been hoping for some practical advice but when we got to her house she told me she had devised battery of psychological profiling tests which she wanted me to try.

'How does this help me get a boyfriend?' I asked.

'How can you possibly have a mature relationship with someone else until you know your true inner self?' Liz countered.

'Don't want a mature relationship. Just want a boyfriend to stop the stupid rumours.'

But Liz was adamant and eventually, just to shut her up, I gave in.

'So,' Liz said, showing me pictures of fruits on

separate cards, 'if you could be one of these four fruits – an apple, a pear, a grape or a banana – which would you rather be?'

'Don't want to be a fruit.'

'But if you *had* to choose, which fruit would you be?' Liz persisted.

'OK, um, a date, I think.'

'That's not one of the choices,' Liz complained crossly. But then added curiously, 'But, erm, why a date?'

'Most people don't like them so I probably wouldn't get eaten.'

Liz sighed and explained with exaggerated patience, 'Look, you idiot, fruits don't know they're fruits: they're not aware of existing, so they've absolutely no fruity consciousness. Therefore they don't care about being eaten. OK?'

'So what does it matter what kind of fruit I am then?' I asked reasonably.

Liz screamed, 'Just choose, OK! An apple. A pear. A grape. Or a *banana*!'

'All right, all right. A banana.'

Liz wrote down my answer and moved on to the next test. 'So if you could be one of these shapes, which would you be? A circle, a square, a star or a triangle.'

I didn't argue. 'A triangle.'

'Good.' Liz noted my response again, then handed me a piece of paper with an ink stain on it. 'Look carefully and tell me what you see.'

'Hmm – an ink stain?'

Liz sighed. 'I know it's an ink stain – you're supposed to say what it looks like.'

'Doesn't look like anything.'

'But if it *did*, what would it look like? Use your imagination. Only people with serious personality problems have no imagination,' Liz warned.

I looked more closely at it. There was a long spiky bit and what looked like smoke curling out the bottom. 'OK, a rocket then.'

Liz smiled happily and noted my answer down. 'I think a pattern is beginning to emerge.'

'What pattern?' I asked suspiciously.

'Well,' she said, 'maybe I shouldn't tell you.'

'And maybe you should. It's *my* personality after all.'

'OK then, I suppose you *do* have a right to know,' Liz agreed. 'The thing is, you, erm, seem to have an obsession with boys and sex.'

'Don't be stupid. Of course I don't.'

'Well, you're probably not *consciously* aware of it, but deep down, *unconsciously*, you're thinking about boys' penises all the time.'

'I so do not. Yuck. I don't think about them at all,' I protested.

'Do too,' Liz said. 'The tests don't lie the way people can. Every single thing you chose – the banana, the triangle and the rocket – is a phallic symbol.'

'Phallic symbol?'

'Shaped like a boy's penis,' Liz explained.

This was mental. Probably something dreamed up by that nutcase Freud again. 'That's totally mad, Liz. How is a banana like a penis? It's nothing like it.'

'Well, it's long and kind of tube-shaped. Unlike, say, an apple, which you *didn't* choose – although you could have.'

'Bananas are also bendy and yellow,' I pointed out incredulously. 'I think boys might be a bit worried if they had a penis like that. Anyway, what about the triangle? A triangle is definitely, totally, no way like a penis.'

'More like a penis than a square, or any of the other shapes though, isn't it?' Liz said. 'I mean, OK, if you'd chosen a square, then fair enough, I'd have to say that's not shaped like a penis, but—'

'Finally you're talking sense—'

'But you didn't,' Liz went on, ignoring my sarcasm. 'And then there's the rocket. Rockets are a lot like penises if, OK, maybe a bit bigger than most.'

'A bit bigger! And what about the smoke? Anyway, the ink blob didn't look like anything else other than a rocket.' I passed it to her. 'So what does it look like to you?'

Liz stared at it for a moment. 'Honestly?'

I nodded.

'A penis!'

Liz has offered me psychological counselling to prepare me for dating but I've turned her down. I mean, how difficult can it be? Have decided to ask Osman to go out with me. I like him and he's a fantastic footballer. Although he's skinny like me he's got nice black skin and white teeth. Don't like his dreadlocks much but maybe I could persuade him to get a number two cut. He'd look good like that.

Cornered Osman at lunch time today and told him I needed to speak to him in private. He looked a bit nervous, probably because he still remembers the time when I punched him for saying there was no way girls could play football as well as boys, but that was way back in first year when I wasn't the mature and controlled teenager I am today. However, he agreed anyway, so as soon as we'd found a quiet spot behind the large school bins I decided to get right to the point.

'I really like you, Osman, and we've got so much in common. Like we both support Man U and hate cricket. Would you like to be my boyfriend?'

Osman said, 'Bloody hell, Kelly Ann.'

This wasn't really the response I was hoping for but he hadn't said definitely no so I tried again. 'Look, Osman, the bell's about to go and these bins stink anyway, so I can't hang about for ever while you make up your mind. Do you want to be my boyfriend or not?'

Osman looked down at his toes. Shoving his hands in his pockets, he kicked a discarded Coke can against the bin before mumbling, 'I'm really sorry, Kelly Ann. Don't get mad at me. I mean, I like you and everything and, um, respect you.' He glanced up at me. 'You're better at football than any girl I know and you've a mean right hook, but I just don't think of you in that way.' His gaze slipped away from my face again. 'You know, the, um, chemistry isn't quite—'

'You mean you don't fancy me? Why not?'

'Well, um, honestly? You won't hit me or anything?'

I shook my head, depressed.

'You're just not really my type.'

'What is your type then?'

'Well, a bit curvier, I suppose, and, um, blonde. No offence.'

It was hopeless. There was no way I could possibly be described as either. Liz was lucky.

Then he added, 'Like Shelly.'

'Shelly! But she's horrible.'

He shrugged. 'Seems OK to me – and anyway, she's hot.'

Boys are really so stupid. Just because a girl looks nice doesn't mean she *is* nice. Why can't they see that?

The bell rang so I made my way over to maths. Osman had PE next, which is in the opposite direction, so we left it at that. He looked relieved.

Met George on the way back. She invited me over to

her place again but added, 'Look, I like you, Kelly Ann, but don't worry – I'm not gonna try and snog you. I don't fancy you or anything. You're not my type.'

'What is your type then?' I asked curiously.

'Well, kinda curvier and, er, blonde.'

I suppose I should have felt relieved that George wasn't going to stalk me or anything, and I was, kind of, but couldn't help feeling a bit disappointed too. It's depressing that even if I were lesbian I might still have trouble getting someone to go out with. Wonder if that's why some people are bi and date anyone. I suppose it sort of doubles your chances. Seems a bit desperate though.

THURSDAY FEBRUARY 4TH

Moaned to Liz about Osman yesterday. She said I'd look stupid as a blonde but why didn't I just stuff toilet paper down my bra to look curvier. Loads of girls did it.

Told Liz I'd feel stupid with toilet paper down my bra but eventually agreed to try it. Just once anyway.

Didn't notice any boys drooling over me like Liz had promised but had to admit I did look more girl-shaped and everything was OK until last period, waiting outside maths, when Shelly said suspiciously, 'You look different today, Kelly Ann.'

Oh God. But I managed a careless shrug. 'Do I?'

Her eyes narrowed as she looked me over, then

smirked and said loudly, 'You've stuffed toilet paper down your bra, haven't you?'

I blushed but said casually, 'Yeah, like I'd bother to do something that pathetic.'

Since most people know I'm not into girly stuff I got away with it, but later I told Liz, 'Right, that's the last time I try that. It's stupid.'

But Liz was horrified. 'Kelly Ann, you'll have to keep it up now. Every day. If people see you flat again they'll know you were lying. You'll be a laughing stock.'

Brilliant.

FRIDAY FEBRUARY 5TH

Mrs Conner, our English teacher, was wittering on about Valentine's Day today. She says that as this is the most romantic month of the year we're going to focus on the two great themes of literature: love and passion. So for the next four weeks we'll be discussing poems, short stories, novels and plays that focus on these themes.

Sounds boring. Especially as we've already been doing lots of stuff like that in English. Especially novels. Why can't we read interesting stories for a change? Like ones that have plots where stuff actually happens without a hundred pages of description just to tell you it's raining. And then another hundred to tell you how the character feels about the fact that it's raining.

Oh well. There's no arguing with Mrs Conner though
– she's not a teacher to cross. She might go on about
how she believes in interactive education and involving
students in every step of the learning process but you do
what she tells you or else.

Still, for most of the period we talked about the story
of Romeo and Juliet, which was quite interesting if a bit
depressing at the end. Was gobsmacked when Mrs
Conner told us that Romeo and Juliet were only about our
age. Bloody hell. OK, I understand fancying people and
wanting to snog them and stuff, but topping yourself
over some guy? It's a bit much.

Maybe teenagers in those days didn't have enough to
do to take their mind off things. I mean, if Romeo and
Juliet had had PlayStations, DVDs and chocolate Creme
Eggs to cheer themselves up, they mightn't have got their
knickers in such a twist when things got a bit iffy on the
romance front.

And let's face it – PlayStations and DVDs are a lot
more interesting than some idiot singing to you outside
your house.

We packed up early and I was hoping we'd just get to
chat but Mrs Conner used the last ten minutes to talk
about her own experience of romantic love and passion.
Wish she hadn't bothered.

She told us that she and her husband were 'soul mates'
– as much in love now as the day many years ago when
they took their marriage vows.

Pass the sick bag. This was bad enough but it got worse. She went on to say that every day their love got deeper and their passion for each other was as fresh and alive as the first day they met. Emotionally *and physically*.

I mean, she as good as announced to everyone that she was still having sex with him. Gross. She can't be that much younger than my mum – definitely well past thirty.

Might not have been so bad if her husband was OK but we've seen him come to pick her up after school some-times. Though he is a successful businessman and drives a really nice Mercedes, he's short, fat, almost totally bald and looks a bit like Danny DeVito.

Thinking about teachers like Mrs Conner having sex with people like that is almost as bad as imagining your parents doing it. Hope she shuts up about her soul mate – at least until next Valentine's.

I was talking to Liz about it at break. She agreed but then pointed out, 'They must have done it though, mustn't they? Parents, I mean. In your parents' case, at least twice.'

Gross. But I suppose they must have. It's difficult to believe, even if it did happen a long time ago when they were young.

Can't get what Liz said about my parents out of my mind. Unfortunately. I was watching and listening to them arguing at dinner time tonight.

DAD: Pass the salt, love.

MUM (*bad temperedly*): It's right at your flaming elbow.

DAD: OK, keep your hair on, I didn't see it.

MUM (*annoyed*): Maybe if you took your eyes off the sports page of the paper and looked, it would help.

DAD (*pissed off*): There's no need to jump down my throat.

MUM (*totally annoyed now*): Sorry, you're right. Look, you go on reading your paper and I'll cut up your dinner and feed it to you so you don't have to make any bloody effort at all. It's the least I can do after cooking it for you. Then you just lie down and I'll fan you while I hook you up to an intravenous drip so you won't have to bother drinking your cup of tea afterwards.

Dad sprinkled the salt on his dinner and then calmly went on reading his paper, ignoring her.

No, I just can't believe they've ever done what Liz says. It doesn't seem possible, even a long time ago.

Maybe I'm adopted.

SATURDAY FEBRUARY 6TH

Actually, the more I think about it, the more it makes sense. Fact is, for quite a while now I've felt that I can't possibly really belong to this family. I mean, I have absolutely nothing in common with any of them.

Specially not Angela. But my parents haven't even hinted never mind told me that I'm adopted, so I suppose it's unlikely. Though it seems more believable than them doing what they would have to do to have me naturally.

Hmm . . . but then maybe they didn't want to tell me I'm adopted in case I got upset. Yeah, that could be it. Although I'm not their real daughter they probably still love me and want to spare me any pain or psychological damage.

I'd have been totally cool about it. They really should have told me.

SUNDAY FEBRUARY 7TH

If I am adopted I wonder who my real parents are. Maybe like Romeo and Juliet they were totally in love with one another but their families disapproved, so they made my mum put me up for adoption then she probably killed herself because of a broken heart.

Or maybe my real mum is a foreign princess who fell in love with a commoner. They wouldn't let her marry my dad because though he was . . . erm, yeah, a famous footballer, he was still a commoner, so they made her give me up so she could marry a royal. Since that day she's thought of nothing else but me and lives for the time I'll come looking for her.

OK, I suppose the foreign princess bit isn't very likely

– don't think there are that many of them around now –
but my dad might have been a footballer. After all, I'm
pretty good, even if our sexist PE teacher won't let me
join the school team.

THURSDAY FEBRUARY 11TH

Have been thinking about this all week and I've become
more and more convinced that it's at least possible I
might be adopted. It could explain so much. I have
nothing in common with the family I'm living with. And
anyway, Mum and Dad hardly look at each other, never
mind anything else. I've never seen them so much as snog
(thank God!) and can't imagine they ever did. As for
doing it with each other? No, it's totally impossible. I
must be adopted.

Decided to tell my adoptive mum that I'm old enough to
know the truth now.

I waited until she was in a good mood – that is, after
watching *EastEnders* and drinking a mug of tea while
puffing on her fourth fag in an hour. I decided to come
straight to the point.

'Mum, am I adopted?'

She was obviously shocked as she choked on her tea
and dropped her fag on her lap but quickly found it again
before it got a chance to burn her. Poor Mum.

'Don't be upset, Mum,' I said kindly. 'You see, I've suspected the truth for quite a while now and I'm old enough to cope with it. And while of course I want to find my birth mum, I won't stop loving you, and I'll always be grateful to you for looking after me as I grew up. I'll never forget my humble beginnings.'

All this time my adoptive mother had been staring at me literally open-mouthed, but now she seemed to have recovered enough to speak and I waited bravely to hear the truth about my real background at last. But I was wrong. She didn't say anything. Just screeched with laughter. At first I thought she might be hysterical at the suddenness of my confrontation but I was wrong again because when she did manage to speak, it wasn't what I expected to hear.

'You, adopted? You must be bloody joking. I suppose you think your sister's adopted as well. My arse. Like I'd actually go *choose* the pair of you.' Here she broke off to laugh again. 'Aye, that *will* be right. I'll just have these two, thanks. Yeah, that's right, the boring one who couldn't crack a joke if her life depended on it, and, yeah, the wee skinny one who's always moaning about something or other. Aye, that's the one.'

'So,' I said, 'I'm, erm, not adopted then?'

'Duh. No, you eejit. You're not adopted and I've got the droopy boobs, blancmange abs and stitches in places you don't want to see to prove it. The pair of you ruined my body and put me through bloody hours of agony, and what thanks do I get for it? Now go and bring your birth mother another cup of tea from your humble beginnings kitchen. Adopted. That's a laugh.'

Feeling a bit stupid now, I did as she asked. When I got back she was still on about it. 'Wait till I tell your dad about this one. And yes, before you ask, he's your real dad as well.' She laughed. 'Or that's my story and I'm sticking to it.'

FRIDAY FEBRUARY 12TH

Just two days until Valentine's, and of course every shop is full of hearts and flowers to remind anyone who might possibly have forgotten that if you don't have a boyfriend then you are a sad, unloved loser.

I've never had a Valentine card unless you count the one from my Aunt Kate last year (I recognized her very badly disguised handwriting) or the one the year before from my mum (I found it in a kitchen drawer the week before Valentine's) – which I don't of course. I suppose it was nice of them to bother so I pretended to be surprised and excited but really it just made me feel pathetic.

I suppose as I've never actually wanted a boyfriend before, I shouldn't complain, but it's always nice to know I could get one if I did, and a Valentine card is definite proof of that. And it just seems so unfair that some people always get loads of Valentines when other people never get any. Like me for instance.

At school people seemed to talk of nothing else, which was depressing. Shelly was behind me in the lunch queue, showing off two early Valentines to anyone who'd listen to her. She even tried me.

'Want to see my Valentines?'

'No thanks.'

'Too jealous? Oh, never mind, Kelly Ann,' she said, in an annoyingly pitying tone. 'Maybe you'll get one tomorrow. There's still time.' She laughed. 'And maybe my granny will take up break dancing and run off with a rapper. Or perhaps my pet goldfish will win the hundred metres hurdles at sports day. About as likely.'

I flushed. 'So? I hope I don't get any Valentines. The whole thing is just commercialized rubbish.'

Shelly sneered. 'Funny, that's what people who haven't a hope of getting one always say.'

I stomped off with my lunch tray and looked round for Liz, who'd been kept behind by Miss McElwee for eating in class, but she still wasn't there so I sat at an empty table and waited for her.

Was scanning the dinner hall again for Liz or one of my other friends when I spotted Michael looking for a table. As usual, he was being stalked by a group of good-looking fourth-year girls and even a couple of fifth years. Michael has jet-black hair, green eyes and (God knows how in Glasgow) an all-year tan. He's so good looking, he seems almost fake and is definitely seen by everyone as the hottest boy in the fourth year. Maybe even the whole school.

Noticed that his admirers were all smiling at him with their heads tilted to one side and bobbing about like a Barbie doll whose neck had been broken. The thought made me grin but he must have thought I was smiling at him as he waved, smiled back and made his way over to our table, followed by his hopeful harem.

'Hi, Kelly Ann. These seats free?'

I nodded. He sat down and after a while we started to chat about Rangers' chances against AC Milan next month and also whether they might win next week's play-off with Celtic (not great and no) – to the annoyance of his groupies as he wasn't paying any attention to them.

'So,' one of the most determined fourth years interrupted, 'do you two know each other?'

'Yeah,' Michael said. 'We were in *Jack and the Beanstalk* together.'

'Oh, you were fabulous as Jack,' she gushed. 'Didn't notice *her* in it though.'

Michael smiled. 'Kelly Ann was playing a supporting role.'

I grinned back at him. Although he'd been playing the lead and I was just the back end of his cow, he'd been really nice to me and sometimes talked to me during breaks. When I moaned about being cast as a cow's arse, he told me acting was a team effort and that every part was important to the success of a play. This was decent of him, even if it was hard to believe, but it got us chatting anyway and we've been quite friendly ever since. You'd think someone as popular as him would be really big-headed but actually he's not up himself at all. And he still stops to chat to me sometimes when we happen to bump into each other. Much to the surprise and annoyance of his fan club.

'So, Michael,' the determined fourth year said, trying to get his attention again, 'what are you doing on Valentine's Day? I just love Valentine's, don't you? So romantic.'

'Actually, I think it's mostly commercialized rubbish,' Michael said. 'A cynical ploy by big business to con idiots out of money.'

Next thing, all the Barbie dolls' heads were bobbing in agreement.

Hmm, obviously it's only people like Michael who can get away with saying stuff like that without being sneered at.

SATURDAY FEBRUARY 13TH

Got a Valentine. Yeah, right. It was from Mum or Aunt Kate of course, although they must have got someone else to do the usual cheesy *Guess Who?* inside as I didn't recognize the handwriting. Well, at least they made a bit more of an effort at disguise this year, but, c'mon, just how stupid do they think I am?

SUNDAY FEBRUARY 14TH
VALENTINE'S DAY

At least it's not a school day so I don't have to listen to people like Shelly boasting about how many Valentine cards they got. Hopefully by tomorrow it will have died down a bit – everyone will have phoned, emailed, texted and talked about what cards they did or didn't get by then.

Chris came over today. For a laugh he brought me a rose 'because it was Valentine's'. He handed it to me with an exaggerated flourish, saying, 'For my Valentine.'

I took the rose from him, saying, 'Why, thank you, My One True Love. I shall treasure this floral tribute for ever.' We laughed, then went into the house, where I got us both an Irn Bru before popping the rose in a pint glass as I couldn't find a vase, where it lolled drunkenly.

As we sipped our drinks Chris asked, 'So did you get a card yesterday?'

I said, 'Nah. Just the usual from Mum. I mean, who would send me a card? Not that I'm bothered. You get one?'

'Don't know about that. Why wouldn't someone give you a card?'

'Suppose,' I said, pleased.

'After all, you're not *that* ugly.'

He ducked to avoid the swipe aimed at his head. I grinned and took another slurp of Irn Bru. 'Anyway, you didn't answer my question. Did you get a Valentine?'

Chris reddened a bit. 'Yeah, I did in fact. Two. But I don't know who they're from.'

'God, two! You're popular all of sudden. Not that you're interested in girls anyway.'

'What do you mean, not interested? I'm not gay, Kelly Ann. Of course I'm interested.'

'Course you're not gay,' I soothed. 'And I suppose you will start thinking about girls sometime. But not now. I mean, you're too busy with schoolwork and football to be bothered with all that dating stuff right now.'

'Well, no, not really. I'd make time. For the right girl, anyway.'

Chris seemed really sincere and the thought depressed me. I'd heard there were quite a few girls in our year who fancied him – like Linda, for instance, who's not bad looking and quite nice. This probably meant I was going to lose another really close friend because they had started dating and weren't interested in my company any more.

Chris said, 'You look upset, Kelly Ann. Don't tell me you're jealous?'

'Of course not. It's just that if you start dating, well, you'll still have time for me, won't you? We'll still meet up and do stuff? Still be best friends?'

'I suppose so. I mean, I'm like a brother to you, right?'
'Yeah.'
'Then we'll always be friends.'

God, I hoped so. Apart from Liz, Chris was the best and closest friend I'd ever had.

MONDAY FEBRUARY 15TH

Liz had got a Valentine from Peter Campbell, a boy who left our school at Christmas when he turned sixteen and now has a job in a supermarket. He didn't bother to disguise who it was from and even put his mobile number on the card. She called him and they're going to meet up this weekend.

Couldn't help being impressed. Imagine having a boyfriend who's that old and has a real full-time job.

Liz's dad is not impressed though. He says the whole Campbell family – father, mother and seven kids – are a bunch of dodgy chancers, every last one of them, and besides, sixteen is too old and there is no way Liz will be allowed to go out with Peter.

Of course this means Liz will have to keep the whole thing secret from her parents, like Romeo and Juliet. As she said, it made everything so much more exciting and romantic.

SATURDAY FEBRUARY 20TH

Liz is out on her date with Peter, although she told her parents she's at the pictures with me. She's not the only one out with her boyfriend – nearly everyone I know has a boyfriend now.

Called Chris but he said he was too busy to come over. When I asked what he was doing he was really vague about it and quickly got off the phone.

Hmm. This wasn't like Chris. Just know he's hiding something from me. But why? Hope Chris isn't going to be one more friend who grows up and is no fun any more.

Wish people would just stay the same and never change. Like me.

MONDAY MARCH 1ST

Chris's friend Gary walked home with Liz and me today, which is pretty unusual as he lives in the opposite direction from us. After Liz went into her house and it was just Gary and me, the reason for this sudden friendliness became obvious.

'So how's your pal Rebecca these days?' Gary said. 'You two still go to ballet classes together?'

'She's fine,' I said suspiciously. 'And no, I stopped going to ballet five years ago. Refused to wear that stupid tutu. You know Rebecca packed it in two years ago too.'

'Oh yeah, forgot. So, I was wondering, is Rebecca seeing anyone these days? Just curious.'

'Not since she chucked Adam. Why?'

'No reason. It's just, well, she's a really nice girl, that's all. Nice legs too. Fantastic bum. Oh, and, um, great personality. That's what I really like about her.'

'Sorry, Gary, don't think she fancies you.'

'Who said anything about fancying? Just want to be friends. Get to know her.'

'Yeah, right.'

'C'mon, Kelly Ann. Help me out here. I'm sure if she got to meet me out of school – you know, in a more sort of social, relaxed kind of place, like my house for instance – and if she could see me out of this naff uniform, bet I could change her mind.'

'No way.'

FRIDAY MARCH 5TH

Rebecca and I are going over to Gary's house to watch a special edition of the *Dirty Dancing* DVD which he told us contains material never seen before and interviews with the actors. Rebecca couldn't resist as it's her favourite film of all time. Mine too actually – I love the dancing in it. So does Rebecca, but the main reason she likes it is that she thinks Patrick Swayze looked really hot in it.

God, Gary must be keen on Rebecca to get this movie for us. He normally watches stuff like *Fight Club* and kung fu action movies and his friends have been slagging him off all week.

I hoped for Gary's sake it would be worthwhile. Thought he might have a chance as he's not bad looking and I know Rebecca likes guys who dress right so maybe she'll fancy Gary when she sees him wearing the new K-Swiss trainers and Levi's he bought last week.

We got to Gary's at seven. Couldn't believe my eyes when he answered the door. He'd no shoes on and his long toes poked out from skinny jeans so tight they clung to his ankles, thighs and bum like cling film. Gross. But even worse than this was his top. A white vest. No, really – a tight white vest made of thin cotton so that you could see his nipples. I mean, really, who wants to see them? Have never seen the point of boys' nipples anyway.

He'd also done something stupid to his normally straight hair: it had a huge wave in the middle which flopped at us as he nodded a welcoming, 'Hi, girls.' Though compared to the jeans and the vest it hardly mattered.

I think he might have been trying to look like Patrick Swayze – he knows Rebecca has a thing about him – but, as she whispered to me as we made our way upstairs, 'Oh my God, he looks like a rent boy.'

Didn't really enjoy the film as I was too mortified for Gary, who seemed to imagine he'd made an impression on Rebecca. He had, but not in a good way. Especially when he got up and tried to imitate Patrick Swayze dancing. Gary can't dance like Patrick Swayze. In fact, Gary can't dance at all, which was embarrassing enough, but when he tried to do a particularly energetic jump-and-twist manoeuvre and his tight jeans split up the back to reveal red boxers I thought even someone like Gary would never recover from the humiliation.

I was wrong. Rebecca nearly wet herself laughing but Gary just smiled and bowed before going off to get changed into his Levi's.

Rebecca's dad picked her up about ten but I stayed on for a few minutes, intending to ask Gary why on earth he'd made such an idiot of himself.

However, as soon as she'd left Gary turned to me and said, 'Thought that went really well tonight. Make a girl laugh and you're halfway there.'

I opened my mouth to explain how totally wrong he was but then closed it again. He'd find out soon enough.

SUNDAY MARCH 7TH

Gary called round today and asked me to find out if Rebecca might be interested in going out with him.

'Why don't you ask her yourself?' I grumped.

'I would, but, erm, I thought it might be better coming from you. You can maybe talk me up a bit first. Say what a great guy I am when you get to know me. That kind of thing.'

'Lie to a friend, you mean.'

Gary laughed. 'Lie *for* a friend.'

Although I knew it was useless, I phoned Rebecca later.

'So what do you think of Gary?' I asked. 'I know he was a bit of an idiot on Friday but he's really—'

'Oh, Gary's a laugh but I don't fancy him,' Rebecca interrupted. 'Actually it's his friend Ian I really like. Do you think I've any chance with him?'

'Hmm, I, erm, don't know,' I lied.

Know for a fact she's wasting her time. Ian, who's six foot three, is always complaining he can't find a girl tall enough for him and won't look at any girl under five foot ten. Rebecca is five foot. Enough said. God, things were much easier when we were all at primary school and no one fancied anyone.

MONDAY MARCH 8TH

Was chatting to Michael in the chip-shop queue. He's got an audition for a part in a TV commercial and didn't know whether he should go or not.

'I don't know, Kelly Ann. I want to be a serious actor one day. Maybe this wouldn't be a good move.'

I thought getting on TV was totally cool even if it was just a commercial and was telling him so when I heard a familiar voice behind me say, 'Hiya, Kelly Ann.'

Shelly. And smiling at me like we were best pals.

I just sneered at her. Suppose Michael must have found my silence awkward because when I didn't reply he looked at Shelly and said politely, 'Hi, how's it going?'

I expected Shelly to get right in there, chatting him up, but to my surprise she just stammered, 'Aayah-sh-sh. I, um, dunno . . . um, yeah.'

Her face had gone all red and blotchy. Then, when she tried to talk again, all she could manage by way of conversation was a few more high-pitched strangled squeaks which sounded like a mouse being garrotted. Not that I've ever heard a mouse being garrotted but, well, if I had it would probably have sounded like Shelly.

It was weird the way Shelly got all shy and stupid around Michael, but maybe even queen bitches like her lose their cool when confronted with someone as totally gorgeous as him. Suppose one of the few good things about being a flat-chested brunette like me is that boys like him are so totally out of my league it doesn't matter what I say or do. So I can just be, like, totally cool about it.

MONDAY MARCH 15TH

Liz has decided that it's definitely time I had a boyfriend and snogged someone. It would finally kill all the rumours about me being gay, so annoy Shelly, and it would be good for my psychosocial development, what-ever that is.

She says the new boy William who started in January has told his friend Dave, who told Gary, who told

Beth and Melissa, who told Liz, that he fancies me.

Hmm, William. He's a bit freckly and thin, but not totally ugly, so I wouldn't be embarrassed to be seen with him. Don't know that I really want to snog him though, but I suppose I could manage it if I closed my eyes and thought about something else. It's not as though he's so ugly I'd throw up or anything. Anyway, as Liz says, I don't have to marry him and have his kids, I just have to be seen snogging him a few times, and I think I could manage that.

Yeah. Told Liz OK, I'd do it.

TUESDAY MARCH 16TH

Liz spotted him in the corridors at break time heading towards the boys' toilets. 'Quick, Kelly Ann, he's on his own and if you hurry you could catch him.'

I ran off after him and managed to reach him just before he got to the door. I grabbed him by the arm. He turned round, startled, then stepped back away from me until he was right against the wall. I moved closer and smiled in what I hoped was an attractive and reassuring manner but felt my expression turn into a grimace as I became aware of the more-than-slight pong that always seems to hang about the entrance to the boys' toilets. Decided to come straight to the point: 'My friend Liz says you like me.'

He flushed but didn't deny it, mumbling something which sounded a bit like, yeah, he thought I was OK. That would have to do.

'So do you want to be my boyfriend then?'

He looked from side to side – I suppose to check if anyone was nosing in on our conversation – then said quietly, 'Erm, well maybe. I don't know.'

This didn't sound too promising and wasn't what Liz had made me think. She'd told me he was dead keen. 'What's *maybe* supposed to mean? Aren't you sure? Why not?'

He held his palms out towards me defensively. 'No offence, Kelly Ann, it's just I'm not certain whether we're suited or not.'

Hmm, wondered what he'd been hearing about me. Maybe Shelly and her lot had got to him already, spreading their poison. 'I'm not a lesbian if that's what you think. You really shouldn't believe everything you read in the girls' toilets, you know.'

A couple of first-year boys passed behind me on their way into the toilets and looked at us curiously, so I bawled at them to get lost and stop being so nosy before fixing my smile back in place and trying not to breathe through my nose.

William put his hands back down, then stared at me strangely. 'I don't read stuff in the girls' toilets.'

'No, well, I suppose not, but anyway, I'm definitely not gay just so you know.'

'Right. Good. But, er, maybe we should get to know each other first before deciding whether we'd like to be boyfriend and girlfriend. OK?'

'Well, all right. What do you want to know?'

'Um, I'm not sure exactly. Look, could I go to the toilet now? *Please*?'

Glanced over at Liz, who was smiling encouragement at me but also pointing to her watch. William was trying to sidle past me, but obviously I couldn't let him go without getting something definite arranged to report to Liz, so I stayed right in front of him and put my arm against the wall to his right, blocking his way.

'The thing is,' I explained, 'it's not that important. I mean, we're not getting married or anything. We don't have to go out for long – just a week or two maybe, and then we can split. You can say you dumped me if you like, although I'd kinda rather you didn't. Maybe we could just say it was sort of mutual and we just drifted apart.'

'Well, I hadn't really thought about splitting up since we're not actually going out together yet. And I still think we need to know a bit about each other first.'

He said *yet*. This was more like it. 'So,' I said again, 'what do you want to know?'

'Look, Kelly Ann,' he said, sounding a bit desperate, 'I'll meet you after school. OK? We'll talk then.'

'Fine,' I agreed happily. 'Where should we meet? Here maybe? Hmm, perhaps not. A bit pongy. At the school gates? Nah, too crowded. What about across the road by the park entrance?'

'Anywhere, I don't care,' he kind of squeaked, clutching himself now. Bloody hell, he must have a weak bladder or something. Decided I'd better let him go before he embarrassed both of us. There was no way I could date a boy who still had 'accidents' after all.

I took my arm away from the wall and he raced into the loo. I shouted after him, 'Four o'clock by the park gates then!'

'Yeah, OK, see ya,' chorused some boys from the loos. By the sounds of their high reedy voices, probably the first years who'd been gawping at us a minute ago.

Ignored them and made my way back to Liz, giving her the thumbs-up sign and smiling. Yes, job done!

Met him at the park entrance as promised, though he took a while getting there and must have gone at the pace of an arthritic tree sloth. He was probably nervous. Maybe, just like me, this was the first time he'd done this kind of thing. I suggested we go for a walk in the park as it wasn't raining and there were loads of frogs in the pond last time I looked. Maybe we could catch some.

As we walked I chatted away quite easily to him as I'm used to boys' company. 'Last time I was here I caught twelve frogs – two were really big ones. I put them all back in the water of course, but one of them got eaten by a seagull as soon as I let him go. He was called Freddie –

he was my favourite. The frog, that is, not the seagull. Maybe I should have taken him home after all but the last time I took frogs home Mum freaked out when she saw them in the bath and made me take them back. Two escaped on the way. One jumped down a drain but the other got knocked down on the road. It's quite a dangerous life frogs have, isn't it? They're not very tough with their soft squidgy bodies. But being a tadpole is worse, I suppose. Then again, not many tadpoles get knocked down on the road.'

He'd been a bit quiet during all this. Maybe he was shy with girls. Or maybe he was having trouble getting a word in edgeways as it's true I do go on a bit sometimes – not that I'm the Bionic Mouth like Mum says, but when I'm interested in stuff I just like to express myself. What's wrong with that? Besides, if he was shy, then my talking would put him at ease so there would be no awkward silences.

Finally he said, 'I'm not that interested in frogs.'

'Oh, right, OK then. Want to climb the tree by the bench? Race you.'

I sped off and after a pause he ran after me but he was pretty slow and I had a head start so I reached the tree way before him, scrambled up, then sat on a branch to wait for him.

When he finally got there I dropped down suddenly, meaning to land right in front of him to give him a bit of a surprise and a laugh, but instead I miscalculated and kind of landed on top of him, which meant we both crashed to the ground. My fall was broken by his body so I was OK, but he was pretty winded so I suggested we sit on the bench until he recovered.

After a few minutes he seemed OK so I suggested climbing the tree again but he just said, 'No thanks. I don't like heights.'

'You're scared of heights? But that tree isn't very tall. Can't be more than ten metres and we don't need to go all the way up.' I grinned reassuringly. 'It's not exactly the Empire State Building or anything. If you did fall out of it you wouldn't end up looking like a squashed tomato like you would if you fell off the top of a skyscraper.'

But this didn't seem to reassure him – in fact he went quite grey and sweaty so I reckoned he must have one of those phobias Liz talks about. Decided to stop talking about falling from heights altogether, which seemed to work as he calmed down a lot, although he still looked a little shaky. And maybe a bit embarrassed at me seeing him looking so scared.

I tried to make him feel better by saying, 'Look, it's OK. My friend Liz says lots of people have stupid irrational fears about something or other. It doesn't mean you're a wimp or anything. Well, it might but it's not definite. You've probably just got a psychological problem.'

'Are you saying I'm a nutter? Thanks a lot.'

'No, of course not,' I soothed. 'You've just got a phobia.

Loads of totally cool people have phobias. I've probably got one too. In fact I have. Yeah, definitely.'

'You have?' He sounded interested and less annoyed. Good. 'What are you scared of?'

'Me? Oh, erm, lots of things. Yeah, um . . .' God, what could I say? Desperately tried to remember Liz talking about daft stuff people freaked out about. Ah yes! 'I'm claustrophobic actually. You know, scared of being trapped in small, confined spaces. Yeah, I'm dead scared of that.'

'Oh, yeah,' he said sympathetically, 'that's an awful feeling.'

'Yeah, it is,' I said. However, not wanting him to think I was a basket case, I thought I'd better water it down a bit. 'Of course it doesn't usually affect me much. I mean, I'm fine going in lifts, even if I get stuck in one occasionally, and I don't mind when I'm in the car with Dad and he drives through tunnels. One time, when I was little, Dad took us on the train through the Channel tunnel, which was pretty cool. Imagine being under thousands of tons of earth and millions of gallons of water for miles and miles above you . . . You OK?'

He looked a bit pale and sick again. Maybe he was aquaphobic – scared of water like dogs with rabies. Decided it was best to change the subject and steer clear of watery stuff.

'I don't fancy potholing though – sounds boring – but

I went down an old mineshaft when I was on holiday in Wales once and it was cool.'

'Doesn't sound like you're claustrophobic at all then,' he said sceptically. He sounded annoyed too.

'Oh yeah, I definitely am. Well, a bit anyway. I mean, I'd hate to be buried alive in a coffin. Can you imagine it? People think you're dead but you've actually been in a coma and when you wake up you discover you're trapped in a coffin under the earth. You try and push the lid up but all you can do is scratch the surface with your nails so you start screaming but no one can hear you. That would really scare me.'

He said, 'Please just shut up about it, OK? Please.' He got up and started to walk away from me.

I hurried after him. 'Hmm, maybe you should sit down again. You don't look very well. You didn't have the chicken nuggets for lunch, did you? They looked pretty minging. Maybe you've got food poisoning.'

He said, 'I'm claustrophobic.'

Trying to lighten the mood, I giggled. 'Bloody hell. Maybe it would be easier just to tell me if there's anything that doesn't scare you so I know what to talk about.'

He didn't sit down but after a while he seemed to recover, and with his hands in his pockets he started moodily kicking an empty twisted Coke can that had been lying at his feet.

'Hey,' I said, 'watch this!' I got my right toe under the can and flicked it up onto my head, then bounced it off my chest and back down to my left foot. Flicked it to the right foot then left and right again. Managed to do another fifteen keepie-uppies before I missed one. William was staring at me, well impressed. Good. Hopefully this had made him forget about being trapped in coffins or splattered on pavements.

I kicked the can towards him. 'Your turn. Let's see how long you can keep it up. Think you can beat me?'

'No, I'm, um, not that good at it. Not with a can anyway.'

'Bet you are. Go on, try it.' I flicked the can onto his head. It bounced off so I headed it right back to his chest and it fell onto his toe. 'C'mon, don't be a wimp.'

He tried to kick the can up onto his other foot but missed by a mile and it skidded off the path into the duck pond. Bloody hell, he really was useless.

Trying to make him feel better, I said, 'Look, yeah, you're right, cans suck. Let's go borrow a ball and have a proper kick around. We can use our bags as goal posts and play penalties. Bet you're shit-hot at that.'

'Nah, I think I'll just go home now.'

I hurried after him. 'Right, OK, yeah. I'm off too. Don't know about you but I'm starving. So, erm, are you my boyfriend now?'

He turned to me. 'No, Kelly Ann. I don't want to be your boyfriend.'

'But why not? You said you liked me. It's because I'm not blonde, isn't it?'

'No, it's not that.'

'Too skinny?'

'Nah, it's just, well, um, no offence but, you know, I want a girlfriend and you're just, well, not sort of girly enough. More like a boy really.'

'Oh.'

'You're not upset? I mean, I never promised to go out with you. Today was just a sort of trial. It's not like I'm dumping you or anything.'

I flushed. Bloody hell, he wasn't feeling sorry for me, was he? I put on a totally unconcerned, happy voice. 'God, no, it's cool. No worries.'

'Right, well, see ya.'

'Yeah, see ya,' I said brightly.

I trudged home, depressed. Things hadn't gone too well. What was I going to tell Liz?

WEDNESDAY MARCH 17TH

I'd avoided Liz's phone calls and emails last night but she got me this morning at break. 'So how did it go with William? C'mon, tell all. I want to know every single detail. Did you snog him? When are you seeing him again?'

'Hmm, well, no, not really. I don't, er, think we'll be meeting up again. The thing is, we sort of, erm, drifted apart.'

Liz stared at me sceptically. 'Don't be stupid. You can't "drift apart" when you've not even snogged once. Drifted apart my arse. Tell me what happened!'

'It's private, Liz,' I said with quiet dignity.

But privacy and quiet dignity are impossible when your best friend is the nosiest person in Scotland and pretty soon she'd dragged the whole story from me. Every embarrassing detail. Oh God.

Liz was disappointed and unimpressed. She shook her head. 'I'm sorry, Kelly Ann, but really I think you haven't yet reached the necessary level of psychosocial development to deal with boyfriends.'

Liz could be a pompous pain in the arse at times. I wasn't putting up with this. 'What's that supposed to mean? Are you saying I'm not grown up enough? You've a nerve, given that you still play with the same My Little Pony Santa got you when you were six.'

'That's just a memento of childhood. Perfectly well-balanced, psychologically sound, mature individuals keep mementos.'

'And the Barbie doll you got for your seventh birthday.'

'Also a childhood mem—'

'Whose hair you washed and braided last week.'

'Hmm, well, OK, I still do *some* childish stuff but really you need to grow up a bit with boys. I mean, you beat William at running, climbing and football. Couldn't you have let him win at one of them at least?'

'Deliberately, you mean? Why would I do that? No boy would respect someone who just let them win.'

Liz sighed. 'Yeah they would. Boys only don't respect you if you let them do stuff like groping your boobs on a first date or—'

'Yuck! I'd never do that. On a first or any other date.' Then I laughed. 'Mind you, I don't suppose any of them would want to. Not with me anyway. Would you ever let a boy do that?'

'Well, not on a first date. Obviously. But maybe when the relationship has shifted to a deeper, more committed phase and mutual trust has been established.'

'When's that?'

'Third date.' Liz giggled. 'Guess what?'

'What?' I said, giggling as well now.

'Peter's asked me out for a meal. A proper meal. In an Italian restaurant with candles and cloth napkins.'

'Oh my God. That's so cool,' I said, genuinely impressed.

Liz has had boyfriends before although none had lasted this long and most finished after one or two dates. Probably because she spent the whole time psycho-analysing them, which usually meant telling them how pathetically weak, neurotic or nuts they were. However, unlike me, she has snogged quite a few boys, and one had bought her chocolates afterwards. And she's even been on a date to the movies twice, though not with the same boy. But out for a meal? And at a real grown-up restaurant, not just Burger King or McDonald's? It just seemed so sophisticated. I wouldn't let anyone grope me but I wouldn't mind being asked out to a posh restaurant. Provided the boy paid of course.

Hmm, good point. Peter wasn't known for being generous. In fact, he'd a reputation for being a bit mean and it was rumoured that when he was at school he used to charge people to borrow a rubber because of 'wear and tear'. Don't really believe that but I do know he recycled a previous year's birthday card for his mum, hoping she wouldn't remember. She did and gave him a black eye. Social work found out and got involved but I don't think they were that sympathetic towards Peter, and his mum got off with a warning.

'Are you sure Peter is treating you, Liz?'

'Of course. He's not at school like me. He's got a proper job. A salary. Anyway it'll cost me a fortune getting clothes and stuff for it so it's only fair.'

The rest of the time Liz chatted about what she was going to wear – she would need new shoes, skirt, top, jewellery and make-up – and what she was going to tell her parents, who don't like Peter and think he's pretty shady.

Officially Liz was going to be at my place and sleeping over. That's the great thing about a mobile, which Liz's parents bought her for safety reasons so they could always keep in touch: you could be absolutely anywhere and your parents will never know, but the fact that they can call you means they don't check.

Well, except for Gary last month, who said he was at Chris's but had actually managed to con his way into a pub with the help of two older cousins. When his parents called they heard the background noise of clinking glasses, music and the barman shouting last orders. Disaster. Why can't parents text, for God's sake?

SATURDAY MARCH 20TH

Chris called and asked me to go into town with him this afternoon to help him choose the new football boots he'd been saving up for, but I told him Mum was making me help clean the house and then I'd planned to go to Liz's.

He said, 'No problem, we'll go tomorrow. Most of the sports shops are open then.'

Went over to Liz's this afternoon an hour before she was due to meet Peter. I expected her to be looking fantastic by this time, as I knew she'd been preparing all day, but when she opened the door she was still in her dressing gown with white gunge on her face and a pair of pink knickers on her head. She also smelled bad.

I came in and said – stupidly, I suppose, 'Aren't you ready yet?'

Liz said, 'Yeah, actually I am. I decided on a casual look tonight but I'm not sure about the knickers. Maybe black would be classier.'

Very funny. As we climbed the stairs to her bedroom

she told me Peter had texted her to say he'd had to reserve a table an hour later than he'd hoped so she wasn't running late. Oh my God. He'd *reserved* a table. Couldn't help being impressed. Imagine having a friend who had a boyfriend who reserves tables in restaurants. Knew Liz was pleased too but was trying not to smile because of her face-mask thing.

'What have you got on your face?'

'Egg white. It's supposed to be good for the complexion but you have to leave it on as long as possible for best results. I've had it on for six hours now. And I've got the yolk on my head. I read somewhere that egg yolk makes a fantastic conditioner for blonde hair. The knickers are to stop the egg white and yolk mixing. Don't want to be covered in omelette.'

We went into her room and Liz cleared a space on her bed for us both to sit down. Close up, in the confined space of her bedroom, the smell was awful. 'Are you sure you used a fresh egg, Liz? You smell a bit like Terry Docherty's stupid stink bombs.'

'Oh God, do I? I never noticed. Got a bit of a cold today.'

Liz went off to shower, thank God, and I opened the windows to let out the smell before I gagged. How could she not have noticed? When she got back she looked a lot better without the egg white and knickers. Smelled better too.

* * *

Two hours later and Liz was finally ready. She was wearing her new skirt, tight black top, drop earrings and high heels. She looked really old and could easily have passed for eighteen. Well, sixteen anyway. Definitely.

We crept quietly down the stairs and Liz was just about to grab her jacket from the hall and scurry out with a quick 'Bye, see you later,' when her dad came out of the living room and spotted us. Or Liz anyway.

'And just where do you think you're going dressed like that? The red-light district? I know finances have been a bit tight recently since those sodding insurers didn't pay up, but your mother and I don't plan on sending you out on the streets just yet. Now go back up those stairs and put on some decent clothes.'

Liz of course refused, which had her dad going all red and ranting at her, so her mum came out to see what all the fuss was about.

Her dad turned to her mum. 'Would you look at the sight of her dressed like a bloody prostitute!'

Liz's mum shrugged. 'It's just the fashion. They all look like that.'

'All look like hoores?' spluttered her dad.

'More or less,' Liz's mum replied calmly. 'When they're dressed up anyway.' But then she frowned suspiciously at Liz. 'I thought you were just going to Kelly Ann's to watch a DVD tonight? Why are you all tarted up?'

Liz stared innocently back at her mum. 'I think it's, er,

important not to take friends for granted. Why shouldn't I take the trouble to dress up for my best friend now and then? It, um, shows respect for our long and, um, loyal friendship.'

Liz's mum raised her eyebrows in disbelief at this lame excuse but eventually Liz was allowed to go, along with a promise she would ring them later and a threat that one or both of her parents might ring *her* later.

Everyone was out so I had the house to myself tonight. Mum and Dad were at Aunt Kate's for 'dinner' (takeaway curry with a bottle of Bacardi and eight pints of beer) so they wouldn't be back until eleven at the earliest. They say they are just five minutes away and I've to call if I need them. Yeah, right. Like I need two drunk parents stinking of onion bhajis rolling up. Had just settled down to watch the football when the phone rang. Hoped it wasn't Liz's parents checking up on her by calling her here instead of on her mobile but it was Liz's mobile number. Good. The match wasn't very interesting and I was dying to hear how her date had gone. I snatched up the phone.

'How did it go? Did you snog him ag—?'

'I'm being held hostage, Kelly Ann,' Liz screamed. 'I need thirty-six pounds or they won't let me go.'

'Peter's holding you hostage?' I asked, totally gobsmacked. Maybe Liz's parents were right and he was a really bad person. But then I couldn't see Liz putting up with this.

'No, you idiot. The restaurant staff.' Liz was nearly sobbing with frustration and fury now. 'Tosser only paid half the bill and I didn't have any money so he just left me here.'

Oh God, thirty-six pounds. How did Liz manage to eat that much? Stupid question. Especially if she thought Peter would pay.

'I can't ask Mum or Dad,' Liz wailed. 'They don't know I'm here and they'd go mental if they did.'

'Don't worry, Liz. I'll be right there with the money. No problem.'

I put down the phone. Bloody hell. Why had I said that? I suppose I just wanted to sound reassuring but where would I get thirty-six pounds? I checked my purse and turned out my pockets. Four pounds and seventy-five pence. So, just thirty-one pounds and twenty-five pence to go. Feverishly I checked down all the cushions and under the bed. Another three pounds twenty-two pence. Also ten euros and twenty-nine cents. Just a pity Britain hadn't joined yet.

So, just another . . . well, a lot to go. Wish I'd paid more attention at mental arithmetic. Also I'd have to subtract my bus fare into town. Bollocks. I'd have to call Liz's parents after all. Or my own. Oh God. Wish I'd someone else I could ask for lots of money.

But I had. Chris. A good pair of football boots would cost over thirty pounds easily. Yeah, that was it. I'd ask Chris. He would be sure to help. Only thing was, Liz had sworn me to secrecy about her date with Peter, and anyway I knew she wouldn't want anyone to know how he'd humiliated her. Not even Chris.

I picked up the phone and dialled. 'Chris, don't ask why, I can't tell you, but I need money right now ... about, um, thirty pounds – well, maybe just a bit less, I haven't worked it out yet. Can you come over right away with it *please*? It's a matter of life and death – well, not quite, but very, very important, though I can't tell you why as I'm sworn to secrecy. All I can say is I desperately—'

Chris said, 'OK.'

'OK?' I said, relieved.

'I'll be over right away.'

Oh God, how I love Chris at times like this. He's just the best friend a person could ever have.

In ten minutes Chris was over and had handed me the thirty pounds. He didn't ask me any questions as I knew he wouldn't (sometimes it's so nice having an un-nosy friend) but looked worried. I shooed him away with a quick 'Thanks, Chris. Sorry about the football boots. I'll get this back to you soon as. Trust me.'

As soon as he was out of sight I checked my watch. Ten fifteen. Should be able to make it there and back before eleven if I hurried. I grabbed my coat and ran for the bus into town.

When I got to the restaurant, I found Liz in the hall by the kitchen, being guarded by a snooty waitress and a scary-looking guy with tattoos on his arms, which were folded over his chest and resting on his beer gut. After I'd paid the bill they released her.

On the way back to my house Liz fumed about Peter the whole time. Apparently, not sure what to order at first, she had looked at the menu and said, 'Oh, Peter, everything seems so expensive.'

He'd smiled and said, 'Hey, special occasion. Our first meal out together. Go mental.'

So she'd ordered everything and had had a great time until the bill-paying stage when Peter had made it clear he was expecting Liz to pay for her share, put £30 on the dish (£3 less than his own bill when the service charge was added) and buggered off, leaving Liz with the rest.

Once Liz and I got back home I called Chris and assured him I'd repay his loan soon (Liz had told me it would take three weeks of her allowance to pay him off). He said not to worry, and whenever, although I know he really needs new boots as his old ones are totally done.

Eventually I went off to sleep thinking about Liz and her horrible date. Have come to the conclusion all guys are totally selfish, mean and useless. Maybe it's as well I don't have a boyfriend after all. Not that anyone seems to want me.

THURSDAY APRIL 1 ST

April fool's day. This time I am not going to get caught out like all the other times. So if anyone tells me that there are pink daffodils in the park, chocolate-flavoured chicken nuggets on the school dinner menu or that eating twelve melons a day makes your boobs grow (I can't stand melons now), then I will so *not* believe them.

It's only ten o'clock and already I've been told that hidden CCTV cameras have been installed in the cubicles of the girls' toilets, that the government has increased the school leaving age to twenty-five, and that in an effort to improve the school ethos all pupils will have to curtsey or bow to teachers if we meet them in the corridors. Yeah, right. Like I'm really stupid enough to believe any of it.

Mr Smith has just come on the tannoy to tell us that the rumour school is closing today at eleven a.m. is not true and anyone found truanting will be severely dealt with.

Since corporal punishment is now allowed in all state schools at the discretion of the head teacher, this is likely to be a very painful experience.

Passed Michael as I was on my way to the shops with Liz to buy some chocolate. As usual he was surrounded by nice-looking fourth-year girls, who were all trying to pull him, judging by their constant superglue-fixed smiles and tilted heads. He spotted me so I waved a quick 'Hi' to him and hurried on as the queue would be building up. But to my surprise he broke free from his group of admirers and caught up with me.

'Hi, Kelly Ann. Look, could I have a quick word with you?'

'Sorry, Mike, not now – I'm in a bit of a hurry. Chocolate starvation has set in and you know what the queues are like.'

However, he turned to Liz and gave her a dazzling smile. 'Maybe you could go ahead and keep Kelly Ann's place for her. Or' – he took some change from his pocket and handed it to her – 'if we don't make it by the time you're served, just buy her a Cadbury's Creme Egg.' He turned to me. 'That's what you usually like, isn't it?'

I nodded, puzzled. Liz took the money, then, giving me a look that said she'd expect me to fill her in later on what Mike was up to, *every single detail*, she ran on ahead.

I said, 'How do you know I like Cadbury's Creme Eggs?'

'You told me one time. Don't you remember?'

I shook my head, then shrugged. 'No, not really, but anyway, what did you want to talk to me about?'

He paused for a moment and seemed for once to look a bit unsure of himself, but then he went on, 'Look, Kelly Ann, I was just wondering if you wanted to meet up after school today. We could go to the café for a Coke and maybe have a pizza later. What do you think?'

I stared at his gorgeous face, puzzled. 'What for?'

'Well, I don't know. I mean, it's just that I really like talking to you. You're different from most girls. Interesting. And, well, fun.'

'Are you asking me for a date?' I asked incredulously.

He smiled. 'Well, yeah, I suppose so. Yeah, I am. So can I see you after school today?'

'But why would you want to date someone like me? You could have anyone.'

'Don't want just anyone. You're, well, special. You're not like most girls I meet – always giggling and talking rubbish. I feel you really listen to what I have to say. That you're interested in me as . . . well' – he reddened – 'as a person, I suppose. That's why you're the only girl I ever sent a Valentine's card to. Bit cheesy, I know.' He grinned. 'Did you never guess who it was from?'

For a moment I almost fell for it. How embarrassing. God, Michael really was a good actor. But then I remembered it was April 1st. Aha! Like I'm really going to fall for that one. I smiled back. 'Sorry, Mike, I'm busy today.'

'OK, well, fair enough. I suppose it is kinda short notice. What about tomorrow then?' he said, still giving me his nice-guy Colgate grin.

'Busy tomorrow too.'

His smile wavered a bit. Maybe he realized his April fool wasn't working. But he persisted anyway. 'So, is there any time you've got free when we could meet up? Maybe next week?'

'Nah, sorry. Fact is, I don't think of you in *that way*. You're way too ugly for me.'

He flushed. *Hmm, so it's OK for him to play jokes on people but he can't take it when it's the other way about.* 'I'm not ugly.'

'Course you're not,' I said, mock soothingly. 'You're just not my type, that's all. Not, um, blond enough. Yeah, I only date blonds, I'm afraid.'

'You don't want to go out with me because of the colour of my hair? That's it?' He looked at me contemptuously. 'Well, in that case I'm glad you said no. I thought you were different from other girls. There's no way I want anything to do with a girl so totally shallow.'

Then he turned and marched off.

As I watched his retreating back I realized the horrible truth – that, oh my God, he'd been serious. The hottest guy in the whole school had just asked me out and I'd said no.

I could have been the envy of everyone. At the very least no one would be calling me a lesbian or Ikea Girl again. And Shelly would have been sick with jealousy. But no, I'd turned him down.

'****!!!'

FRIDAY APRIL 2ND

'Just imagine, Kelly Ann,' Liz said, trying to comfort me, 'when word gets out you've actually *knocked back* the school's total sex god, everyone's going to think you're, like, beyond cool. Bet you'll have every fit guy for miles around desperate to date you.'

'Don't need loads of fit guys. Just one, so people stop going on about me being weird and leave me alone. And I could have had that.'

'Well, why don't you try explaining things to Michael then? Tell him you thought it was an April fool's joke. Might work.'

Spotted Michael heading off to the toilets at lunch time. Wouldn't have been surprised if his groupies had followed him there, but fortunately even they must have decided that was a bit OTT so I was able to catch him on his own as he came out again.

Took a deep breath and marched up to him. Thought he might just ignore me but he didn't. Instead he looked at me in a kind of hurt way and said, 'Hi. You wanted to talk to me?'

I stared at his gorgeous film-star face and gazed into his deep green eyes, then I squeaked, 'Aayah-sh-sh. I, um, dunno . . . um.'

It was hopeless. Michael gave me a bored look, shrugged and walked away.

Oh God. Never thought I'd have anything in common with Shelly but, unfortunately, this one time I did.

MONDAY APRIL 5TH

Didn't notice any fit guys paying me much attention. Did notice a new graffiti message in the girls' toilets that said KELLY ANN IS DEFINITELY A LES.

Brilliant. This month was not starting out too well. Still, at least since Liz is not going out with Peter any more, I can stay over at her place Saturday and won't have to endure the company of my sister and her nerd, who have pointedly told me they intend to stay in. I mean, why can't they go out clubbing and getting totally wasted like normal people their age?

After school I went to see our school team play Shawbridge, who we beat last year by a crushing six–nil and who've since vowed revenge. Rumour has it they're better now, with a lot of new players, but I think we'll still win.

Liz reluctantly agreed to come with me even though

'watching a crowd of idiot boys kicking a ball about in the mud' was not her idea of fun.

I was surprised to see Linda and her friends Beth and Sue there, as I thought they were about as keen on football as Liz; however, from the remarks I overheard when I passed them on my way back from the toilet, it soon became clear why they'd come.

'Mmmm, isn't he gorgeous?'

'Oh yeah, he's OK, but look at the other one – the goalie – now he's hot.'

Wouldn't have been so bad if Beth and Sue weren't talking about Shawbridge boys, although Linda only seemed to have eyes for Chris. Hmm, the rumours about her fancying Chris must be true. Don't think Chris knows though, or if he does he's not interested.

Our team won easily, three–nil. I like watching football but I'd much rather be playing. I've asked Mr Ferguson twice this term to give me a trial but he's always found some excuse not to. It's just totally sexist and so unfair. I'm as good as any boy. Better than most. That's it: I'm going to see Ferguson again and force him to take me seriously.

TUESDAY APRIL 6TH

Found Ferguson at lunch time. I knew he was supposed to be taking the sixth-year boys for a cross-country run this lunch time as they are training for a charity marathon, but as usual this meant taking them to the gates of the park and waving them off while he went to the pub for a pint to wait for their return. My plan was to head him off before he got to the pub and speak to him about joining the football team.

I was in luck as he'd stopped for a fag by the park gates. When he saw me he threw the butt away, muttering something about having confiscated it from a pupil and what a filthy habit it was.

Yeah, right. I suppose he must have confiscated the nicotine-stained fingers from a pupil too. He looked annoyed at having his fag break interrupted but I pressed on anyway, begging and pleading to be on the school team.

At first he just said no way, he'd told me before, but I wouldn't let up. He kept looking at his watch, conscious, I suppose, of his lost drinking time, until at last he gave in. 'All right, Kelly Ann. Come to the practice at four o'clock today and I'll give you a trial. Now I've really got to get on with some lesson preparation and important administration.'

At that he hurried off to the pub without even acknowledging my shouted, 'Thanks, Mr Ferguson. Thanks a million. I won't let you down.'

Turned up at the playing field at four. Didn't have any kit so had to play in my usual school clothes and trainers but

I hoped Mr Ferguson would make allowances for that. The whole school team were there doing various exercises and practice stuff, but also keeping an eye on what happened with me. Chris jogged up to wish me a hurried 'Good luck' before moving off again to practise penalty kicks at the other end of the pitch.

I was quite nervous as I hadn't played any football in ages. Used to play five a side with Chris and his pals until Ian, who is over six feet and, as my dad puts it, built like a brick shit house (very well built), fell on me and crushed my ribs. Dad wouldn't let me play again after that but I think he'll be OK about the school team as there's no one as big or clumsy as Ian in it.

Mr Ferguson turned to me and smiled, which was really unlike him and a bit menacing somehow. Then he told me to give him fifty. For a moment I thought he was asking me for money as some sort of joining fee, so I hoped he meant pence and not pounds, but then he pointed to the muddy ground and made it clear he meant push-ups. And he wouldn't accept knees-on-the-ground, girly push-ups, like Miss Paterson, our gym teacher, does, but toe and hand contact only. There was no way I could do this and he knew it, but he made me try anyway. After the tenth push-up I collapsed face down in the mud, so he just barked 'Failed' and started to walk away.

I ran after him. 'Wait, Mr Ferguson, this is just so unfair!' He ignored me and carried on but I managed to get in front of him. I walked backwards facing him, which forced him to slow down. I knew this was a bit cheeky but he'd been just *so* unfair and I wasn't going to let him get away with it, teacher or not.

'You're not being fair,' I gasped. 'I'm not unfit. I'm not. I can do the splits. Look.' I did a perfect splits right there in front of him so that he nearly tripped over me. I scrambled up again. 'I bet no one else on this pitch could do that. And anyway, no one needs to do press-ups to play a game of football.'

'No one needs to do the ruddy splits either,' Mr Ferguson pointed out. 'But OK, fair enough. Let's have a football test instead.'

He dropped a ball at my feet and told me to take it to one of the goal posts. Then he instructed me to kick it as far as I could. If it got to the other goal I was in. He gave me three tries but there was no way I was powerful enough. I argued with him some more but he wouldn't listen, just called Osman and Chris over. He told Osman to 'give him fifty', and right away, even though he is small and skinny like me, Osman dropped to the ground and did fifty press-ups, no bother. Osman said, 'Sorry, Kelly Ann.'

Then Mr Ferguson told Chris to kick the ball to the other goal. At first Chris kicked it way short but Mr Ferguson just barked, 'Stop fannying about like a big girl's blouse and kick the ruddy ball or you'll be off the team faster than you can say "Please, sir, that's no' fair." '

No one seemed surprised at a teacher using this sort of

language as apparently Mr Ferguson has said that his outside school hours work is voluntary so he'll talk any sodding way he ruddy well wants and if anyone doesn't like it they can just sod off.

Chris kicked the ball to the other net, then muttered, 'Sorry, Kelly Ann.'

At this Mr Ferguson turned to me and said, 'What part of the word no don't you understand?'

It was hopeless. Ferguson wasn't ever going to let me on the team. Looks like I'm never going to succeed at boy stuff. But I'm useless at girl stuff too, like getting boyfriends. Brilliant.

WEDNESDAY APRIL 7TH

Liz's dad has found out that she was going out with Peter 'behind his back', so has grounded her and docked her pocket money for a month. He says the month is to reflect the amount of time she'd lied to him about Peter. Actually it was five weeks but Liz wisely didn't correct him.

I've told Liz I'll save up from my allowance to pay back Chris, then she can give me the money when she starts getting pocket money again.

Was feeling bored today so when Rebecca invited me over to her house after school, I agreed. Her two best friends, Debbie and Nicola, came too.

Rebecca's got a really cute hamster called Ben. Found myself spending most of the time playing with Ben as all Rebecca and her friends wanted to do was talk about make-up and boys.

In an effort to change the subject I asked if anyone had heard Smashed to Pieces' latest album. They all had – though instead of talking about the music, which was really good, they all started on about the boys in the band and which one was the hottest. There's a new guy now called Jason Donnelly and he's got a fantastic voice, but all they could talk about was how he looked and whether he was fitter than Zach the drummer and Matt the lead guitarist. They agreed he was – except for Debbie, who is 'in love' with Matt.

No, really, she's totally obsessed with him – even knows his shoe size, birth weight and rising sign. All her school books are covered with pictures of him and she's had his face lasered onto her knickers. Mental.

Oh God – except for Liz, can't help finding girls' company boring now. I mean, for God's sake, what did it matter what these guys in the band looked like? It wasn't as though any of us would ever have a chance of meeting them, never mind dating them. Most girls my age are just so stupid.

THURSDAY APRIL 8TH

Liz's dad has told my dad that I was Liz's alibi with that 'wee shite' Peter so Dad has grounded me and docked my pocket money for a month, which I think is totally over the top and completely unfair. I wasn't the one having any fun after all. Honestly, parents are such copycats sometimes.

Looks like Angela and Graham are going to have the pleasure of my company again on Saturday. Also looks like Chris is going to have to wait a while for his football boots. Just as well he's patient.

THURSDAY APRIL 15TH

Liz's mum says it's all very well Liz's dad saying she's grounded for a month but he's off to London with his work for the next fortnight and won't have to share the house with a moaning teenager 24/7 so her grounding is lifted. But if Liz so much as speaks to a boy without getting her parents' written permission first she'll be sent to a nunnery for the rest of her life whether she's Catholic or not.

Mum says there's no way she's putting up with a weekend of me moping around the house with a face like a buffalo with piles so my grounding's lifted but I'd better not tell any more lies or she'd batter me up and down the house.

She did seem pretty desperate to get rid of me so I decided to push it a bit. 'Thanks, Mum, but I'll just be staying in tonight all the same as I've no money to do anything.'

Mum threw a tenner at me. 'Away to the pictures or something and take your moaning face out of my sight.'

Really, sometimes my mum isn't too bad. Called Liz telling her that Mum had given me money to go out – did she want to come with me? At first, instead of being pleased, she went on about how bad it was for me that my mum was not consistent about sanctions (yeah, like her mum was) and how this would negatively affect my psychological development, but when I told her I'd enough for both of us she quickly changed her mind. After all, as she said, adult human beings' behaviour was not always fair, consistent or rational so this would help me learn to deal with the flawed nature of humanity and so really Mum was teaching me a valuable lesson. Liz would be ready in half an hour.

As it turned out though, Liz's mum had also given in over pocket money withdrawal when she heard mine had caved in (sometimes the copycat behaviour works to our advantage) so as well as going to the pictures we were able to afford a bucket of toffee popcorn, a pound of pick-'n'-mix plus a hot dog and two large Cokes, although Liz had Diet Coke as she is trying to lose weight.

MONDAY APRIL 19TH

Liz and I were talking to Gary about the film we'd seen last night. Gary said he'd wanted to see that film too and had suggested it to Chris but he'd been broke and Gary hadn't wanted to go by himself. We should have called him.

Gary looked at us. 'Why have your faces gone all red? It isn't a dirty film, is it? Bloody hell, if I'd known that I'd have loaned Chris the money to go with me.'

Oh God, felt so guilty. So did Liz, though she later pretended she didn't.

'Of course I don't feel guilty,' she said. 'Guilt is a negative, useless emotion. Well, not totally useless, I suppose. Without it we'd be psychopaths and cool about slaughtering innocent people, then eating pizza and watching *Doctor Who* straight after. But we've not done anything like that. Slaughtering people, I mean.'

'We should have paid some money back to Chris, Liz,' I said miserably. 'How much have you got left?'

'Twenty-six p,' Liz replied, flushing. *Knew she felt guilty.* 'You?'

I looked in my purse and checked my pockets but I knew the answer anyway. 'Twelve p. That makes, um, thirty-eight p. Not much point in giving that to Chris now.'

'Hmm, no. But we could donate it to charity.'

'How does that help Chris?'

'It doesn't, but doing a selfless good deed will help us feel better – er, less guilty.'

'So how is it selfless then?'

'You're right. Let's buy a Freddo to cheer ourselves up. Chocolate contains mood-enhancing chemicals, you know.'

'OK.'

FRIDAY APRIL 23RD

Liz's gran has come down to stay over for the weekend and as usual on these visits she gave Liz money to buy herself 'something nice'. Normally Liz would have spent all of it that day but this time, as we were walking home from school, she held the thirty pounds out to me and said, 'Take it quick, Kelly Ann, before I change my mind. Don't want to feel guilty about Chris again. Guilt is a very negative emotion, you know; it can lead to feelings of self-hatred.'

I reached for the money but Liz was still holding it in a tight grasp.

'I would probably try to blot out these feelings,' she continued, 'by abusing alcohol and drugs. Of course, this would eventually only make me feel worse and I would be drawn into a vicious downward spiral of guilt, shame and addiction so that finally the only way out was suicide.

'Of course, if Chris found out he was responsible for my death he'd feel guilty too, which would lead to feelings of self-hatred and—'

I yanked the money from Liz's grasp. 'Thanks, Liz, I'll see Chris gets this.'

SATURDAY APRIL 24TH

Called Chris today with the good news that I could return the money I borrowed. Then I said, 'How about we go to the shops today and I'll help you choose a pair? Maybe we could get a burger for lunch while we're there, then—'

'Sorry, Kelly Ann, I can't today. I'm, erm, going to the pictures. Maybe some other time.'

'Even better,' I said. 'Wasn't really in the mood for shopping anyway. A movie's a much better idea.'

'I'm, um, going with a friend.'

'Yeah, so? That's cool.' I laughed. 'I don't mind Gary or Ian coming.'

'She's a girl.'

'Oh.'

I put the phone down. Don't know why I should feel so surprised and depressed but I do somehow. Just wish my friends wouldn't keep changing all the time and would just stay like they've always been. It's annoying. And scary.

WEDNESDAY MAY 5TH

Chris's girlfriend isn't Linda like I'd thought, but Emily, a girl in Chris's geography class who lives near Liz. She's small and slim like me but has bigger boobs (doesn't everyone!). Unlike me she's a really girly type who wears heart-shaped pink earrings, covers her jotters in shiny lilac paper and brings her Tampax to school in a special flowery silk bag that smells of lavender. I suppose she's nice looking, but other than that I don't know what Chris sees in her. Neither does Linda, who is rumoured to be gutted, although she's pretending not to care. Not very successfully.

I still find the idea of Chris having a girlfriend wrong somehow. Maybe she isn't really a girlfriend but just a girl who he's got friendly with.

SATURDAY MAY 8TH

Was skateboarding home from Liz's when I spotted Chris snogging Emily on her doorstep. Surprised, I stopped and gawped at them. It just looked so weird somehow. I must have been staring at them for a while before Chris noticed me and broke away from her, embarrassed. When Emily saw me she looked annoyed and shouted over at me, 'Hasn't anyone ever told you it's rude to stare?'

Felt my face flush as I hurriedly skateboarded off. Oh God, I must have looked like a pervert or something but it had just been so strange seeing Chris snog a girl like that. I always kind of thought he would be too, well, intelligent and serious to like snogging, but he must do. I mean, she hadn't been forcing him and he hadn't looked as though he was going to throw up exactly. No, he'd been enjoying it.

I suppose she must be his girlfriend and not just a girl who's a friend. Still seems so wrong somehow.

FRIDAY MAY 14TH

Haven't seen or even spoken to Chris all week. I suppose he's too busy now he's got Emily. They seem to be super-glued to each other these days. So much for his promise always to be friends no matter what.

MONDAY MAY 17TH

Spotted Chris at break today as I was hurrying off to get my Cadbury's Creme Egg from the newsagent's. For once he wasn't with Emily. She probably had to go to the toilet – the only place she can't take him along. He saw me too and waved over to me but I pretended I hadn't noticed and walked on.

'Wait, Kelly Ann!' he called.

I slowed down a bit and he caught up with me.

'I'm in a rush, Chris. What is it?'

'Nothing really, but yeah, I was just thinking, the thing is, I haven't got my football boots yet. Been, um, too busy.' He reddened. 'So maybe we could go into town and buy them like we talked about. And, you know, go for pizza afterwards or something.'

Was tempted. It would be so nice to meet up with Chris again without his barnacle stuck to him. But no, he was probably just being polite as he seems to want to be with Emily all the time now, so I muttered a quick 'Yeah, maybe,' then turned to go but he caught my arm.

'So is next Saturday OK for you? Say one o'clock?'

'No, look, it's OK. Emily can go with you. She seems to do everything with you these days.'

'She doesn't know anything about football boots – or football in fact. Besides I, er, I just want to see you. Spend time with you again. We're still friends, aren't we?'

I looked up at his face. Earnest and familiar. Chris

was staring at me anxiously. 'I've missed you, Kelly Ann.'

'OK, next Saturday then,' I decided.

'Great. So, you want to come to the gym with me now? They've got volleyball set up.'

'No, I gotta go now, Chris. Break's almost done and I haven't had my Creme Egg yet. And you know how bad-tempered I am when I don't get my Creme Egg.' I made a scary, murderous face, then did an impression of the *Psycho* film's stabbing-in-the-shower scene by holding an imaginary knife up high above him and bringing it savagely down again and again while mimicking the bloodcurdling, dramatic music – '*Hink! Hink! Hink!*'

Chris clutched himself, staggered about, then sank to the ground, pretending to be the victim of my homicidal assault. We were both doubled up, laughing helplessly, when Emily crept up on us and looked at me like I was a piece of dog turd attached to her shoe. Decided it was time I went. Honestly, don't know what Chris sees in her. Except that she's very nice looking when not scowling like a vampire bat that's been force-fed lemons, I can't see what the attraction is.

SATURDAY MAY 22ND

Was really looking forward to seeing Chris today. God, it had been so long since we'd hung out together just by ourselves without his stupid girlfriend trying to snog his face off every time he opened his mouth.

But no such luck. When I met Chris at Central Station, there she was standing with him.

'Oh, hi, Kelly Ann,' she said, all casual friendly even though we've hardly spoken to each other before. 'Just decided at the last minute I might as well tag along with you two as I'd nothing planned for this afternoon. You don't mind, do you?'

Yeah, right. Last minute my arse. It was obvious she must have spent all morning getting ready. Her hair, normally quite frizzy like mine, had been straightened so that it was totally smooth and hung down to her shoulders like a gleaming curtain. Plus she was wearing full make-up, including foundation, three different shades of eye shadow, mascara, lipstick, lip-liner and gloss.

And she was dressed like she was going to a party or something. Pink high-heeled shoes (for trailing round the shops – I ask you!), a white crop top and a very short pink skirt which sat low down on her hips so that you could see she'd a matching thong. Don't know what Chris thinks of short skirts, high heels and thongs, since it wasn't the sort of thing we ever discussed, but I hoped he'd be too intelligent to be impressed by them.

Really wished she wasn't here today, but what could I say? *Yeah, actually, I do mind so just push off?* Or maybe, *If it's all the same to you I'd prefer to talk to my friend without someone trying to hoover his tonsils every five minutes.*

Instead I muttered, 'Yeah, no worries,' like the total coward I am.

Chris said nothing but gave me an apologetic glance when she wasn't looking, like the total coward *he* is. This was going to be a long, dismal afternoon.

We went to the sports shop first. Couldn't help noticing on the way, and in the shop, how loads of boys looked at Emily admiringly and glanced at Chris enviously. No one looked at me at all, like I was invisible or something.

Stared at myself in the shop mirror. No, definitely not invisible, but maybe it would be better if I were as I had to admit I wasn't looking my best.

My trainers were old and grey. My jeans were frayed at the bottom, which might have looked quite stylish if most of the hem on the left leg hadn't worked its way off, so that it trailed in a dirty rope along the floor. The slight tear on both knees which had looked fine just a couple of weeks ago had widened to two gaping holes through which my bony knees poked unattractively.

At least my striped T-shirt looked OK – except that I appeared only to have only one breast as the toilet paper I'd stuffed down my left bra cup had fallen out sometime when I wasn't looking. Might not have been quite so noticeable if the stripes over my left breast weren't so obviously straighter than the tissue-stuffed right one. Wished now that I'd at least worn a plain top.

Fortunately I'd my baseball cap on, so although I

hadn't washed my hair this morning – it somehow managed to be both greasy and frizzy at the same time – only the bits that stuck out the bottom could be seen.

Still, yeah, maybe I should have made more of an effort today.

When Chris tried on the football boots Emily went on about how fabulous they looked on him. I mean, for God's sake, they're football boots – i.e. boots to play football in – not the latest 'must have' fashion statement.

Chris said, 'What do you think, Kelly Ann?'

'Ooooh,' I said, 'they're just sooo you, Chris. Totally cool. But, erm, I'm not sure about the colour. I mean, black is rather last season, don't you think?'

'Stop it, Kelly Ann,' Chris said, but he was smiling. 'What do you really think?'

I examined them seriously now. 'Yeah, looks like a good fit.' I felt the material. 'Flexible but strong and water resistant too. Go for it.'

By the time we'd queued and paid I was starving but Emily wanted to look in Accessorize for a bag. I waited outside, thinking she couldn't take more than five minutes to find something. After all, you don't have to try on a bag to see if it fits or anything. All you really need to decide is whether you want a big bag to carry lots of stuff or a small bag to carry not very much. Then maybe pick your favourite colour.

But no such luck. After fifteen minutes I was still waiting so, fed up with standing, I hunkered down on the pavement with my back leaning against the wall, which was much more comfortable until a seagull shat on my head. Fortunately most of it went on my cap, which I took off and put on the ground in front of me while I tried to wipe the bird mess off my hair and shoulder with a bit of tissue I'd surreptitiously removed from my right bra cup. At least I would be symmetrical if flat-chested again.

Had almost finished when an old lady with large thick glasses approached me and dropped a 10p into my hat. 'Go get yourself a cup of tea, son.' Oh my God, I really should have made more of an effort today. I was about to return the money and explain I wasn't a homeless tramp – or a boy, come to that – but just waiting for friends, when Emily and Chris came out of the shop. Didn't want them to know what had happened, especially not Emily, so just mumbled a quick 'Thanks' and stood up. Felt bad about practically stealing from an old lady, but it was only 10p after all and not nearly enough for a cup of tea anywhere. Don't old people know about inflation?

Finally we went for pizza but Emily chattered all the way through the meal, mostly about her bag purchase (very interesting – not) so I hardly got to talk to Chris at all. Afterwards she wanted to do some more shopping and told me I was welcome to tag along. So it's me tagging along now, is it? Well, no thanks, especially as, though her voice was all nice and friendly, her narrowed eyes made it obvious my company was about as welcome as a head-lice infestation.

Headed off home, depressed. On the way I passed a beggar, so, feeling guilty about keeping the old lady's donation, I dropped the 10p I'd been given earlier into his outstretched torn polystyrene cup. Wish I hadn't bothered as he slagged me off.

He said, 'Whit's this supposed to be fur, hen, if ye don't mind me asking?'

Without thinking I just repeated what the old lady had said: 'A cup of tea.'

'A cup of tea? Aye, right. This widnae buy me a cigarette butt, never mind tea. Or the pint that I'm pure dying fur by the way. Ye widnae happen to have the price of a pint on ye by any chance?'

'I don't think alcohol is a good idea,' I replied, genuinely concerned. 'It's very bad for your health.'

However, my advice just seemed to annoy him. He put on a false snooty voice and said, 'Awctually, yir ladyship, alkihole in modirition is viry good fir one's hilth.' Then he laughed wheezily. 'No' that I've ever tried it, mind. Moderation onyway.' He tossed the 10p coin back at me. 'Here, hen, ye look as though ye need this mair than me. Away and buy yersel' a new pair o' troosers.'

Bloody nerve. Still, it has to be said he *was* probably better dressed than me. Today anyway.

When I got back home I went to my room and examined myself in the mirror again. Now, OK, I suppose it could be said I needed some decent clothes, a top-class hairdresser and possibly breast implants, but I wasn't really ugly, was I? My face was OK. Definitely. And at least I wasn't plagued by spots like some people in my school. OK, sometimes I get a few but they usually clear up pretty quickly if I zap them with Clearasil. Yeah, I'd really nice skin actually. Well, except for that one tiny spot on my forehead, but so what?

SUNDAY MAY 23RD

Correction. Six rather large spots on my forehead, two on my chin and a pimple at the end of my nose. Brilliant. Just when I'm starting to care how I look, I turn into pizza-face.

Decided to have a rummage in my sister's room for her Clearasil. She hasn't had any spots for ages now but I know she's too mean to throw anything away. Sure enough, I found the bottle in her make-up bag in her chest of drawers. Also found condoms. Gross. I suppose this must mean she does actually do it with her sad boyfriend Graham – or at least intends to anyway.

I stared at the condom packet. Maybe there was some other explanation. Perhaps she's keeping them for a friend, but then why would she? Or maybe she planned to use them for something other than having sex, like, erm, a disposable shower hat for instance. Yeah, could be.

* * *

Put this point to Liz later that night when she came round, but she was sceptical.

'Honestly, Liz, I've heard there are loads of uses for condoms other than sex.'

'Such as?'

'Such as, well, um, guerrilla fighters. Yeah, fighters in places like the Amazon jungle use them to keep bandages and rifle butts waterproof if they have to wade through rivers and swamps and stuff.'

'Hmm, suppose so, but I can't see Angela wading through the Amazonian jungle. It's too messy for her. She won't even use the school swimming pool in case boys have peed in it.'

'Yuck. Do boys pee in the swimming pool? No, don't tell me, Liz.' I put my hands over my ears. 'I won the pool bubble-blowing competition last year. I so don't want to know.'

When I was sure Liz wasn't going to say any more about the pool thing, I took my hands from my ears and continued, 'Anyway, OK, I'm not saying Angela uses condoms to keep guns and bandages waterproof. I'm just saying the fact that she has condoms in her drawers doesn't mean she definitely uses them for sex.'

'Of course it doesn't,' Liz agreed. 'Maybe she cuts the ends off and uses them for, um, leg warmers or—'

'Leg warmers? I don't think—'

'Or,' Liz continued, 'wet suits for leprechauns. Yeah, that's the most likely.'

I giggled but Liz had made her point. The truth is, my sister is almost certainly not a virgin any more. It's horrible to think what she and her nerd boyfriend had been up to behind my back in my own home. Still, as Liz said, it's probably better behind my back than *not* behind my back.

MONDAY MAY 24TH

Spots have not faded and in fact are even worse. Maybe the Clearasil isn't going to work any more. I know it's only a day, but still.

Saw Emily with Chris at lunch time today. Couldn't stop thinking about Saturday and how all those boys kept looking at her. And how Chris looked at her too. I wasn't jealous of some girly idiot like Emily, was I?

WEDNESDAY MAY 26TH

Didn't want to go to school today because of spots but Mum said I had to and no one looks at me anyway.

Aunt Kate says beauty is only skin deep, whatever that's supposed to mean. Yeah, maybe I've got gorgeous guts and fabulous-looking liver and kidneys, but who's going to see them?

THURSDAY MAY 27TH

Scotland play Italy in Milan tonight and Chris has asked me and some other pals over to his place to watch the match on Sky. Am so excited. Hope we won't be totally humiliated though: Italy are just so good, but at least no one is expecting us to win. Imagine we did though. OK, I know it would take a miracle but they do happen, don't they?

Chris's parents will be watching the game at the pub so we'll have the house to ourselves. Yay.

Went over just after seven. Gary and Ian were already there. Unfortunately so was Emily, who was dressed all in pink and wearing false eyelashes so long and thick that she had to squint to see out of them. Come to think of it, Emily always wears false eyelashes, even at swimming lessons, but never ones as big and bushy as these; she looked like she'd glued two furry caterpillars to her lids.

Chris's parents were just getting ready to leave. His dad has said we can help ourselves to snacks and drinks but if we touch the beer we're dead. Chris's mum repeated the warning and added that she'd be popping back at half-time to check up on us. Hmmm, nice to be trusted.

Since Chris's dad is a police detective, even Gary isn't going to chance it.

'He'll probably breathalyse us then dust every bottle for prints,' he moaned.

'Won't need to,' Ian said. He turned to look at Chris. 'Bet your mum could probably tell just by looking at our pupils or something. Better stick to Irn Bru.'

Chris's mum is a nurse. It's just as well Chris is super smart or he'd never get away with anything with parents like that.

After his parents left we switched on the TV and chatted for a bit while we waited for the game to start. I tried to talk to Emily but she just gave me a tight smile about as welcoming as a shark's grin, then ignored me. Don't understand why she dislikes me so much. OK, we don't have anything in common, but I've never done anything nasty to her.

Don't understand either why she agreed to watch a game she'd obviously zero interest in. Once the match started she spent most of the time playing with her hair, re-doing her make-up, or asking Chris for the umpteenth time to explain the offside rule to her, then giggling when she didn't get it, like this was cute instead of totally moronic. Mind you, from the indulgent, superior smiles the boys gave her, maybe they *did* think it was cute.

They weren't so pleased when Italy scored and she cheered by mistake.

Just before half-time she picked up her make-up bag and disappeared into the bathroom, probably to brush her eyelashes or something equally important – then it happened: Scotland scored an equalizer. Couldn't believe it. I mean, Italy has the best defenders in the whole world. Scoring a goal against them is like trying to break into a tank with a feather duster. But we did it!

We all leaped up at once, screaming and waving our arms in the air. 'Goal! It's a goal!' Then we were hugging each other, laughing and screaming. Chris lifted me off the ground and spun round with me as we started chanting, 'Easy, eeeaaasy!'

Just then, Emily returned, scowling like a gargoyle. At first I thought she was gutted at missing the goal but soon realized it was just me and Chris she was glaring at, like she'd just caught us snogging or something.

What an idiot. I mean, Scotland had just scored against Italy, for God's sake. In Milan! Even Ian and Gary were hugging, and yeah, Ian had lifted Gary off his feet too and was swinging round with him.

Chris quickly set me down. It was half-time so I decided to go to the toilet and leave Emily and Chris to sort things out.

Just before I got to the living-room door Emily called after me, 'Oh, Kelly Ann?'

I turned round. Her gargoyle glare had gone but she still stared at me with eyes so narrow her lashes nearly stuck together. She waved her make-up bag at me and said, 'Want to borrow my concealer for your spots? You've got quite a big one on your chin.'

Before I could answer she put her bag down again.

'Oh, I forgot, you don't worry about your looks, do you? Must say, I really admire that. It would be fantastic to be so totally confident that you don't care how awful you look.'

'What's that supp—?'

'Not that you do, of course. Look awful, I mean.'

Yeah, right.

I trudged off to the bathroom and examined my face. She was right about the spot on my chin. It was practically the size of a grape. And there was a crop of smaller ones growing on my forehead. Oh God, I did look awful. I wasn't stupid and vain like Emily but I didn't want to look like my face was erupting either.

When I came out, Chris's mum was just opening the outside door and coming into the hall. She was smiling, but when she saw me she frowned and said, 'What's the matter, Kelly Ann? I thought you'd be happy Scotland equalized.'

'Yeah, I am, but, well, it's these.' I pointed to my spots. 'They're worse than ever, no matter what I do.'

I thought she'd just nod sympathetically, or maybe even tell me not to moan because I didn't have a horrible disease like cancer or something, like the people she works with, but she was really nice. She took me back into the bathroom and handed me a tub of blue paste stuff, which she told me to put on my face every day for a month, leaving it on as long as possible. 'It doesn't work for everyone, Kelly Ann, but it's worth a try.'

When we went back into the living room, Emily was practically in tears. Turned out one of her false eyelashes had come unstuck and fallen into Gary's Irn Bru. He fished it out and handed the soggy thing to her but it was ruined.

Chris's mum wasn't as nice to Emily as she'd been with me. 'It's not the end of the world, Emily,' she said. 'Just take the other one off.'

Emily did look stupid with just one false-lashed eye but, bloody hell, now I knew why she always wore fake ones. Her own lashes were stubby and so sparse you could count each one.

She insisted on going home so, with a sigh, Chris's mum offered her a lift back even though that would make her late back to the pub for the start of the second half.

But I had a fabulous time after that. It was great to be with Chris again without Emily spoiling things. Even when Italy scored again, winning two–one, it didn't totally spoil things. It had been a fantastic game and we'd played really well against a shit-hot team. I even forgot about my spots.

When I got back home though, I put on the blue paste stuff that Chris's mum had given me. I looked a bit like the Cookie Monster, but if it works it will be worth it.

FRIDAY MAY 28TH

Went to watch our football team play Elmwood after school. Emily was there – I guess because Chris was playing, since I now know for sure she's not remotely interested in football. It was a great game and we won three–nil but Emily looked bored. She also threw me a dirty look when I talked to Chris afterwards.

Honestly.

I ignored her furious scowl which, if she'd only known, made her face look as attractive as a chewed toffee, and continued talking to Chris, but he seemed uneasy and cut me off: 'I'd best go get changed, Kelly Ann.'

Thinking it over, I was quite annoyed with Chris and called him tonight to tell him so but he wouldn't listen.

'Look, Kelly Ann, Emily's my girlfriend. It's only natural she gets jealous sometimes if I talk to other girls.'

'Jealous? But that's stupid! Totally mental. Just tell her—'

'Maybe,' Chris interrupted, 'but that's how it is. She's no different from most other girls. Look, people change. Move on. It's part of growing up.'

'Yeah, well, if growing up means ignoring your best friends, then you can count me out,' I said, slamming the phone down.

Chris called back but I refused to talk to him. I'd let

him stew for a while before accepting his hopefully grovelling apologies. Wish he'd get rid of Emily. Why can't he see she's just a stupid, boring girl who stops him having any fun?

SATURDAY MAY 29TH

Was on my way to Liz's when I bumped into Emily, for once not with Chris. I just nodded hello and was going to walk on when she surprised me by smiling and saying, 'Oh, hi, Kelly Ann. You know, this is weird, I was just thinking about you.'

'About me?'

'Yeah. Actually, this is great because I was kind of hoping to get the chance to talk to you about things.'

'What things?' I asked, puzzled.

'Well, erm, I hope you won't take this the wrong way, Kelly Ann, but the thing is, you see, Chris is getting a bit embarrassed with you always hanging around him now.'

I glared at her. 'That's rubbish. Don't believe you.'

'It's true.' She paused and stared at me in a concerned kind of way. 'Oh God, don't tell me he hasn't said *anything* to you? Not even kind of hinted?'

I flushed, remembering the phone call yesterday. Is that what Chris had been trying to tell me? Surely he wouldn't do that to me. He was my best friend, after all.

She waited, obviously expecting me to say something, but now I wasn't sure what to think any more.

When I didn't reply she went on, 'I mean, he likes you and everything. But, you know, he feels it's kinda time to move on. No offence.'

She paused again. Still I said nothing.

'Oh God,' she said, 'I hope I haven't upset you.'

Felt my eyes start to tear up but blinked them back. I would *not* let her see me cry. At last I said a bit shakily, 'Why didn't he tell me himself if that's really how he feels?'

'Oh, you know boys.' She laughed. 'Total cowards about stuff like this. And anyway, Chris is such a nice guy. He wouldn't want to hurt anyone. Asked me to have a word with you, sort of girl to girl.'

'Oh.'

'So, you OK then?'

'Oh God, yeah, of course.'

'Cool. You know, Chris was convinced you'd be gutted.' She chuckled. 'Boys. They're so big-headed. Always thinking they're way more important to us girls than they really are.'

'Yeah.' I attempted to laugh too but it came out more like a maniacal cackle so I stopped abruptly. 'Actually, the truth is, I was meaning to speak to Chris about this myself.'

'You were?'

'Yeah, um, in fact I was just going to say it was time we

sort of cooled the friendship a bit. I mean, we're not kids any more and, well, him always being around is kind of putting boys off asking me out and stuff.'

'Yeah, totally. It must do.' She smiled at me. 'So, actually, you must really be relieved about all this.'

'God, yeah.'

'So, do you want me to tell Chris what you said? You know, how you were just going to ask him to stop hanging out with you? Or do you want to tell him yourself?'

'No, you do it. It's fine.'

She looked at her watch. 'God, is that the time? I've got to get a move on. I'm meant to be meeting Chris in ten minutes. It's been great talking to you. See ya.'

'Yeah, nice talking to you too.'

Yeah, bloody fantastic.

SUNDAY MAY 30TH

Chris came round to my house this afternoon. When I opened the door he didn't come in and I didn't ask him. His face was grim. Hmm, maybe he was annoyed that I'm not as gutted as he thought I'd be. Honestly, Emily's right. Most boys are so up themselves.

'Emily told me what you said. Did you mean it? You don't want us to be friends any more.'

'Oh, that,' I said casually. 'No, of course we're friends. I mean, we haven't fallen out or anything. It's just that, yeah, we've been spending too much time together. And, you know, I'm busy with other things these days. You are too.'

'I haven't done something to upset you?'

'God, no. You didn't upset me at all. It's cool. Just, you know, time to move on.'

He was silent for a moment, then he said, sounding a bit puzzled, 'So you're still talking to me?'

'Yeah, course I am. God, we're not primary kids falling out over nothing any more.' I looked at my watch. Of course, I didn't actually have anything planned, but looking at my watch wasn't lying. 'Anyway, glad that's out the way. So' – I put on a pleasant, formal voice – 'was there anything else?'

'Well, um, no, I suppose not.'

'Fine.' I stretched my lips into a smile. 'See ya.'

Then I closed the door. I climbed the stairs to my bedroom feeling very pleased with how I'd handled the whole thing. Calm, mature, dignified.

Passed Angela coming down the stairs. She said, 'Aren't you going to take that blue stuff of your face yet? You've had it on for more than an hour now.'

Oh God.

FRIDAY JUNE 4TH

Chris and I are still friends. Sort of. We talk to each other at school and he called me once to remind me about a Man U versus Chelsea game on the TV that night. It's all very mature and civilized but nothing's the same any more.

Difficult now to imagine that he was once my closest friend and that I shared all my secrets with him. Well, not all my secrets of course, like the fact I have to shove toilet paper down even a trainer bra to get it to fit properly and that I still can't use tampons, no matter how many times I try, because the diagrams they give you along with the instructions are so totally useless and look nothing like me. Not that I actually know what I look like down there – I'm not a contortionist – but I'm pretty sure no one really looks like the diagrams. So, yeah, not *all* my secrets, *obviously*, but still lots of stuff.

Now it's all kind of false, polite conversation. Seems

unreal somehow. If this is being grown up like Mum wants me to be, then it sucks.

Gary is having a sort of party at his house tomorrow and has invited loads of people. I say 'sort of party' as Gary's parents don't know about it – they are going to be at a dinner-dance thing in Edinburgh and won't be back until around one in the morning. I've told Gary I don't want to go. Just don't fancy the idea of any more polite conversation with Chris – or Emily come to that, as they are both likely to be there – although that's not what I said to Gary of course.

Liz can't go as she's been grounded this weekend because her mum found a bit of leftover Christmas pudding and two sausage rolls from the New Year party mouldering under her bed, which she says is proof that Liz hasn't cleaned her room properly for nearly six months.

Her mum seems to have forgotten that they were in Aberdeen over the Christmas holidays last time so the stuff was from the Christmas and New Year before that. Liz didn't point this out and is hoping her mum won't remember.

SATURDAY JUNE 5TH

Gary called me again, trying to get me to change my mind.

'C'mon, Kelly Ann, it'll be great.'

'No thanks. Like I said, I'm busy,' I lied.

'OK, yeah, right. But, erm, do you know if Rebecca's definitely coming? Has she said anything about it to you?'

God, hasn't he given up on this yet? He's wasting his time with Rebecca – she's only going because she fancies Ian, who I know for a fact won't be interested in her because of the height thing.

Honestly, life is so complicated once people start to fancy other people (or not) instead of just being friends. Everything was fine until all this 'who's hot and who's not' and 'who wants to snog who or not' started up.

I suppose I should warn Gary and Rebecca that they've almost no chance but they probably wouldn't listen to me.

Instead I just said, 'Yeah, she's definitely coming. But for God's sake don't wear gross tight clothes. Rebecca doesn't like them. And ditch the tsunami hairstyle.'

Gary hung up soon after and I decided to spend the rest of the afternoon on my PlayStation. Yeah, I was glad I wasn't going to the party. I'd have a nice quiet time just doing exactly what I wanted. After all, I was quite capable of amusing myself for one day, wasn't I?

Mum and Dad are at the pub and even Angela and her sad boyfriend have gone to the pictures and won't be back until ten so I'm in by myself. There is absolutely nothing on the TV (all fifty-eight channels), no one is on MSN, and I am just so totally bored. Have been on my PlayStation for hours but I'm sick of it, and anyway my eyes are red and thumbs nearly numb.

To amuse myself, tried seeing if I could drink a bottle of Irn Bru while standing on my head (yes), whether I could do a no-handed cartwheel (no), and counting the number of freckles on my face (sixteen). Decided to join up the freckles with a felt-tip pen to see what kind of pattern they made. Actually a lot like an aeroplane. Hmm, interesting.

Called Gary. He didn't answer for a while, and when he picked up the phone I could hear loud music playing and the sound of people laughing. Had to shout to make myself heard.

'I've changed my mind, Gary – can I come over?'

'Yeah, course.'

'You want me to bring something? I can't bring beer. Dad's only got two cans left so he'd notice.'

'That's OK. Just bring loo paper.'

'Loo paper?'

'Too many girls. Don't know what you lot do with it. OK, don't answer that.'

Quickly splashed some water on my face, put on my favourite pair of jeans and a clean T-shirt, grabbed a couple of toilet rolls and ran off to Gary's.

Loads of people had come so the place was crowded, even the hallway and stairs. Don't suppose holding out two loo rolls was a very classy way to make an entrance, but Rebecca, who'd been locked in the toilet for ten minutes waiting for supplies, was relieved and grateful. So were the people queuing outside.

Noticed that there were almost twice as many girls as boys at the party and I don't think this was accidental. Probably Gary trying to stack the odds in his favour. The music was really good though, so I was soon enjoying myself dancing in the living room with a large group of girls. Most of the boys just hung around watching or drinking beer.

After a while I got thirsty so Rebecca and I went to the kitchen to get some Cokes. When we got back to the living room I spotted Chris and Emily, who must have just arrived, talking to Gary.

They both nodded 'Hi' to me and I nodded back, meaning to ignore them, but Gary waved us over, no doubt so he could chat up Rebecca.

He'd taken my advice about tight clothes but had gone a bit OTT with it: his jeans were so loose and low they exposed nearly all of his pants while the crotch hung down around his knees so that he had to walk like a toddler who'd just wet himself. He'd also dyed his hair purple (Rebecca's favourite colour) and gelled it into spikes.

Rebecca wasn't impressed. As she whispered to me on the way over, 'All he needs is a pair of braces and he'd get a job as a circus clown.'

After a quick 'Hi, girls,' Gary practically ignored me so

he could hit on Rebecca, who kept looking longingly over at Ian (who literally didn't see her as he scanned the room for tall girls), so I was left to make awkward conversation with Chris and Emily. After, oh, about sixty seconds of this I'd had enough, but they didn't move off, so eventually I interrupted Gary's desperate chat-up attempt.

'So, Rebecca,' I said, 'how is Ben? Is he better now or are you going to have to take him to the vet again?'

'No, he's fine now,' Rebecca said happily. 'It was just an abscess, which cleared up with antibiotics. Vet said they're quite common in hamsters.'

'Ugh,' Emily said. 'You own a hamster?' She shuddered. 'They're rodents, aren't they? Like rats. I think rabbits are much nicer. I've got a white rabbit with big floppy ears. He's called Flopsy and he's gorgeous.' She looked up at Chris. 'Isn't he, Chris?'

Chris looked embarrassed, but dutifully nodded his agreement.

Bloody hell. How can Chris fancy someone so totally wet? I looked at Emily's simpering face. 'I'm not that keen on rabbits. Did you know,' I said casually, 'that they eat their own poo?' I glanced at Chris, who was trying to suppress a grin. 'Don't they, Chris?'

'Yeah,' Chris said. 'It's so they can digest their food twice. More efficient use of, um, resources.'

He was grinning openly at me now and I smiled back. Emily's simpering expression vanished and she scowled at me. Then she came closer and stared hard at me.

'Did you know,' she said, 'that you have an aeroplane on your face?'

Oh God.

I checked in the bathroom mirror, and sure enough, there it was still. A very faint but, if you looked closely, definite outline of an aeroplane. Washed my face again, but although I scrubbed until it was red, the ink marks wouldn't come off completely. I'd have to wait until they faded away.

Decided to go home early. On the way back I thought about Emily. She likes to give everyone the impression that she's sweet and delicate like a meringue but I was beginning to think she was as hard as a gobstopper. Maybe I should warn Chris. But no, he probably wouldn't listen. Boys never do.

SUNDAY JUNE 6TH

At least my spots have nearly cleared up. The blue stuff must be working. Feel guilty now about being nasty to Angela when she had an outbreak of acne last year and I called her a pimpled, pilfering piranha. But in a way she had asked for it as she'd eaten my last Creme Egg. Well, OK, they were actually bought by Mum at the supermarket in a pack of three and could possibly therefore be seen as 'family' Creme Eggs, but Angela knows they're my favourite. Still, I vowed never to insult anyone who had spots ever again if God would just make sure mine never came back.

MONDAY JUNE 7TH

Saw Shelly and her friends at lunch time. They were eyeing me and Liz the way a pack of vicious velociraptors size up prey before moving in for the kill, and sure enough they started making their way towards us.

'Oh, Kelly Ann,' Shelly said, 'I hear you and Chris have fallen out.'

'Well, you heard wrong. We're just too busy to hang around together much any more.'

'Oh yeah, that's right. You need some space so all these boys who fancy you can ask you out. Right? So, er, how many so far? Bet you're totally inundated.'

They all giggled like she was really hilarious or something. I glared at her. Then I noticed it. The normally perfect Shelly had a spot. No, several spots. Quite a lot in fact. They were small and mostly disguised with concealer and foundation but still noticeable if you looked closely.

I said, 'Loads actually, but not nearly as many as the number of spots on your face. Yeah. If only I'd got that many boys asking me out I'd be the most popular girl in Scotland. In the whole universe maybe.'

I laughed and we walked away, leaving Shelly fuming. Yes! Felt great for about three seconds until I remembered my promise to God about not slagging anyone off for spots. Oh no. Maybe He would punish me with a plague of spots of my own.

On the way home Liz tried to reason with me. She told me that a guy called Richard Dawkins, who's a totally brilliant genius professor, has proved that God probably doesn't exist, and says people who think that He probably does are probably ignorant or stupid or completely bonkers.

'Honestly, religion's just childish, totally illogical stupid rubbish,' Liz said, stepping onto the busy road to avoid walking under the ladders that stretched over the pavement.

A motorist blasted his horn then shook his fist at her as he swerved to avoid knocking her down. Liz tutted. 'Road rage syndrome. An increasingly common psychological phenomenon.'

I yanked Liz back onto the pavement. 'Get off the road, you idiot.'

She ignored my comment and instead returned to her argument about God and spots. 'Anyway, Kelly Ann, even if He does exist, then someone who created the entire universe – like, *come on*, billions of stars and gazillions of planets – well, He's not going to be bothered about you slagging off Shelly for being spotty, now is He?'

Yeah, it made sense. Surely if God the Creator of the Infinite Universe cared at all about how we humans behaved, then He'd concentrate on really wicked people like rapists or mass murderers. Genghis Khan or Hitler maybe. Not me.

Hoped so anyway.

TUESDAY JUNE 8TH

Spots haven't come back. Maybe Liz and Professor Dawkins are right after all and there is no God; either that or He doesn't care about me. Thank God for that. Drew a face covered in red dots on Shelly's English folder when she went off to the toilet near the end of the period and called it 'Smelly Shelly the Spot Snot'. He he – childish, I know, but very satisfying.

THURSDAY JUNE 10TH

Spoke too soon. The spots are back, even though I'm still using the blue paste, and there are even more than before. So much for Professor Dawkins and his brilliant theories.

Moaned to Liz about it. 'You're wrong, Liz. God does exist and He's got it in for me. Just after I broke my promise and insulted Shelly my spots came back. He's punishing me.'

'Don't be stupid. There's probably some simple explanation. Maybe it's psychosomatic.'

'What's that?' I asked, hoping it wasn't some fatal
disease.

'Well, that's when you think you're going to get spots
so your brain tells your body to make them.'

I gawped at her. 'That's mental, Liz.'

'Not as mental as thinking God gave you spots.'

Maybe Liz is right. Not about the psychosomatic stuff,
but I suppose the spot rash could just be coincidence. I'm
going to keep my promise to God next time though, just
in case.

MONDAY JUNE 14TH

'So, Kelly Ann,' Shelly said halfway through biology, 'I
suppose you're still having trouble fighting off all these
boys who're constantly begging you to go out with them.'

I know I should have just ignored her and walked
away but I was totally fed up with her rubbishing me so
found myself saying, 'No, it's fine actually. I just tell them
I've already got a gorgeous boyfriend, thanks, and I'm not
the kind of slapper who'd cheat on anyone.'

Shelly flushed with annoyance about my reference to
cheating slappers, which she knew was meant for her, but
then her mean little mouth tightened and she said, 'Don't
believe you. Who is this gorgeous boyfriend then?'

'He's, um, called' – I glanced at the poster on the wall showing a family of lions – 'Leo.'

'Leo? I don't know any Leos.'

'He's not at this school. He goes to, um, private school actually. His parents are loaded but he's not a snob. He says he doesn't care if mine are poor. He likes me anyway.'

Oh God, this was getting complicated. What had I done? Fortunately the biology teacher told us all to shut up and get on with our work so I was saved from any more interrogation by Shelly.

TUESDAY JUNE 15TH

Of course word got round the school about the gorgeous new boyfriend I'd been keeping secret, and practically everyone wanted to know about Leo.

Found lies falling out of my mouth like the big ugly toads in the cursed princess fairy tale.

Leo had black hair and deep blue eyes. He played rugby and the electric guitar. We'd met in town when he bumped into me, knocking over my ice-cream cone, so he bought me another. We got talking, and he asked me out. On and on.

On the way home from school Liz got at me. 'For God's sake, Kelly Ann. What are you doing? You're bound to get found out.'

'Oh God, Liz, I don't know. But I can't take it back now. I'll just have to leave it a few days then say we fell out and I dumped him or something. I'll sort something out.'

'Hmm.'

THURSDAY JUNE 17TH

Our first date was to Pizza Hut. We had pepperoni and spicy chicken pizza, with chocolate ice cream to follow. Leo insisted on paying for both of us because he gets fifty pounds pocket money a week and more if he needs it.

We didn't snog on our first date because Leo respects me too much, but after our third date at a proper Italian restaurant with tablecloths and candles, I let him kiss me. Now he can't keep his hands off me he fancies me so much.

The lies are getting easier – it's actually quite fun. Some people are a bit jealous of course, but everyone wants to hear about my perfect boyfriend. I'm starting to really like him too.

FRIDAY JUNE 18TH

'You've got to stop this stupid Leo thing, Kelly Ann,' Liz said. 'You need to focus on finding a real boyfriend.'

'Why? Leo's much better than a real boyfriend.'

'That's mental. How can he be better than a real one?'

'Well, he never tells fart jokes for a start, his room doesn't smell of sweaty socks and he wouldn't ever cheat on me. Bet you don't know any boys like that.'

Liz sighed. 'OK, but there is just one tiny problem with Leo.'

'What?'

'He doesn't exist.'

I shrugged. 'Nobody's perfect.'

SATURDAY JUNE 19TH

Was dreaming about Leo when Liz called to see if I wanted to watch a DVD at her house.

I said, 'Sorry, Liz, Leo and I are going to the pictures tonight.'

'Right, that's it, Kelly Ann. This has gone too far. I'm coming over to sort this out right now.'

'You have to stop this Leo thing, Kelly Ann. It's totally insane.'

'Why? I'm really enjoying it. Leo's fun.'

'It's lying. Which is, well, immoral,' Liz said huffily.

I shrugged.

'It's not good for your psychological health. You could totally lose touch with reality, then you'd turn psychotic and have to be locked up like Hannibal Lecter.'

'Bloody hell, Liz, I'm just making up a few stories about a boyfriend. That doesn't mean I'm going to start slaughtering people then eating their livers with fava beans.'

'You're bound to get found out,' Liz warned. 'Shelly's already asking people how come no one has ever seen this Leo and saying you're a liar. If this gets out then you'll be the laughing stock of the whole school.'

Felt my face flush scarlet and my stomach twist at the thought of it. It was true. Sooner or later people were bound to get suspicious. If they ever found out I was a sad person who'd invented a pretend boyfriend I'd die of shame. Liz was right. I'd have to get rid of Leo.

MONDAY JUNE 21ST

Told everyone Leo had died suddenly in a tragic skiing accident and I was too upset to talk about it. People were really nice to me – except for Shelly, of course, who said, 'Skiing accident! In June? Yeah, right.'

I said, 'Water-skiing accident.'

Shelly still doesn't believe me but she can't prove anything. As Liz said, 'It's difficult to prove someone never existed after all. That's the problem with being an atheist too.'

People seem to have forgotten all about me and Leo already. No one mentions him any more or even gives me sympathetic looks. Like he never existed or something, which I know he didn't, but they don't know that, do they?

Moaned to Liz, 'I really miss Leo, Liz.'

Liz sighed. 'Leo wasn't real, Kelly Ann. Tables and chairs are real. You and I are real. Leo was a figment of your imagination. A total fantasy, like pixies, leprechauns, Santa and lipstick that stays on for sixteen hours without smudging.'

'Yeah, I suppose so.'

'What you need is a real boyfriend.'

'No one seems to fancy me.'

'Rubbish. Somebody will. Even really ugly, stupid people manage to find someone eventually.' I scowled at her and she added hurriedly, 'Not that you are, of course.'

'Thanks, Liz.'

Liz wisely changed the subject: she started talking about her birthday tomorrow and the iPod her mum had promised her. I wasn't all that comfortable talking about this in case I somehow let slip the secret celebration plans.

She's been told she won't be having the usual big family party with all her aunts, uncles and cousins coming round as everyone's too busy this year. However, for her fifteenth I know her parents are actually planning a surprise party bigger than all the rest but they have sworn me to secrecy. Her mum has asked me to take her to my house after school until six o'clock, then make our way over. When we get into the living room everyone will be hiding. I have to say, 'You must be disappointed you're not getting a birthday party this year, Liz.'

After Liz answers, everyone will leap out from their hiding places and shout, 'HAPPY BIRTHDAY!'

Sounds easy enough. And fun. Wish my parents would bother to do something exciting like that for me.

THURSDAY JUNE 24TH

We arrived at Liz's at exactly ten past six. Liz wanted to go straight upstairs to her room but I persuaded her to go into the living room first to look for the TV guide.

When we went in I could see a man's shoes poking out under the floor-length curtains and the tip of a yellow party hat peeking over the sofa, but Liz didn't notice anything – probably because she wasn't expecting anyone to be there. I knew that some of the guests would be hiding under the kitchen table but I couldn't see any of them.

I said loudly, 'You must be disappointed you're not getting a birthday party this year.'

Liz shrugged. 'Not really. I think I'm getting too old for that kind of stuff now. I'd rather spend my birthday getting totally wasted at a club in town, then snogging the face off some really hot guy.'

'You don't really mean that, Liz,' I said, desperately pointing with my eyes to the feet under the curtains.

But Liz didn't notice my attempted warning. 'Yeah I do. And anyway, I won't be sorry to be missing that awful birthday cake Aunt Marian makes every year. About as light and airy as a doorstep – don't know who ever told her she could bake.'

'But you love Aunt Marian's birthday cake. You know you do,' I said, frantically jerking my thumb in the direction of the yellow party hat behind the sofa.

'Yeah, right,' Liz said sarcastically. 'About as much as I like Aunt Grace's crap presents. Honestly, they get cheaper and crappier every year. I mean, it's not as though she's mean with her own kids. Total spoiled brats, the pair of them. Thank God I won't have to put up with those two toni—'

'HAPPY BIRTHDAY!' Liz's mum screamed, leaping from behind the couch before Liz could say anything else.

Oh God.

Even though Liz pretended she'd noticed the hidden guests and was just winding people up for a laugh, the rest of the evening was pretty awkward. Liz forced herself to eat four huge heavy slabs of birthday cake while saying 'Mmm, delicious!' after practically every bite but I don't think her Aunt Marian was fooled.

Liz also made a great fuss over the saucer-sized orange plastic earrings her Aunt Grace had got her. 'These are gorgeous. Thank you so much.' She put them on and wore them all evening even though her earlobes turned green. But it was no use and everyone left early looking totally pissed off.

God, surprise birthday parties are an awful idea. Hope I'm never, ever involved in one again.

FRIDAY JUNE 25TH

At the last assembly before the summer holidays our head teacher, Mr Menzies, told us we had won the prize for the most environmentally aware school in Glasgow. This is because we recycle nearly all our rubbish and last year the biology department started an organic garden project beside the football pitch. Our prize would be ten sacks of organic compost.

This is going to be a pretty useless prize as Mr Smith is having the garden concreted over because he got fed up with boys peeing on the compost heap and pretending they were recycling when they just couldn't be bothered with the two-minute walk to the toilets.

Don't blame Mr Smith but I do think recycling (within limits) to save the environment is so important. Unlike Mum. Caught her this morning just shoving all the rubbish into one bag. I had to fish it out again and put it into separate paper, glass, plastic and metal containers. When I complained about it she just said, 'I'm throwing rubbish out, not sodding filing.'

Typical.

We finished at lunch time. Liz, Gary, Ian and I all went to McDonald's to celebrate but Chris went to Pizza Hut with Emily. Don't suppose I'll see him all summer now. Wish he'd never met Emily, but I suppose if it wasn't her it would have been some other stupid girl he'd dump all his friends for.

SATURDAY JUNE 26TH

The only thing worse than not going anywhere on holiday is going on holiday with your embarrassing parents, especially if you are the only daughter tagging along behind like a totally sad teenager who has no life and no friends.

Angela has refused to come this year, saying she is too old to go on holiday with parents and can be depended on to look after the house by herself while Mum and Dad are away. And they've agreed. I mean, what other self-respecting seventeen-year-old could be trusted to spend a fortnight in a parentless house without hosting wild parties full of gatecrashers, traffic cones and policemen's helmets?

Can't say I blame her for avoiding two weeks of trying

to pretend you are not remotely related to your drunken parents, but what about me? Without anyone else there it's going to be so much harder to convince people that my parents don't belong to me. Who's going to think I'm in Spain on my own?

My parents, as usual, have been totally unsympathetic. My dad says I'll make friends my own age and have a great time. Yeah, right. Like I'm three years old or something and can bond with some other infant while playing in the sandpit. Don't they realize I'm a teenager now? What am I supposed to do? Saunter up to a crowd of people I've never seen before and say casually, 'Hey, you don't know me and I've absolutely no idea who you are, or what you're like, but would you like to be my friends please?' I mean, *as if*. I'd rather be a sad loner than a laughing stock.

My mum, if anything, is worse than Dad. She says that she and Dad work their fingers to the bone for me and what thanks do they get? Then she tells me to shut my moaning face or she'll shut it for me.

Really hate my parents sometimes: they just so totally do *not* get it.

SUNDAY JUNE 27TH

Moaned to Liz about it today, but she wasn't very sympathetic: her parents have told her they're not going on holiday this year because of having to replace everything after the burglary.

'Honestly,' she grumbled, 'why can't they just get a loan like everyone else? Their meanness is probably due to being toilet-trained too early, but that's hardly my fault, is it?'

Don't know what toilet training had to do with anything but decided not to argue about it – Liz was in a really bad mood, especially as she'd bought flip-flops and sunglasses with her pocket money last week. 'And for what?' she moaned. 'Like I'm going to get any use out of them in Glasgow. I'd have been better off buying an umbrella and wellies.'

We spent the rest of the afternoon slagging off our parents, who we agreed were totally mean, insensitive and uncaring. Wondered if we could put ourselves up for adoption, hopefully to find parents who were never embarrassing and always generous and let us do whatever we liked.

WEDNESDAY JUNE 30TH

My mum has been talking to Liz's mum, and guess what? Liz can come on holiday with us!!

I was so excited when Mum told me that I actually threw my arms around her and hugged her voluntarily for the first time since my fourth birthday, when she bought me a two-wheeler bike without stabilizers. Can still remember how fantastic it felt riding a proper bike for the first time. Just a pity it got trashed later that day because I left it in the lane where the garbage truck was reversing. But still, I'd had a whole morning riding a proper bike without the shame of stabilizers (which I *so* never needed in the first place) and the bin men kindly took it to the dump for me without telling Mum so I could pretend someone had stolen it.

Anyway, Mum was quite moved by my show of affection today, I think, although all she said was, 'Still as flat as an ironing board then. Bloody hell, Peter Pan right enough. We'll need to put you on hormones.'

But nothing she said could possibly annoy me now. At last, a proper holiday with a real friend instead of my sad boring sister. So love my parents sometimes.

Also, as Liz has pointed out, it might be the perfect opportunity to get a real boyfriend and lose my (now shameful) virgin lips status.

Feel this is going to be the most exciting holiday of my whole life.

SATURDAY JULY 1OTH

Went shopping for holiday stuff with Mum. Didn't need
to go bikini shopping unfortunately as the one I got two
years ago still fits, sort of. Still, at least it's the first bikini
not bought at the children's department and there's
another week to go before we leave. Maybe my breasts
will grow a bit in that time or in the heat of Spain.

WEDNESDAY JULY 1 4TH

Was really surprised when Chris called me today and
asked if I wanted to go into town with him to check out
the new game shop that had just opened and maybe get a
burger or something.

I said, 'Why me? Won't Emily go with you? Or Gary
maybe?'

'Emily and I have split up. I haven't asked Gary.

Thought it might be nice for us to go. I haven't seen you since school ended. And, well, like you said, we're still friends, aren't we?'

Felt a rush of relief. Yeah, now that Emily wouldn't be hanging around him any more maybe he'd have time for me.

But I said, 'Oh, I'm sorry, Chris. What happened?'

'Nothing really. Just, I don't know, it was time to move on, I suppose. So, you want to come? They've got a sale on.'

Hmm. Time to move on. Chris seemed to be doing a lot of 'moving on' these days. And I bet as soon as he's got a new girlfriend it will be time for him to 'move on' again so he won't want to be bothered with me. There was no way I was going to let him humiliate me a second time.

'Sorry, Chris, but I'm really too busy for town today. Maybe another time.'

And maybe not. I put the phone down before he could answer. Chris was right. It was time to move on.

THURSDAY JULY 15TH

Just one more day to our holiday. Can't wait. It's going to be so great going with Liz instead of boring Angela. I mean, who wants to go on holiday with someone who always packs an umbrella and diarrhoea tablets, listens attentively to the safety instructions on the plane and spends the entire vacation writing postcards which – get this – she actually puts stamps on and posts. God knows what she finds to write about as she never actually does anything.

Liz and I have talked about nothing else but our holiday for weeks now. We can hardly believe it's finally nearly here. Only problem is, Liz constantly going on about my finding someone to snog.

'Doesn't matter that much, Liz. I mean, being a virgin lips isn't all that shameful, is it?'

But Liz was determined. 'Of course it is. It's like, well . . . like still riding a tricycle when everyone else is on a bike.'

'That was you, Liz.'

'Or, um, still wearing mittens tied together with wool and threaded through your coat sleeves when everyone else wears proper gloves and loses them.'

'That was you too.'

'Or getting a spit wash from your mum in front of the whole school.'

Oh God, that was me. When I was in primary six, Mum met me at the school gates at home time and 'cleaned' a dirty mark on my nose by spitting on her thumb and using it to wipe the mark away. In front of the whole school. I blushed at the memory.

'So,' Liz said, 'it's way past time you had your first snog.' She laughed. 'This holiday you're going to kiss goodbye to your virgin lips.'

Yay, finally!

At the airport the check-in person wasn't able to find us four seats together. Dad said, 'Thank God for that. Can you put them as far away as possible so we can pretend they're not with us?' Then he looked at Liz and me and smiled. 'Only joking, girls.'

Hilarious. I mean, as if *we* actually wanted to be associated with *them*.

Parents made for the airport lounge so Liz and I wandered off to look at the duty-free shops. Saw a nice pair of sunglasses which I thought I might buy as spares since I usually lose mine. Only £2.99, so a good bargain too. However, when I took them to the cash desk the assistant told me quite snootily that they were £299 and was I sure I really wanted her to ring this up.

Bloody hell. £299! Still, how was she to know I couldn't afford them?

'Oh, um, no, actually, they're um' – I squinted at the label – 'Emporio Armani and I'd wanted, er' – I paused, desperately trying to think of some other expensive brand they hopefully didn't stock – 'Gucci actually.'

'I'm sorry, miss, but we don't have any in stock at the moment.'

'Oh, what a pity,' I said, in what I hoped was a convincingly disappointed tone.

'Aye, right,' the woman laughed.

Bloody nerve. It's not as though *she* could have afforded them either. She was just a shop assistant person like Mum.

Unfortunately once we got on the plane I discovered we were seated right across from my parents. Liz bagged the aisle seat so I had to sit in the middle between her and a woman so fat her flesh flowed under and over the arm rest into my seat. Just as well I'm skinny.

Liz and I tried our hardest to act as if we weren't really with my parents, especially as they were intent on drinking their way to Spain, laughing and giggling like geriatric school kids while singing (if you can call it that) 'Summer Holiday'.

At least they stopped their embarrassing tuneless braying when the dinner came. This sounded really nice and kind of classy: 'Boeuf bourguignon with pommes sautées and petit pois'. It was disgusting though, with a kind of yellowish circle of mashed something, which I think was supposed to be potato, some green gunk (peas?) and brown stuff which looked like dog turd. Also I was uncomfortably squashed, and even though I'm small I still had to eat the meal with my elbows tucked in and my hands in front of my chin so I probably looked like a praying mantis.

Can't wait for this flight to end and our holiday to really begin.

SATURDAY JULY 17TH

Liz and I woke around eleven o'clock with the sunshine streaming in our window. We decided to go to the pool right away and put on our bikinis. I examined my reflection in the mirror but unfortunately my breasts hadn't grown in the week or in the heat of Spain. Having said that, the room was air conditioned. Maybe when I went outside . . . Everything expands in the heat after all.

However, Liz dashed this hope for me too. 'Breasts aren't made of mercury, Kelly Ann, so I don't think going outside will make much difference. Here' – she pulled some pink toilet paper from the roll – 'use this. It's the same colour as your bikini. Just remember to take it out before you go into the pool.'

I folded the paper into two wads, which I used to pack the cups of my bikini top, then eyed Liz's double-D breasts enviously. 'You're so lucky, Liz.'

'Stop looking at me like that, Kelly Ann, or people really will think you're gay. Anyway, you're the one that's lucky. Loads of boys fancy slim girls. And you can eat anything you want. Talking of eating' – she took two chocolate Creme Eggs out of her bag – 'I bought our breakfast at the airport yesterday.'

After we'd had 'breakfast' I knocked on Mum and Dad's door, but they were still in bed, probably sleeping off a hangover because of all the booze they'd drunk. Mum called grumpily through the door that we could go down to the pool by ourselves and told me to grab two sun loungers for her and Dad.

The place was already crowded but luckily there were four loungers left so we bagged them. Well, actually, only two definitely free but the others only had towels on them, which we quickly removed then stashed under a table by the pool café.

Liz wanted to sunbathe for a while, which I find kind of boring.

'I've got to work on my tan first, Kelly Ann.'

Yeah, like it really takes a lot of effort just to lie and bake, but I didn't argue as I know Liz loves getting a tan because she thinks it makes her look slimmer. 'If you can't tone it, tan it' is her motto, so I settled down to read the magazine she had loaned me while I waited for her to decide when she'd toasted enough.

Was just reading about this season's 'must have' strawberry-pink pumps, banana-yellow tops and tangerine skirts when Liz whispered, 'Oh my God, Kelly Ann, look at that.'

I followed the direction of her gaze and saw a blonde, skinny woman who must have been at least as old as my mum bathing topless. Yuck. And she was with her two sons, one of whom looked about the same age as me and Liz. Oh God, how embarrassing. Yet the woman was behaving as though nothing was wrong at all; like it was, I don't know, totally normal to flash your breasts at everyone, even complete strangers and your own sons. Gross.

I stared at her, horrified, as she sat eating a baguette; when some of the crumbs fell onto her boobs she just brushed them off with her hand like you would if you had your clothes on.

I suppose she must have noticed me gawping at her as she smiled at me. I looked away hurriedly and saw Mum coming towards us, fortunately wearing a proper swimsuit, so even though she had a fag in one hand and a Bacardi and Coke in the other, I smiled at her gratefully. Yeah, some people had even more embarrassing parents than me.

Mum settled in alongside us, leaving a space for Dad, and I went back to reading Liz's magazine. As soon as Mum finished her drink and another two and a half fags she fell asleep with her mouth open like a basking shark as usual, then started to snore loudly. Normally I'd have been quite embarrassed but not now. As long as she kept her clothes on I didn't care.

Tried to concentrate on the magazine as Liz has said I really do have to learn something about girl stuff like fashion and make-up, but it was just so boring. I mean, who really cares or can be bothered to line their lips and put on three coats of mascara? And only a total masochist would wear 'killer heels' that you can't actually walk in without excruciating pain and probably permanent foot deformity.

I tossed Liz's magazine aside and picked up my copy of *PSW*. Was happily reading reviews of the latest games when I was interrupted by Liz saying very loudly and clearly, 'You know, Kelly Ann, it was so good of *your* parents to invite me on this holiday, especially as I have absolutely no connection to your family and am totally unrelated.'

What was Liz on about? I looked over at her but she was staring at something to the left of me; from her expression, it was something pretty disturbing. I followed her gaze and saw my dad walking towards us. At first I couldn't see why Liz was bothered. He was wearing a T-shirt as his white skin burns in the sun, and a stupid-looking straw hat which was too big for him, but so what? Then my gaze travelled down. Oh. My. God. Instead of the normal navy blue, baggy boxer trunks that he's worn on every holiday since I was six, he had tiny red lycra pants which were very, very tight and showed well, EVERYTHING!

I covered my face with the magazine, desperately hoping that if I couldn't see him maybe he'd somehow magically disappear.

No such luck. 'Hi, girls. Enjoying yourselves?' He settled himself in the lounger next to me. 'Your mother's been working hard again I see, Kelly Ann. Don't know how she keeps up the pace.'

'Dad,' I hissed, still hiding my face behind the magazine, 'where are your trunks?'

'Bloody hell, don't tell me I forget to put them on,' Dad joked. 'I knew there was something else I should have done this morning.'

'You know what I'm talking about!'

'Oh aye, the *new* trunks. They were your mother's idea. Seems they're all the fashion now because of some James Bond film. You don't like them?'

I stood up and dropped the magazine on his lap, not very gently. 'Cover yourself up, for God's sake.'

Boiling with rage and shame, I stomped off and dived straight into the cool, blue pool. Oh God, that felt so good. At first anyway, but then I had to spend the next fifteen minutes straining bits of pink toilet paper from the water. A bunch of young kids helped me and seemed to enjoy the game, yelping and screaming as they caught tiny pieces of sodden tissue and brought them to me, making sure that absolutely everyone by the pool was aware of what had happened.

Finally a little blonde English girl of about four or five brought me the last pink shred, then advised me solemnly, 'Toilet paper is for your bottom, not your boobies.'

Well, thanks for that. Still, as Liz said later, at least she is the first person to acknowledge that I *do* actually have breasts.

SUNDAY JULY 18TH

Gave in yesterday and asked Mum to buy me a bikini from a children's shop as I don't want any more embarrassing pool episodes. Actually, the top is a bit small for me so what little cleavage I have is more noticeable. Also I am hoping that with a different bikini, baseball cap and dark glasses people might not recognize me.

Persuaded Dad to buy a huge, outsize and, more importantly, very long T-shirt for himself which I hoped would cover him up when he wears those disgusting lycra swimming trunks again.

Sorted.

Mum and Dad were sleeping off their hangovers again this morning so Liz and I went down to the pool by ourselves. Think my disguise worked as no one seemed to be staring at me and sniggering. Liz was disappointed there weren't any boys around the pool with 'snogging potential'. I think she meant for me rather than her as she is still determined I'm to lose my virgin lips this holiday.

After Liz had 'worked on her tan' we had a great time messing about in the pool and even got talking to a couple of boys from Liverpool who, though they were totally unfanciable (freckly and skinny) and had a weird accent, were a good laugh. They probably thought the same thing about us.

We had just been joined by some pals of the boys, one

of whom was older and really good looking, when Liz nudged me. 'Look, Kelly Ann.'

I glanced over and saw a very tall, well-built woman in a short white dress and straw hat walking towards us. She had the hairiest legs I'd ever seen. 'God, yeah. I mean, she really should wax her legs.'

I started chatting to the boys again about Liverpool's chances in the Premier League when I heard a familiar voice say, 'So, girls, enjoying yourselves?'

I looked up. Dad! Oh my God. The 'woman' in the white dress was actually my dad in the very long T–shirt, which reached to mid thigh.

Dad gave the boys a hard, suspicious stare, which looked stupid rather than menacing, given his outfit, but luckily didn't say anything to them or ask who they were. Instead he just said, 'I'm off to get a beer. Want me to bring you two back an ice cream?'

'No thanks!' I said quickly, which drew an annoyed look from Liz but I didn't care. Just wanted Dad to go away quickly and not come back.

'Fair enough,' he said and mercifully sauntered off.

As I sighed with relief the hot Liverpool guy asked, 'Who was that?'

Oh my God, what to say? 'No idea.'

He looked at my dad's retreating back with disgust. 'Pervert.'

* * *

'Oh God, Liz,' I whispered later, 'I've publicly disowned my own dad. What kind of a person am I?'

Liz shrugged. 'A totally realistic one. He was wearing *a dress*, Kelly Ann. Bloody hell, what else could you say?'

MONDAY JULY 19TH

Finally my parents agreed to go to the beach today, although Mum moaned about how she couldn't stand the sodding sand, which went sodding everywhere – even in unmentionable places which, in fact, she did mention. The good news, though, is that Dad was wearing a normal T-shirt as Mum had told him she wasn't going anywhere with him 'dressed in sodding drag'. He was also wearing his old, decent, navy blue trunks as she also said, 'I bought you those red ones for a laugh when I was drunk, you eejit. Can't you take a joke? Now cover yourself up and don't affront me. You're no James sodding Bond.'

The brochure had said the beach was a 'stone's throw' from our hotel. Yeah, right. It took us nearly twenty minutes to walk there. Not even an Olympic discus champion could throw a stone that far. It also took us ages to find a shady spot for Dad as Mum refused to spend thirty euros on a 'jumped-up umbrella' and Dad doesn't like the sun. Don't know why my parents booked a beach holiday in Spain when they don't like sand or sun, but there's no understanding adult thinking sometimes.

Still, Liz and I had a great time there – well, we did after Liz had finished working on her tan, which meant when her skin changed from pink to red and started to peel.

After we'd had lunch Liz wanted to sunbathe again so I wandered off down the beach by myself. Suddenly found myself thinking about Chris, of all people, and how great it would be if we were friends again and he was here with me and Liz. While she sunbathed Chris and I could have kicked a ball about. Or maybe swum over to those rocks down the beach to look for crabs.

I shook my head and sighed. He's probably too grown up now to look for crabs. Most likely he'd have spent the whole time looking for girls and ignoring me.

Oh well, I supposed I could just investigate the rocks on my own. I put my hand above my eyes and squinted over to get a clearer view. Spotted a group of Spanish boys a bit older than me, who were diving off a large flat rock which jutted out into the sea. Decided to walk towards the rocks to get a closer look.

Unlike most Scottish guys, the Spanish boys all had dark brown skin and looked strong and muscular as they competed with each other to see who could jump from the highest rock or stay under the water the longest.

Mmm. Must say I really enjoyed looking at those boys. Especially the tallest one, who was also the best swimmer. Wonder what it would be like to have a boyfriend like that . . .

Later, they moved onto the beach near me and started to kick a football around. The ball rolled towards me at one point. I kicked it back to the tallest guy, who smiled and said, '*Gracias*.'

I watched them play for a while. After a few minutes the ball rolled in my direction again. Was going to kick it back to them but this time, for a laugh, I decided to make off with it.

They chased me, but though they soon caught up with me, I managed to keep the ball away from them for a while. They were impressed with my football skills, I think, so they let me join in their kickabout.

I was having a great time until three really posey girls arrived on the beach. They were all wearing totally ridiculous bikinis, which hardly covered anything and looked as though they'd dissolve if water touched them. Their sandals had heels (on the beach – I ask you!) and they all wore loads of make-up. I suppose they would have been really nice looking if they hadn't looked so stupid – especially the way they walked, sort of wrapping one ankle round the other, which made their bums wiggle stupidly. No wonder one of them tripped and fell. Idiot.

But instead of laughing at how daft their get-ups were, the Spanish boys stopped playing and rushed over to see if the girl who'd tripped needed any help. I mean, she'd only fallen on sand, for God's sake – how hard can that be? But the tallest guy made a huge fuss of her and rubbed her ankle while his friends got chatting to the other two girls. They were all smiles, the football and me forgotten.

I kicked the ball over to them, none too gently, but they didn't even notice so I wandered off to find Liz, who had now fallen asleep.

I nudged her awake. She rubbed her eyes and grumbled, 'What's wrong?'

I said, 'Do you think I'm ugly, Liz?'

'Of course not.' She sat up. 'Bloody annoying waking me up but not ugly, no.'

'So would you say I was, well, quite nice looking then?'

'Yeah, but that doesn't mean I fancy you. What's up with you anyway?'

'God. I've just seen the most gorgeous Spanish guys on the beach. I think maybe you're right about the sex-drive stuff. It is really, really important.'

'Erm, Kelly Ann—' Liz said, looking over my shoulder.

'You can't see them from here,' I interrupted. Then I continued, 'But really. You're definitely right. I mean' – I giggled – 'I wouldn't shag a headless person like a praying mantis but I wouldn't mind sucking the faces off those Spanish boys. Mmmm.'

Heard a voice behind me say grimly, 'Glad to see you've got some standards, Kelly Ann. Now put on your T-shirt and let's get back to the hotel.'

Dad.

WEDNESDAY JULY 21ST

There was a pool party tonight for adults and older kids with a free buffet and cheap drinks. Everyone went.

Had a great time until two of the reps announced the start of the karaoke.

Oh my God. Not karaoke. Please, God, don't let my parents volunteer.

They were first up. Dad sang 'Sex Bomb' while thrusting his hips back and forth energetically. Mum didn't sing. Instead, she circled round him, writhing about suggestively and waving her sarong.

I am never, ever going on holiday with my parents again. Even if social services have to take me into care for two weeks and I'm beaten to a bloody pulp every night by the other kids because my mum isn't on methadone and I know my dad's name. Never.

FRIDAY JULY 23RD

I am also never going to drink alcohol. Not after witnessing my parents making yet another total public spectacle of themselves.

Started out fine last night when we went to a really classy restaurant, with proper tablecloths and candles on the table, plus polite waiters who held out our chairs for us and called me *señorita*. So nice.

We ordered a fish and rice dish called paella, which was delicious, and everything was fine until Mum, after drinking several glasses of red wine the size of buckets, complained about the soft guitar music being boring – didn't they have something a bit livelier?

Next thing I knew she and Dad were screeching along to some stupid 'Viva España' song; then, oh my God, Mum got up on the table to dance. Oh God. Not again.

I begged her to stop but she just laughed at me and continued stamping her high heels and flailing her arms about in what was supposed to be an imitation of Spanish flamenco dancing but looked more like she'd trodden on an invisible wasps' nest and was trying to fight them off.

Finally she tripped and tumbled face first into a large plate of paella.

Thank God we'll be leaving the country next week. Obviously none of our family will ever be able to show our faces in Spain again.

THURSDAY JULY 29TH

Last day and we went to the beach. Saw the Spanish boys again. They were with the posey girls and it was obvious they'd all paired up already. None of them noticed me. Like I was invisible or something.

Wondered if I could get their attention if I lined my lips, put on three coats of mascara and wore a nearly–not-there bikini with high heels. Hmm. Probably have to grow breasts first.

Have refused to go out to a restaurant with my parents tonight as I just can't bear the mortification. Mum and Dad have said we can stay at the hotel provided we 'behave ourselves'.

Bloody nerve. Like Liz and I were the ones making arses of ourselves every night!

It's the last night for a lot of other people too and the holiday reps have organized an under-sixteens disco from eight o'clock until ten thirty. Mum says it's fine for us to go but Dad was more worried. 'Will there be young lads at this do?'

I mean, duh. 'No, Dad, it's a gay club. They're very broad-minded in Europe.'

'Aye, right, don't give me any of your snash, young lady. You can go, but don't be having anything to do with any boys, mind. Just you and Liz stick together.'

Hmmm, Dad seems to think that every boy in Europe is just dying to get his hands on me. *As if.* Honestly, if only he knew how little he had to worry about. Most of the boys my age are totally so not hot, and the very few who are remotely fanciable wouldn't notice me if I danced starkers in front of them. OK, well, not quite true. I guess they would notice me but probably not in good way.

Rather than attempt to explain all this to Dad, I sighed and promised to behave myself.

Mum screeched on her way out, 'Right, have fun, you two, but don't do anything I wouldn't do.'

Yeah, right. Suppose Liz and I won't be able to go ahead with the bank heist or international terrorism we'd planned – but hey, just about anything else was still possible.

Then she added, 'And don't do anything I *would* do either.'

Hilarious. She cackled loudly at her own joke and made for the door. Dad just said, 'Mind what I said now. No boys. Any problems, just call us at the restaurant. You've got the number.'

Then they left. Finally.

Liz and I got ready for the disco. She suggested I wear my one skirt (the pink one) so I'd look a bit more girly just in case a miracle happened and there were nice-looking available boys there. Even though it's our last night, Liz hasn't quite given up on the idea of me losing my virgin lips status on this holiday. She wore a low-cut white top (to show off her tan and other things) and a red skirt.

As usual at parties like that, there were twice as many girls as boys, and none of the boys were remotely fanciable except for two, who were OK looking and of course already surrounded by a large group of girls. So, just as I thought, there was nothing for Dad to worry about. Unfortunately.

But the music was good and I like dancing. I'm good at it too, probably because Mum used to send me to ballet classes for ages in an attempt to make me less boyish. I'd hated the naff dresses and stupid shoes but I loved the music and dance, though I prefer modern stuff now. Tonight, as usual, none of the boys were dancing so Liz and I just got started on our own.

I was having a good time but Liz was disappointed that there wasn't any food at the party, just cans of Coke and fruit juice, so after about an hour she suggested we go off to our room and finish off the chocolate we'd stashed there, then come back.

We were just passing the boys' toilets, which had a large OUT OF ORDER sign on it, when two of the Liverpool boys came out and invited us to join them inside for an alternative party. Yeah, right.

'It's OK,' the smallest, freckliest one called Charlie told us. 'There's other girls here already. Look.' He opened the door wide so we could see inside, and sure enough, there were four girls and two boys standing around talking and giggling while drinking something from white paper cups.

The place didn't smell bad like the boys' toilet at school so Liz and I decided to check it out.

Charlie handed us each an empty cup then ushered us into one of the cubicles. Liz and I looked at each other worriedly. He didn't expect us to drink loo water, did he? I'd thought these Liverpool boys were quite normal before but maybe they weren't. Maybe they were really weird English people – members of some disgusting cult who all drank from toilets as a kind of initiation thing. Well, they could forget it.

Was ready to run out when he surprised me by opening the cistern top to reveal a large jug of reddish liquid with bits of fruit mixed in, sitting in the water. 'Great place to keep it cool,' he explained. He pulled the jug out with a flourish. 'Sangria. Give us your cups here.'

I shook my head. 'No way. That's got alcohol in it. It must do 'cos I've seen my mum drink it.'

'So?' He poured the sangria into our cups. 'That's what makes it good. Brighten up this boring party a bit. Drink up before someone else grabs it!'

Liz looked hungrily at the fruit at the bottom of her cup. 'I suppose we could just eat the fruit. That's not alcoholic. Fruit's good for you. Healthy.'

Hmm.

In the end I agreed to try it. The fruit didn't taste like proper fruit as it was kind of mushy, but it didn't smell disgusting or taste really gross like beer or whisky. The juice didn't stink either, like proper alcohol would, so we decided we might as well drink it. Everyone else was, and they seemed to think it was OK. Like the fruit, the juice didn't taste quite right but we downed it anyway and Charlie filled our cups again.

Funny thing was, the second cup tasted much, much better than the first. So good in fact that we demanded another two before heading back to the party.

And what a fantastic party it was. Everyone seemed

friendlier and funnier, the music was brill, and I did my best dancing ever. So good in fact that I got up on the pool table so everyone could see me. Unfortunately one of the boring reps insisted I get down in case I damaged myself or the table. Honestly.

Liz argued with him. 'Holiday weps are shupposed to be extwoverts, not misherable shocks and snicker ironin' intwoverts.'

But the guy didn't seem to understand her. You'd think they'd hire reps with better English, for God's sake.

Still, getting back on the floor allowed me to try out some break dancing. I've never tried it before as I always thought it looked a bit difficult, but it turned out to be a lot easier than I'd imagined. Everyone watched and applauded wildly as I spun round on just one elbow, then jumped up and did a couple of forward rolls followed by two backward flips and a cartwheel.

Some people took photographs; others whistled. Only the rep and Liz seemed to be trying to stop me. Wondered what was the matter with Liz. Maybe she was jealous of all the attention I was getting. Not like her though. Anyway, I was having way too much fun, so I ignored them, concentrating instead on the roars of approval from the rest of my audience.

After dancing on my hands I tried a double forward flip but unfortunately didn't quite make it and fell, bumping my head. Surprisingly it wasn't painful, and though I was now feeling a bit dizzy, I thought I'd give it another try. However, Liz had got hold of me and hissed in my ear, 'Kelly Ann, you're wearing a shirt. Member.'

Shirtmember? What was Liz on about? She must be drunk.

Tried to shake her off but she clutched at me desperately, then pointed to my skirt. Oh my God, I was wearing a skirt. And I'd been dancing upside down.

Pants!

FRIDAY JULY 30TH

Woke up this morning feeling awful. Had a sore head, felt sick, and my tongue seemed to be stuck to the roof of my mouth. Also my whole body felt as though someone had battered me with a baseball bat. Obviously I was seriously ill and someone would have to call for an ambulance.

I opened my eyes but instantly closed them again, drawing the sheet back over my head. The room was bathed in sunlight so bright it hurt my eyes. Must have forgotten to close the blinds last night. And, oh yes, bright sunlight, so I was still in Spain and not back home in Glasgow. Wonder what the Spanish for ambulance is. Wish I'd done Spanish instead of French at school, then I would be able to call for help. Strange to think I might die just because of choosing the wrong subjects in second year.

I twisted round in my sweaty sheets to lie face down on my pillow, but that just made me feel more nauseous so I turned onto my back again, which made my head throb.

Well, I didn't care about dying any more. I can totally see why euthanasia is a really good thing. What is the point of my continued existence when I feel this bad? My quality of life is rubbish and I'd be better off dead.

I suppose my parents would have to fly my body back home but how would they get my coffin onto the plane? There was hardly room for me sitting on my seat, never mind lying out in a large wooden box. Maybe if they laid it across their knees? But no, a coffin on the plane would freak people out. There must be somewhere else to put them.

I stretched over and nudged Liz awake. 'Liz, where do coffins go on planes?'

Liz said, 'Leavemelonengoway.'

Hmm. Maybe they'd put my body in the same place as the luggage, though I've heard it gets very cold there. Also they'd probably lose the coffin and I'd end up in, like, Guatemala, alone and frozen like a large fish finger.

I prodded Liz awake again. 'I don't want to die, Liz. Have you got a Spanish phrase book?'

She groaned and sat up. 'You're not going to die, you idiot. You're just hung over. From the sangria.'

This was a hangover? Oh my God. Maybe I should have been nicer to Mum and Dad in the mornings.

* * *

At last we were on the plane back to Glasgow. Am feeling a bit better now but can't wait to get home to dull grey skies and cans of Irn Bru, which I'd had a craving for all day. Fortunately Mum and Dad didn't notice that anything was wrong with Liz or me. Mum just said we were a pair of grumpy buggers today. Dad laughed and said, 'No change there then.' He was a bit suspicious when we kept our sunglasses on inside the airport though.

Now that I was feeling a bit better I started to think about what an idiot I'd made of myself last night.

'Oh God, Liz,' I whispered. 'I suppose everyone must have seen my knickers.'

Liz nodded. 'Yeah. Everyone. Still, at least they were the same colour as your skirt.'

'What difference does that make?'

'Hmm. None really, except that you looked sort of coordinated. Unlike your dancing.'

'Thanks, Liz.'

Obviously I could never go to Spain again. Or (after Liz showed me the picture Charlie had taken on his mobile – and thoughtfully sent to Liz – of me doing a one-handed cartwheel) Liverpool.

SATURDAY JULY 31 ST

Was awake for ages last night. Couldn't stop thinking about the total embarrassment of my stupid dancing at the party. Eventually I decided that no one there knew me and I never needed to see any of them again.

Exhausted, I was almost drifting off to sleep when the Spanish boys at the beach popped into my head. They were just so gorgeous. Especially the tallest one. Mmmm – just remembering how his strong, tanned body looked as he dived off the rocks into the ocean made me feel all hot and sweaty. In a very nice way.

I really would love to have a boyfriend like that. And not just to shut Shelly up or so I can fit in with friends who've all dated someone by now. No. I wanted a boyfriend just for me. And if I had to wear make-up, five-inch heels and a bikini that looked as though it had been made from three miniature post-it notes and some dental floss, then so be it.

I suppose, at last, I really am growing up. Maybe Mum would be pleased if she knew. Don't think Dad would though.

SUNDAY AUGUST 1 ST

Was passing my sister's bedroom when I heard her sobbing. Bloody hell, what was up with her? She had seemed a bit quiet and moody yesterday but I thought she was just depressed that we were all back and she wouldn't have the house to herself any more. Didn't think she'd actually be crying about it this morning though – after all, she knew we would only be gone for two weeks.

I decided to find out what was up, so I knocked then went in. She was sitting on her bed snuffling into a damp tissue and her eyes were red. Noticed that the duvet cover was slightly rumpled, there was a used tissue lying on the floor by her feet and her T-shirt hadn't been ironed. Things must be really serious.

'What's wrong?' I asked.

'Nothing,' she sniffed, without looking up.

'Oh great, I'll be off then,' I joked, trying to cheer her up.

She looked up at me. 'It's Graham. We're . . . we're finished.'

I put my hand over my mouth to disguise my relieved smile, then spoke through my fingers, trying to sound as sympathetic as possible. 'Oh God, I'm sorry. What happened?'

'I don't want to talk about it,' she said – then proceeded to tell me all about it of course. Every detail.

'Graham was over here sometimes when you were all away on holiday. Not staying the night or anything—'

'Course not.' *Yeah, right.*

'Just, um, to watch TV and, erm, chat. Anyway, last Saturday night he was reading the *Metro* while I ran a bath. I'd just added my peach and passion fruit Pamper Me bath bombs to the bath water and was ready to get in when Graham asked if he could pop into the toilet for a second, so I said OK.'

She started crying again so I sat down beside her and handed her another tissue from the box on the bedside table. Bloody hell, I wondered what Graham could have done to get her this upset. Maybe he attacked her in the bath – but no, though Graham is a tosser, I didn't think he was a psycho and I couldn't believe he'd do anything like that. More likely he'd just forgotten to fold the hand towel properly. You could never tell what stupid little thing might get to Angela.

After a few minutes she'd calmed down again and continued, 'But Graham wasn't in the toilet just for a second. He was in for quite a long time. When I went in afterwards it was obvious he'd sat down on the toilet.'

'Yuck, gross.'

'The stench was awful, Kelly Ann. You couldn't smell my peach and passion fruit Pamper Me bath bombs at all. Totally ruined my bath. And he didn't even apologize.'

'Tosser.'

'I was so stupid. So naive. I should have realized what was going to happen when he took the newspaper in with him.'

She started to sob again, so I patted her hand and said, 'Anyway, you did the right thing dumping him. That'll teach him to crap in your bath.'

'He didn't actually cra—'

'Good as,' I said.

'Anyway, I didn't dump him right away. We . . . we had a row about it. Said terrible things to each other. I . . . I called him an inconsiderate pig.'

'Too right.'

'And he said . . . he said . . . I was a – a fusspot.'

'No!'

'Yes. And so I told him, if he thought I was a fusspot maybe he should just shove off. And then . . . and then . . . he did.' She started sniffling again. 'It's over, Kelly Ann. We haven't spoken to each other for a week.'

'You're better off without him,' I said sincerely.

'Do you think so?'

'Definitely. And you'll soon meet someone else. Someone much better than him.'

'Really?'

'Yeah, well, probably. Maybe, anyway.'

Angela hugged me. 'You're the best sister I've ever had.'

Hmm.

'And I think your boobs have grown a bit.'

I hugged her back. There are times when I really like my sister.

MONDAY AUGUST 2ND

Angela seemed in a better mood today, although now she's decided to give up guys for good rather than try to find someone else.

'You're so right not to bother with boyfriends, Kelly Ann. Dirty, smelly, disgusting things. I never want to have anything to do with them ever again in my life.'

Weird that she's given up on boys just as I'm starting to get interested in them.

Inspected myself in the full-length mirror in my bedroom. Baggy T-shirt, torn combats and greying trainers. And I knew, without looking, that all my other clothes were like that, barring the one skirt Aunt Kate bought me for Christmas. Obviously I was going to need an entire new wardrobe before I could hope to get a decent boyfriend.

Yeah, but with different clothes I would look nice, wouldn't I? I examined my image again. Frizzy brown hair, flat chest and spotty face. Right, OK then, an entire new wardrobe, wig, implants and a face transplant. That should do it.

Trudged downstairs, depressed. Wondered if I'd still get spots after a face transplant. Probably.

Mum and Dad were at work and Angela had gone shopping for stuff she needs for starting college, so I'd the place to myself, which I'd normally enjoy, but not today. Today I felt ugly. Something had to be done.

Looked through the beauty sections of Mum's old magazines but they were useless. Didn't want to look ten years younger and lose a stone. I wanted to look older and grow breasts. Went up to Angela's room. Found some teen mags – neatly bound and catalogued in date order of course – and flicked through them. These were more promising. Apparently you could change your whole image just by some clever application of the right make-up. And they had step-by-step guides which looked really easy. In just a few minutes each day I could create a whole new me. Sounds exactly what I needed. And the model certainly looked fabulous. Wouldn't mind looking like her.

Decided to 'borrow' Angela's make-up. Don't suppose

she'll mind now that she's given up on boys for good anyway. Didn't take me long to find it. It was on top of her dressing table and labelled MAKE-UP, between the jewellery box labelled JEWELLERY and the scrapbook labelled . . . yeah, you guessed it.

I'd never used make-up before, or even played with it when I was a kid, but how hard could it be? After all, some girls at my school with IQs of pond plankton use make-up. If they could do it, so could I.

The magazine advised me to highlight my best features so I decided to do my eyes first as everyone says they're nice. But trying to create a 'dramatic sunset sensation' by blending deep blue, purple and gold shades above and below my lids didn't work out that well for me. I looked more like a victim of domestic abuse.

Washed it off and decided to concentrate on having 'irresistibly kissable' lips instead. Opted for 'this season's sexy scarlet shade', adding a top coat of 'juicy gloss to plump and shine'.

Unfortunately the gloss smudged some of the colour outside of my lips (maybe lip-liner has some use after all) and I even managed to get some lipstick on my teeth. How did that happen? Hmm. Don't know about being irresistibly kissable. Looked more like I'd just finished feasting on a raw, bloody carcass.

Maybe some boys liked that. Or maybe there was more to using make-up properly than I'd thought. The pond plankton girls can't have been quite so dumb after all.

TUESDAY AUGUST 3RD

Not too many spots today, although the one on the end of my nose is getting bigger. And of course everyone knows that one spot on the end of your nose is equal to at least ten anywhere else. It seems to kind of scream, *Hey, look at me, everybody! Here I am! Look, I'm right at the end of her nose, you can't miss me.*

Depressed, I flicked through Angela's mags again but didn't find any new cures for spots, though did see a feature that said boys love girls who have shiny, healthy hair. Examined my frizzy mop in the mirror. Maybe I should just give up now. Unless I dyed it blonde of course. Boys don't seem to care if blonde hair is peroxided to a frazzle and sits on top of a gargoyle – they'll ask it for a date. But Mum won't let me.

Went back to the hair article and read about solutions for 'the dreaded frizz'. Didn't have any of the products they suggested in the house, but then I saw a section that suggested I could use 'cheap natural ingredients you can find in your own kitchen'. Like a hair rinse made with vinegar, and beer shampoo.

Decided to try the vinegar.

* * *

Don't ask. All I'm saying is when the instructions say 'one or two drops of vinegar' they don't mean half a bottle. Don't know about attracting boys, but I've been followed around outside by every salivating stray dog in the place thinking I'm a fish and chip shop.

FRIDAY AUGUST 6TH

Decided to try the beer shampoo in the hope it might disguise the smell of vinegar, which I've been unable to get rid of completely, along with my canine followers.

But Dad is furious. He's refusing to believe anyone would shampoo their hair with beer. 'Pull the other one. Next you'll be telling me you and your mum bathe in sodding ass's milk.'

I've been grounded for a week for stealing and drinking alcohol. Bet he wouldn't have been so mad if it hadn't been his last 'sodding can'. I smell like a brewery so I wouldn't want to go out, but still, it's just so unfair.

SATURDAY AUGUST 7TH

Mum has made me stand in the shower for nearly half an hour until I smelled 'less like an alky and more like a normal moaning-faced teenager'. However, she's also convinced Dad that I'm just a complete eejit and not a budding alky so my grounding has been lifted.

They've got a nerve talking about the misuse of alcohol, if you ask me, but no one does.

THURSDAY AUGUST 12TH

Went over to see Liz today. She'd bought a new DVD of Smashed to Pieces which she said was fantastic so we put it on.

Liz kept going on about Zach, who she fancies big time.

'Mmm,' she said dreamily, 'he's gorgeous, isn't he? And so interesting. I mean, he's just got out of rehab for the fourth time and has attempted suicide twice.'

Zach was OK looking but I hardly noticed him as I couldn't take my eyes off Jason. Watching him somehow reminded me of those Spanish boys on holiday. Not sure why as he has sun-bleached blond hair and blue eyes. Maybe it was because of how he made me feel. Sort of tingles in my tummy. Oh God, yes, Jason was *hot*. Must borrow this DVD from Liz sometime so I can watch it again just by myself.

FRIDAY AUGUST 13TH

Angela enrolled at college today. Feels a bit weird that she won't be at school with me any more and will have no clue what I'm doing during the day. And she'll have nothing to report back to my parents. Yeah, it will be weird but good weird. Finally I'm free of my nosy informer.

She came into my bedroom this morning and woke me up so I could wish her good luck. Told her to sod off but I don't think she heard me properly as she just said, 'Thanks, Kelly Ann. I'll tell you all about it as soon as I get back. What do you think of my new outfit? I bought it especially for my first day.'

Was forced to open my eyes and look just to get rid of her. She was wearing a crisp white blouse buttoned to the neck and tucked into a navy blue pleated skirt. Add a tie and she could have been wearing her school uniform.

I mumbled, 'Cool.'

She totally failed to notice any sarcasm in my voice and skipped out happily, swinging her new, polished briefcase beside her. It's official. I really do have the saddest sister in the whole of Scotland. Maybe the planet.

SATURDAY AUGUST 14TH

Angela actually met some new people at college yesterday and she was invited to a party tonight. Maybe, at long last, she is turning into a normal teenage sister I don't have to be ashamed of.

She didn't look too naff going out either. OK, her jeans did have a sharp crease ironed into them and her T-shirt was kind of stiff, like she'd starched it or something, but she didn't tuck it into her jeans. And she'd nice blue canvas wedge shoes with a matching bag so the leather briefcase would be left at home, thank God.

Was surprised when she set off at six thirty though – it seemed a bit early for a student party but, OK, maybe they would be going to a pub first. Maybe she'd even come back a bit wasted like other people's big sisters do. I could only hope.

Angela returned at 9.45 completely sober and going on about what a fun time she'd had. I give up. Totally.

MONDAY AUGUST 16TH

First day of school. At registration Liz and I were told that there's a new girl called Stephanie who's starting tomorrow and we'd have to look after her for the first week. Not looking forward to this as she comes from a really posh private boarding school and will be totally stuck up, but it's only for a week and then we don't need to have anything more to do with her, I suppose.

There's also a new boy who started today. Everyone –

all the girls anyway – are talking about how fit he is, and he *is* definitely very good looking but Gary says he thinks he's a bit of a tosser. Like Liz and me, Gary will have to put up with the new boy for a week since he's been told to look after him. And maybe longer than that – Ferguson is letting the new boy join the football team just because he says he was in one at his last school. According to Gary he played five a side with him at lunch time and he's useless. Maybe Gary is just jealous though: Rebecca told me loads of girls were watching them play and it was obvious they were all only interested in the new boy.

Saw Chris at break. He was with Gary and Ian so Liz and I wandered up to chat. We talked for a bit about how pissed off we were that the holidays were over and moaned about our new timetables. Chris didn't say much but kept looking at me and smiling, obviously pleased to see me.

Didn't see him again until home time, when he caught up with me at the school gates and asked if I wanted to go to his place and play a new Xbox game he'd just got hold of, *Infernal Invasion Two*. However, I said 'No' as I still haven't really got over how he treated me when he was going out with Emily.

But I couldn't help feeling a pang of regret as I watched him go off without me. Wanted to run after him shouting, 'Stop, Chris, I've changed my mind.' But I didn't.

Felt my eyes tear up as he turned the corner out of sight. *Infernal Invasion One* was a brilliant game with fabulous graphics and I've heard *Two* is even better. Now it would probably be weeks before I'd have a chance to play. It was just so frustrating.

TUESDAY AUGUST 17TH

As well as being rich, Stephanie is really nice looking with gorgeous streaked blonde hair (not a single root showing), a fantastic figure and what looks like a natural tan, although she later told us it was Saint Tropez.

Liz and I disliked her on sight, although not because we were jealous of course. We asked her why someone like her had come to our rubbish school if her parents had money.

Stephanie said, 'Mum suddenly decided she didn't agree with elitist private education.' But then she laughed. 'Actually I was expelled for shagging the gardener's son in the greenhouse.'

I stared at her, shocked. 'You did it with someone? In the greenhouse?'

'Yeah – should have done it in the potting shed.' She giggled. 'Less see-through. But we, erm, got bit carried away. Mmm, he was really hot. Even if he did smell of compost.'

Maybe Stephanie wasn't going to be that stuck-up

after all. I wondered if she'd really had sex with the gardener's son or was just saying that for a laugh. I've never met anyone who's actually had sex and admitted it.

I suppose she might have done it – after all, she's a year older than us. She should be in the year above but apparently her school hadn't bothered about academic stuff, just how to eat posh food and walk like a model, so she was made to start in the fourth year.

Asked Liz about it. She thinks maybe Stephanie was serious. And besides, a lot of posh girls liked sex.

I wondered if we could get her to talk to us about it. Not that I'm interested of course. OK, I'm just a bit curious. I mean, we've had sex education and all that but although Mrs Brown, the biology teacher, said we could ask questions, no one actually asked the kind of stuff you'd really want to know. Like, if you do it with him will he tell all his friends? Also, should you talk to him while he's doing it? If so, what about? And what do you say afterwards? Then there's the whole problem about the next time. I mean, suppose you've done it once just to find out what it's like, will he expect you to definitely do it again even if you're not curious any more? Would it be really rude to say no, given that you're not a virgin any longer anyway and haven't really got anything to lose? And will your parents somehow know you've done it just by looking at you, the way they used to know when you stole the last chocolate biscuit meant for visitors even though you denied it?

Well, you couldn't ask Mrs Brown all that, could you?

WEDNESDAY AUGUST 18TH

It was raining at lunch time today so we had to spend most of our time in the social area, which is a large hall with nothing in it – not even seats – except for an ancient music player and, of course, a CCTV camera to spy on us. Social area my arse.

Stephanie leaned against one of the large blue pillars and scanned the hall, her eyes resting mainly on the boys, I noticed. She shrugged, unimpressed. 'Not much talent here, is there?'

'Not a lot,' Liz and I agreed.

Someone was playing a CD and Stephanie started swaying rhythmically to the music. I asked her if she liked dancing and she said she did. So I asked, 'What kind of dancing? Modern stuff? Ballet? Tap?'

'Pole actually.'

Liz and I stared at her.

'Want to see?' Stephanie continued.

We nodded.

Stephanie told the boy who'd put the music on to turn the volume up full, then turned to the pillar she'd been leaning on and started, slowly at first, to gyrate her hips sexily. Of course everyone turned to look at her, especially the boys.

Gradually her movements became faster and wilder as she worked her way up, down and around the 'pole', swaying, thrusting and flinging her arms back like she was actually doing it with a pole instead of a person. Most of the boys just stood there gawping at her like they couldn't believe their luck, though some whistled and shouted encouragement. The girls mainly watched in silence, but some giggled, and others huffed disapprovingly. Liz and I looked on admiringly. Stephanie could definitely dance. And she didn't seem to care a toss what people thought of her.

Unfortunately old Miss McElwee, the home economics teacher who everyone keeps thinking will retire but never does, marched in and turned off the music. She rounded on Stephanie. What did she think she was doing making a spectacle of herself with this disgusting exhibition? Had she no sense of propriety? This was a disgrace.

On and on she went, but Stephanie didn't seem bothered at all. When Stephanie finally managed to get a word in, she just said coolly, 'Keep your knickers on. It's not as though I did a strip. I was just dancing, for God's sake.'

I thought for a moment Miss McElwee was going to have a stroke: she went all reddish purple and seemed at first to choke on her reply, but eventually she said she was going to report this incident to Mr Smith and Stephanie was never to use that word to her again.

'What word?' Stephanie asked with a wide-eyed innocent expression. 'Dancing?'

Miss McElwee wasn't going to fall for that and be made to say the knicker word so she just said, 'You know very well what word, young lady.' Then she marched off.

Before she got to the door, Stephanie shouted after her, 'Oh, you meant knickers, didn't you? Knickers is the word I've not to say again. Is that right? Is it knickers? It is knickers, isn't it?'

Miss McElwee hurried out of the door as though she hadn't heard. But everyone knew she *had* heard what Stephanie said. And also, of course, the laughter.

After that lots of people, mainly boys, came over to say how impressed they were with Stephanie's performance. However, Liz and I tensed when Shelly and two of her pals wandered by. Shelly didn't say anything directly to Stephanie, just glanced at her; then, turning to her friends, she said loudly enough for people round about to hear clearly, 'Slapper.'

Stephanie didn't respond directly to Shelly. Instead she stared for quite a long while at her mean little mouth, then said, 'Oh, it talks. It must be a mouth. And here I was thinking it was a ferret's arse.' She paused. 'Much the same crap comes out of it though.'

Everyone round about laughed at that and Shelly, unable to better Stephanie insult-wise, stomped off, furious. When we'd stopped giggling Liz and I looked at each other and nodded. Yes, Stephanie was going to be our friend. Definitely.

SATURDAY AUGUST 21ST

Liz and I went over to Stephanie's house for the first time today. It was amazing. Really huge, especially as it was just for her and her mum, who's divorced, although Stephanie told us she also has a brother at boarding school.

Her mum seemed nice but was so glamorous it was difficult not to feel a bit nervous at first. She just didn't look like a normal mum at all. I mean, she was wearing a tight black pencil skirt and high heels with a silky cream top on a Saturday afternoon. Well, you couldn't go to the supermarket or mop the kitchen floor in that, could you?

She was the sort of mum you could imagine actually having sex still. Not that I usually imagine people's mums having sex, of course – I'm not weird – but all I'm saying is, it's possible Stephanie's mum still does it. Maybe more than possible, as Stephanie says she has a boyfriend called Pierre, a French musician, who stays over quite a lot and sleeps in the same bedroom as her mum.

Stephanie's bedroom was fantastic, with a king-sized bed, huge walk-in wardrobe and ensuite bathroom all to herself. Couldn't help feeling a bit jealous and confessed as much to Stephanie, but she said, 'You and Liz are the lucky ones. You've still got your dads living with you. I'm the innocent victim of a broken home.'

Felt awful then and started to apologize. 'Oh God, sorry, Stephanie, I didn't think—'

'Yeah, it's really tough,' Stephanie interrupted. 'Last summer I had to spend two weeks in the south of France with Mum, then another two cruising the Med with Dad. Christmas holidays will be hectic as well: skiing with Mum at Klosters, then off to Tenerife the following week with Dad.' She laughed. 'Bloody exhausting.'

Hmm. Being an innocent victim of a broken home didn't sound too bad. At least if your parents were loaded.

THURSDAY AUGUST 26TH

Home economics was quite fun today. We were making a fruit salad, and since this is dead easy, Miss McElwee said we should try to make it look as attractive as possible, maybe by doing some kind of picture or design with it.

I made a kid's salad with a smiley face, using apples and grapes for the mouth and eyes, with peach slices for cheeks. Liz made an abstract design of whorls of strawberry and chocolate sauce laced over bits of squashed fruit. She refused to identify what it was supposed to be, instead telling everyone it was a psychological test that could reveal loads about the personality of the guesser and give clues to our unconscious mind and deepest secrets.

It just looked a bit of a mess to me, to be honest, and I wasn't keen to guess what it was supposed to be in case it really did reveal some shameful secret about me, like the fact I still sometimes slept with my stuffed toy, Gerry the Giraffe, but Liz insisted.

'To be honest, Liz, it doesn't remind me of anything really – but, OK, maybe, um, a butterfly.'

'Aha! That means you are presently undergoing a huge change in your psychosocial development – a total metamorphosis, no less, which you are very anxious about. Or it could mean you just get bored easily and lack concentration. It's difficult to say. Psychology isn't an exact science. I'll have to run further tests on you.'

'No thanks.'

Johnny, a sleazer who fancies Liz (and every other girl with big boobs), had been listening to our conversation. He said, 'Nah, no way it's a butterfly. Looks like breasts to me. Yeah' – he pointed a finger at two grapes in the bowl – 'see, these are nipples. Right? Definitely nipples.'

Liz scowled at him before replying, 'Hmm, interesting.'

'So what does that mean?' Johnny said, smirking. 'I've got a really enormous sex drive, right?'

'Not quite. It means, *actually*, that you have a fixation with your mum so you'll never be able to form mature sexual relationships with girls. Sorry.'

More people had gathered round our table now to see what was going on and were laughing at Johnny's indignation. 'What's fixation mean? You saying I fancy my mum? That's rubbish. Total crap. Psychology's crap. You can't say stuff like that. It's – it's disgusting. Yeah, disgusting.'

As Johnny is well known for using dirty language all the time, this made people laugh even more as he stomped off, red faced and still protesting. Liz turned to Stephanie. 'Your turn. Let's see what the test reveals about your personality.'

Stephanie examined Liz's creation carefully for nearly a whole minute before saying, 'Looks like someone's been sick in a bowl.'

Everyone looked at it then. We all nodded. Yeah, that's exactly what it looked like. Stephanie's comments put an end to Liz's test as no one could see anything else now. The small crowd was about to wander off when Stephanie said, 'Wait, I've got another test. OK, what does this remind you of?'

She put her hand behind her, grabbed the dessert bowl she'd been working on and held it out in front of us. It consisted of a large peeled banana standing up vertically; it was covered in blueberry syrup and propped up at the bottom by two plums. Of course the whole thing looked totally obscene and we all howled with laughter, which unfortunately brought Miss McElwee over.

She was furious and ranted on at Stephanie. What was

the meaning of this? How dare she make such a lewd and disgusting thing? She wouldn't get away with this. Stephanie would be reported to Mr Smith, who would no doubt want to have a word with her parents. She needn't think she could defile this home economics kitchen with this disgusting pornography. Oh yes, that was what it was. Pornography no less. She wouldn't stand for it.

All the ranting just made everyone laugh more – except for Stephanie, who stared innocently at Miss McElwee, protesting that she had no idea what she was talking about. It was just a banana and plum pudding, her favourite actually. She would have liked to do some fancy design but hadn't been able to think of anything. She'd never had much imagination really.

'Don't play the innocent with me, young lady,' Miss McElwee cut in. 'You know exactly what I'm talking about.'

Stephanie stared hard at her creation, pretending she was trying but failing to make out what on earth Miss McElwee was talking about.

'No, miss. I've no idea. Really.' She stared hard again, then her expression changed to one of pretend shock. 'Oh my God. *Now* I see what you mean. You think it looks like ... Oh God, you didn't think that I would ever ...? I mean, if you hadn't said, I'd never have imagined it could look like a boy's—'

'Right,' Miss McElwee interrupted. 'That's enough. It's

time to clear up, everyone. We'll just forget all about this nonsense.'

Miss McElwee hurried back to her desk, red-faced, and tried to look very busy with paperwork, but we all knew she was mortified: Stephanie had made it look as though *she* was the one with the dirty mind. Oh yes. School was much more fun now that Stephanie was here.

FRIDAY AUGUST 27TH

Chris caught up with me as I was walking home from school today.

'Hi, Kelly Ann. Just wondered if you're coming to the match tomorrow. We're playing St Mungo's. Should be a close thing.'

'No, it's too far away and no one else I know is going.'

'That's OK. My dad will give us both a lift. And we could maybe go for a pizza or burger afterwards.'

Thought about it. We've been a bit friendlier recently and sometimes hang out together at break, but things aren't the same. Having said that, I did let him share his lunch with me today when I forgot my money as there's no point in being stupid about things. Mmmm – turkey and bacon panini with guacamole and mozzarella. Delicious. And I accepted his offer to do my maths home-work for me at break yesterday as I was busy copying my history homework from Liz (who was copying my biology, so it's fair) and I know Chris can forge my handwriting. Wasn't pleased when he deliberately put some mistakes in so I didn't get full marks like him, but eventually accepted his explanation that our teacher would have been suspicious as I'm rubbish at maths. Or 'not always one hundred per cent accurate', as Chris put it.

So yeah, sharing lunch or help with homework is OK. We're both mature teenagers after all. But accepting a lift from his dad and spending nearly a whole day with him? No way. Not after being treated as a nuisance when he had a girlfriend.

Eventually I said, 'Nah, don't think so. I'm kinda busy.'

'You always used to come. To the important ones anyway. This is our last chance to get into the schools semi-final.'

'Yeah, well, I used to do a lot of things, but that was before you got fed up with me hanging round you.'

'*I* got fed up?' Chris said. '*You*'re the one who told me—'

'Only after *you* told Emily to tell *me* to shove off. You might at least have talked to me yourself.'

'Kelly Ann, listen to me. I never said that. Never. Not to anyone. Because it's not true.'

I looked at his earnest, sincere face. Bloody Emily. Stupid little liar.

MONDAY AUGUST 30TH

Didn't punch Emily as Chris asked me not to. Also, have decided to be more mature and feminine. Though I did confront her at break today – told her I knew what she'd done and warned her not to stick her nose in my business again.

But she didn't even apologize. Just said, 'It's not fair. You don't want him but you won't let anyone else have him either.'

Honestly. Some people would never be mature enough to understand that boys and girls can just be really good friends without either of them wanting to play tonsil tennis.

Wished now I hadn't promised Chris not to hit her. However, I did manage to sneak a fake dog turd into her packed lunch box. It was made of brown-coloured damp clay borrowed from the art department and so realistic looking it totally put her off her sandwiches.

They were chocolate peanut butter sandwiches too. Serves her right.

TUESDAY AUGUST 31ST

Stephanie has found a boyfriend already, which doesn't really surprise me. He's not at our school though as he's seventeen and has a job. She won't tell us what he actually does. Just says we'll find out when we meet him sometime soon.

Liz has also started going out with a boy in our maths class. I'm really happy for my friends of course, but honestly, did they both have to start dating at the same time? Couldn't they take it in turns or something so I'd have someone to hang out with at the weekend?

'What's the matter, Kelly Ann?' Stephanie said at break, sounding puzzled. 'You look miserable.'

'Nothing. I'm fine. Perfectly happy.'

Liz glanced at me. 'Yeah, right. About as happy as a turkey who knows it's coming up for Christmas. C'mon, Kelly Ann. Just because we've met some boys doesn't mean we're going to abandon you.'

'Yeah, I know, but I'll have nothing to do at the weekend.'

Stephanie said, 'Why don't you pick up some boy if you're bored? There's plenty of them about.'

'It's not that easy,' I moaned. 'I've tried but no one seems to fancy me. I've never had a boyfriend.'

Stephanie was shocked. 'Never! Oh my God. I mean, what have you been doing for the last five years? Knitting?'

Five years? Bloody hell. Does Stephanie think people should have boyfriends the moment they hit double figures? Hmm, she probably does.

I felt more miserable than ever. Maybe now that Stephanie realized what a sad loser I was she wouldn't want anything to do with me.

She must have noticed my grim face as she said, 'God, I'm sorry, Kelly Ann. I was just so, um, amazed that anyone could, well, survive like that. But it's rubbish that no one fancies you. I'm sure loads of guys do. You're just not giving out the right signals.'

'What signals?'

Stephanie laughed. 'The ones that say you might be a lot of fun if they're ever lucky enough to find out.'

I wasn't convinced it was as simple as that and tried to change the subject but Stephanie has decided she's going to sort out my 'ridiculous boy problem'.

'No really, Kelly Ann, you have potential.' She gazed at my face and nodded. 'Great bone structure. You could be a model.'

'Really?'

'Well, no, not really. You're not tall enough. Still, you've got a nice face. Hmm, of course we'll have to do something about the spots. A good foundation and extra-thick concealer perhaps. And the hair. Nothing a top-class stylist can't sort though.'

'Oh,' I said, wondering if maybe a burka was the answer.

'And you've got a fabulous figure.'

'I have?' I said, smiling.

'God, yeah. Well, except for those.' She eyed my chest area. 'Still, you can always pad up, then I'll show you how to use highlighter and shaders to fake a cleavage.'

'I don't know. I don't think—'

'Rubbish,' Stephanie said. 'Trust me, no one knows as much about make-up and fashion as me. Or boys. We'll start next week.'

It was true. If Stephanie couldn't show me how to get a boyfriend, no one could. Next month might just be a lot more exciting than I could ever have thought.

WEDNESDAY SEPTEMBER 1 ST

Mrs Conner is back. Knew she'd been on compassionate leave since the holidays so I thought at first that someone in her family had died. Was gobsmacked to learn the truth. Her devoted husband has chucked her and run off with his secretary.

Mrs Conner is furious. She used her 'compassionate leave' to cut up all her ex-husband's expensive Italian suits and silk shirts, burn his entire CD and DVD collection along with his golf clubs, and sell his Mercedes to his business rival. We know all this as she's posted all the details with pictures on the Internet, along with a 100,000-word blog saying some very unflattering things about him.

At least we think they are very unflattering things but since Mrs Conner rarely uses words with less than four syllables it's difficult to be sure. However, we're pretty certain calling her husband a *mendacious dissembling canker of putrescent crapulence* wasn't meant as a compliment. She also posted a video clip (called Adonis Slumbers) of him sleeping starkers except for a pair of yellow and black Homer Simpson underpants and red fluffy Santa Claus socks with bells on. His mouth was wide open and slightly drooling, plus he snored loudly the whole time except when he belched or worse. Gross.

We had English last period today. Mrs Conner was in a foul mood and gave half the class punishment exercises, but fortunately only the boy half. She has also said that this term we are going to focus, not on love and passion, but on the truly great themes of fine literature: betrayal, revenge and death. Cool. Sounds like English might be a lot more fun now. Unless you're a boy.

Went to Liz's with Stephanie after school. Liz agrees with Stephanie about my need to get a boyfriend. Or, as she put it, at this stage in my psychosocial development it's time to stop sublimating my sexual urges and start gratifying them.

Told Liz I wasn't a slapper and there was no way I was doing it with anybody yet.

'I'm not talking about actual sex, Kelly Ann, but maybe at least some snogging. You can't stay a virgin lips for ever.'

Stephanie told me I'd have to get an entire new wardrobe and a mobile. I was pretty sure I could persuade Mum to give me some money for clothes, especially if I tell her I'm going to buy a skirt or dress, but didn't know about the mobile.

'Anyway, why do I need a mobile?' I asked.

Stephanie looked at me incredulously. 'How can you possibly have a social life or a boyfriend without one?'

It was true. Not having a mobile is like a social death sentence: how am I ever supposed to get a boyfriend if no one can call me without running the risk of having to speak to one of my parents first?

But my parents have always refused to buy me one. Well, not quite true. They've refused to buy me a mobile *again*. Two years ago they bought me one for my birthday but I lost it the same day. Not really sure where I lost it, but I think it was probably at the billboards near my house – I climbed them that afternoon, then practised my new trick of hanging upside on them. Quite safe really, so long as you hook your hands and feet around the beams.

Anyway, the result was that my parents have refused ever since to buy me another so now I'm just about the only girl in my year who hasn't got a mobile. It's so embarrassing.

THURSDAY SEPTEMBER 2ND

I asked Dad again for a new mobile. Told him I was a lot older and more responsible now and that everyone else on the planet had a mobile. Even ancient nomadic tribes in Outer Mongolia had mobiles these days. Wasn't sure that was really true, but it probably was. However, Dad wouldn't budge.

He just said that a mobile would probably be useful for nomadic tribes in Outer Mongolia to keep in touch over long distances, where there weren't any telephone lines, and that if we lived in such a tribe he'd be sure and get me one. However, he wasn't going to spend a fortune on me just so I could send daft texts about sod all to pals I'd been talking to all day anyway, then lose the bloody thing. And besides, it was bad for my health. Might give me brain cancer.

'Yes, Kelly Ann, love, that's the real reason your mum and me don't want you to have one. We're only thinking of your welfare.'

I'd heard this stupid excuse before and hadn't known how to get round this supposed concern for my welfare but now I was ready for it.

'Oh,' I said, 'in that case why did you let me have one in the first place?'

Dad had no answer to that one but typically Mum did. She laughed and said, 'Truth is, we used not to like you much but you've grown on us since. Now go make us a cup of tea and shut your moaning face.'

Charming. But Mum said she'd think about the mobile thing although I wasn't to nag her meantime.

FRIDAY SEPTEMBER 3RD

Mum said, 'You can have the mobile I bought a while back but never use. You'll have to pay for all your calls though. Don't ask me to bail you out.'

Mum had bought a mobile and never used it? I didn't know that. She probably couldn't handle the modern technology. She can barely manage the TV remote control and still doesn't know what most of the buttons are for. But anyway, this was fabulous news for me.

Dad smiled. 'I'll away upstairs and get it for you, love. I charged it up last night so you'll be able to use it right away.'

Oh God, I so love my parents sometimes.

Dad returned and, still smiling, handed me a large black block that was so heavy it could have been used by a mafia hitman to weigh down a corpse before dumping it into the river, ensuring it would sink for all eternity.

I screamed, 'I can't use this . . . this monster.'

'What's the matter, love? Your mum bought it second hand a good few years ago but I tested it this morning and it works fine. You wanted a mobile, didn't you?'

'Yeah,' I said. 'I wanted a MOBILE! The only way this . . . this *thing* could be called mobile is if you dragged it into your garage and fitted it with four wheels and an engine. Mobile my arse!'

Then I stomped off to my room and slammed the door.

My parents are hopeless. Totally. I'd be a laughing

stock if I was ever spotted with something like that. Why can't they see that?

SUNDAY SEPTEMBER 5TH

Mum is still refusing to buy me a phone but did give me thirty pounds for new clothes when I complained about having sod all to wear. Stephanie said she'd come shopping with me: she didn't look for anything for herself and spent the whole time picking out stuff she thought I'd suit then marching me to the changing rooms with armfuls of clothing.

Unfortunately nearly everything Stephanie liked was way too dear but eventually she found a short denim skirt in TopShop and a deep pink T-shirt in H&M which I could afford and looked really nice on me.

When I got home I tried on my purchases again, this time with my high heels, and inspected myself in Angela's full-length mirror. Yeah, Stephanie was right. The outfit did look much better with heels. Decided to keep it on.

Was still wearing it when Chris came over later to watch Man U versus Chelsea.

He looked at me, surprised. 'You look nice, Kelly Ann.'

'Thanks. Stephanie helped me pick the outfit.'

'It suits you. You look, well, um, very pretty.'

'Good. Maybe Stephanie's plan to get me a boyfriend will work then.'

'Thought you weren't interested in boyfriends.'

'Well, I am now. And I'm totally fed up being the only one of my friends without one.'

Chris frowned. 'I don't think you should date someone just because your friends are, Kelly Ann. You should only go out with a boy because you really want to. Because you think they're special.'

Typical Chris answer but he doesn't understand. None of his friends are dating anyone right now. Hmm, good point. Maybe Chris could help me find a boyfriend.

'Chris, do you think you could find out if any of your friends fancy me? Or maybe the boys from other schools you play football with? It would be great if you could ask around and—'

'I can't believe you're asking me this!'

Bloody hell. Chris looked really pissed off. 'What's up with—?'

'What do you think I am? A dating agency?' he raged on. 'Find your own boyfriend. Shouldn't be too hard as you seem to have absolutely no standards whatsoever.'

Then he shoved on his jacket and marched out, banging the door shut behind him. And the game hadn't even started.

MONDAY SEPTEMBER 6TH

Chris avoided me at school this morning so it seems he is still in a mood. Told Liz about it and she agrees that Chris was totally out of order yesterday. She cornered him at lunch time to offer him 'anger management therapy'. He told Liz he didn't need anger therapy and why didn't she mind her own ******* business.

Hmm. Don't understand why he was so pissed off with me. Maybe he thought I'd meant him to set me up with his best pals Gary or Ian, which I definitely hadn't. But then again, why should Chris care who I dated? Hope this doesn't mean Chris and I fall out for ages again.

I needn't have worried. Chris came over tonight and, once we'd gone upstairs to my room, apologized for his weird behaviour yesterday. He had calmed down a lot and now seemed just embarrassed by the whole thing.

'Don't really know why I did that, Kelly Ann. Sorry.'

'Yeah, well, you were a bit mental but it's not like you normally so let's just forget it.'

'Cool.'

We were quiet for a moment, then Chris said thoughtfully, 'Maybe it's because you seem to be changing somehow.'

I shrugged. 'Everybody changes.'

'Yeah, I know, but, well ... you won't change too much, will you? You'll still be my Kelly Ann?'

'Course, don't be stupid,' I said, puzzled.

'Great.' He looked at my PlayStation console. 'So, do you want a game?' He picked up a controller and held out the other one to me.

'Yeah, but just wait a minute until my nail varnish dries. I'd just put it on before you came and I don't want it to smudge.'

Chris looked at me with raised eyebrows and smiled.

Hmm, maybe he's right and I am changing. But not so much that I'll ever stop being friends with Chris. That would never happen.

TUESDAY SEPTEMBER 7TH

Mrs Conner was ranting on today about how us females have been oppressed by males for centuries. Some people say she's just got it in for men because her husband dumped her but I'm not sure. I think she's dead right about it being totally unfair that girls haven't always been allowed to vote. And I was gobsmacked when she told us that brave suffragettes had to chain themselves to railings and throw themselves under carriages (although not at the same time of course) to force selfish up-themselves male politicians to give us the vote.

Yeah, maybe Mrs Conner is right and we need to keep an eye on guys in case they try and oppress us.

Was talking about the voting thing with Mum at tea

tonight. Thought she'd be outraged like me, but instead she just lit up a fag and said, 'Aye, well, they needn't have bothered their arses. Look what clowns we've got to choose from these days. Greedy, useless, lying buggers, the whole sodding lot of them.'

Honestly, Mum is so cynical about everything. And she didn't take my concern about the oppression of females any more seriously. Just advised me that if any guy ever tried to oppress me I was to knee him hard in the you-know-whats. That's what she always did and it worked for her.

Hmm.

WEDNESDAY SEPTEMBER 8TH

Mrs Conner was still on about male oppression today and asked if anyone had had any personal experience of 'gender-based discrimination'. There were some blank faces so she sighed and said, 'That means boys being unfair to girls.'

There were a flood of complaints after that.

'My boyfriend only bought me a card at Valentine's and I got him a DVD and a box of chocolates.'

'My big brother always leaves the seat up in the toilet.'

'My dad won't let my boyfriend stay over but he's fine about my brother having his girlfriend to stay. Well, since they got married anyway.'

Mrs Conner wasn't interested in any of these but when I told her that Ferguson wouldn't let me join the boys' football team because I was a girl, she was outraged.

She was going to get to the bottom of this apparent injustice. There was no way she was going to countenance sex discrimination in her very own place of work. She would be discussing this issue with Mr Ferguson directly.

FRIDAY SEPTEMBER 10TH

Mrs Conner arranged a meeting to discuss things with Mr Ferguson and me in the English department in the second half of the lunch-hour. I kept my mouth shut the entire time but Mrs Conner had plenty to say as usual.

Mr Ferguson listened politely for a while but finally interrupted her. 'No way!' Seeing Mrs Conner's shocked look, he went on a bit more calmly, 'I'm sorry, Mrs Conner, but that's just not an option. Out of the question, I'm afraid.'

Mrs Conner smiled – a dangerous sign. 'Perhaps we should discuss this later, Mr Ferguson.'

'Nothing to discuss, Mrs Conner. I've made my decision as PE principal and I'm afraid it's non-negotiable.'

Oh my God. Ferguson was either a lot braver or more moronic than I thought.

'On the contrary, Mr Ferguson,' Mrs Conner said in a menacingly polite tone. 'There is, in fact, a great deal to discuss. Oh yes, a great deal.' She put her elbows on the desk and brought her fingertips together in front of her. This was almost always a sign that she intended to talk for a very long time, sometimes for an entire double period.

Mr Ferguson seemed to know this too, and I caught him glance longingly at the door before being forced to focus on Mrs Conner again as she continued, 'Clearly an informed judgement cannot possibly be reached without first considering the social, political, historical and, I hardly need mention, philosophical context of gender discrimination up to and including radical postmodern theory. Don't you think?'

Mr Ferguson muttered, 'Well, um, maybe, I'm not sure.'

'But I *am*, Mr Ferguson. And surely you'll agree that one cannot really have any meaningful debate about equality of opportunity for females in sport without first exploring the concept of gender per se, including its relevance to the issue of identity and whether, as some would argue, it is in fact a social construct rather than a biological phenomenon?'

Mrs Conner paused, supposedly to give Mr Ferguson a chance to say something. Yeah, right. Ferguson obviously had no clue how to answer this and his open-mouthed slack-jawed expression showed it, so Mrs Conner went on relentlessly.

I did what I normally do when Mrs Conner is off on one of her mad ravings and thought about other things, like what to watch on MTV tonight. Mr Ferguson wasn't so lucky though, as she was staring at him the whole time, scanning his face with narrowed eyes, alert for the slightest sign he wasn't giving her his total, undivided attention.

Even though Mr Ferguson isn't exactly my favourite teacher, I couldn't help feeling a bit sorry for him: he stared back at her like a trapped frog eyeing a python. He wasn't sure when she'd strike but he knew he was doomed. Totally.

It wasn't long before she moved in for the kill. 'So, Mr Ferguson, obviously these discussions will take some time. Oh yes,' she added menacingly, 'I think definitely some considerable time. Perhaps we should block out some periods in our schedule now. Let's just take a look at our respective diaries, shall we?'

Ferguson caved in. 'Erm, maybe it would be best if we just gave Kelly Ann a shot with the boys' team.'

Mrs Conner beamed at him. 'What a splendid idea, Mr Ferguson. Absolutely splendid.'

Yeah, go, Mrs Conner! Finally, yes, I'm in the school football team – which is what I've always wanted, isn't it?

When I came out I looked for Chris to tell him the fantastic news but couldn't find him. Instead I met Liz and Stephanie, who didn't seem impressed at all.

Liz said, 'But you'll have to buy a whole new football

kit. The boots alone will cost forty pounds. How are you going to save up for clothes, make-up and a mobile then?'

Stephanie was blunter. 'Ugh. Football boots and thick socks that fall down. You can*not* be serious. And the strip is totally the wrong shade of orange for you. There's no way you'll ever find a lipstick or nail varnish that will go, you know.'

'Seriously,' Liz said. 'Not many guys are going to fancy you if they see you like that. Are you sure you really still want to be in the team now?'

Thought about it. Did I? Actually, I concluded, not really any more. The thing is, I like football but maybe not enough to spend all that time and effort on it. I wanted to spend time doing other things now. Like maybe *dating* boys instead of just playing football and PlayStation with them. Will have to tell Ferguson I've changed my mind. Suppose he'll be pleased. Don't think Conner will be though.

SATURDAY SEPTEMBER 11TH

Stephanie says we can meet her boyfriend if we want and let her know what we think. They're going for a burger at McDonald's today, then off to see a movie. Liz and I could join them for the burger bit.

At first we said no, as we didn't wanted to gatecrash her date, but Stephanie said it was cool. 'We've been going out for two weeks. We don't need to be massaging each other's tonsils every two seconds any more.'

I was still doubtful but Liz was too nosy to turn down the invite so we're going. Must say, I'm a bit curious myself. Wonder what a boyfriend of Stephanie's will be like. Probably really rich and posh, with two second names like Legge-Burke or Fotherington-Smythe.

His proper name was Kenny but he told us we could call him Zombie if we liked. Everyone else did apparently. He wasn't tall but very thick. By thick, I mean his body was wide and solid, and his arms were so muscular they couldn't sit alongside his torso but had to be held out a bit, while his head seemed to merge into his shoulders without an obvious neck. He was also pretty thick in other ways too – he seemed incapable of stringing two coherent sentences together, grunting one-word replies to any polite questions we asked.

Most of the time he just sat silently shovelling large quantities of food into his mouth and demolishing them efficiently while ignoring the conversation around him. However, he did become very excited and enthusiastic when he talked about his job, which seemed to be his only real interest.

Turns out he is a trainee gravedigger – or cemetery operator, as he called it – and was keen to tell us all about it. Unfortunately.

Through Zombie we learned that graves were not 'six

feet under' but usually more like eighteen, especially for a multiple family plot. Digging that far down had its problems: in his first few weeks on the job, for a laugh his older workmates took his ladder and left him in the grave overnight, unable to climb out.

What were they like, his mates?

One time he'd fallen asleep in the grave and they'd tried to lower a coffin on top of him in the morning. He'd had to shout, 'Hawd on a minute there. I'm no' deid!' Which shocked the mourners of course. That was the great thing about working in the cemetery business. You didn't half get a laugh sometimes.

Hmm.

Other facts I didn't want to know included: how difficult it was to dig clay soil and prevent waterlogging; how even expensive oak coffins with tassels got invaded by various grubs over time, especially if people skimped on the lining; how the latest trend was for eco-burials in recyclable wicker coffins interred near surface soil so that the bodies decomposed faster.

Thanks.

When Zombie got up to go to the toilet Stephanie said, 'So what do you think? He's gorgeous, isn't he? Mmmm, those biceps. They're thicker than my waist, you know.'

I said politely, 'Yeah, um, very nice.'

Liz said carefully, 'He's sort of interesting, I suppose, but not exactly what I expected.'

'Why not? What did you expect?'

'Don't know. Just thought, well, someone a bit smarter maybe.'

Stephanie laughed. 'Yeah, he's not too bright but I kind of like that in a guy. I mean, his bicep measurements are probably bigger than his IQ but I'm not going to snog his IQ, am I?'

Suppose not.

Have told my parents that I want to be cremated, but as usual Mum treated my wishes, even on such a serious issue, with a total lack of respect.

She said, 'Right now – or can we finish our tea first?'

Very funny.

My dad said, 'Don't be stupid, Moira. She means after she's dead of course.'

I nodded my thanks to Dad, but he continued, 'Mind you, once we've cremated her, she will be, won't she?'

Ha ha.

MONDAY SEPTEMBER 13TH

Told Ferguson about not wanting to be on the team.

'Bottling out?' he sneered.

I flushed. 'Just changed my mind.'

'Ah, a girl's prerogative,' he said, all condescending. 'I'll just inform Mrs Conner, shall I?' Then he walked off.

Almost ran after him to say I'd changed my mind

again but thought that might look even more pathetic. It hadn't gone too well. But, oh God, what will happen when Conner finds out? She'll be furious.

She didn't say anything to me in English this afternoon so I supposed he hadn't told her yet. However, when I went to the newsagent's to get some chocolate after school, I noticed Mrs Conner looking at magazines in the corner. Was quite surprised as I didn't think she'd read anything that had pictures and wasn't at least five centimetres thick. Then I noticed some of the article headings: 'Expose Your Love Rat Ex'; 'Cheating Husband? Fifty Ways to Make Him Pay'.

She spotted me and said, 'Hello, Kelly Ann. This is fortunate. I was meaning to speak to you earlier. Mr Ferguson told me about your decision not to join the football team.'

'I'm so sorry, Mrs Conner. I mean, I was really grateful and everything but—'

'And I quite understand,' she interrupted.

'You do?'

'Of course. You merely wanted to establish that you had the inalienable right to join the boys' football team. And I think we made that point clearly. Whether you chose to avail yourself of this opportunity was a matter of personal choice. Wasn't that your point all along?'

'Um, yes, miss.'

'Splendid.'

She returned to browsing the mags. 'Crimes of Passion – Women Who Got Away with It'.

Felt I'd just been let off too.

TUESDAY SEPTEMBER 14TH

Bought a cheap mobile in town from pocket money I'd saved up. It didn't have a lot of features on it but it looked OK and had five pounds worth of free calls and texts.

I suppose I can afford it if I use my lunch money for top-ups and just live on scraps.

WEDNESDAY SEPTEMBER 15TH

Oh my God, it's fantastic having a mobile at last so I am no longer a sad technological social outcast. Spent the whole day calling and texting everyone I knew. Even people I didn't know but whom people I know knew. And received loads and loads of messages back. Finally I am a member of the teenage community.

Got into trouble tonight for calling and texting during dinner so was told to switch my mobile off. Put it on silent, finished dinner quickly – or, as Mum said, hoovered the food off my plate – and put it on again.

Was looking forward to a whole evening of texting and

calling friends but by seven o'clock I'd used up all my credit. Was surprised when Dad came up to me while Mum was in the kitchen and handed me a tenner. 'Here, love, this is for your phone. You'll need to buy the next lot from your pocket money, mind. And, erm, don't tell your mother I gave you anything. She'll just get on at me for spoiling you. You know what she's like.'

I said, 'Thanks, Dad.'

Dad asked me to go and make him a cup of tea. Went into the kitchen, where Mum was sitting reading a magazine and smoking a cigarette. Seeing me put the kettle on, she asked for tea as well. She drinks nearly as many mugs of tea in a night as she smokes cigarettes but at least it was better than downing more Bacardi and Cokes, so I agreed – not that I had a choice.

While I was waiting for the kettle to boil she surprised me by handing me a tenner and saying, 'Here, take this for your phone but don't tell your father. He can be a grumpy old bugger sometimes. Tight as a duck's bum. You know what he's like.'

I said, 'Thanks, Mum.'

Mum took her tea into the living room, switched on the TV, sat down and lit up another fag. Dad was reading the sports page of the newspaper, which is the only bit he bothers with. I looked at my parents affectionately. Yeah, they were maybe old-fashioned and knew nothing about the modern world, but they were decent, good-hearted people who loved me. It wasn't their fault they weren't too smart and were totally ignorant about fashion and modern technology. I shouldn't get so annoyed with them. They were more to be pitied in a way. I guess it's up to me to guide them through this new technological age.

Ah, another text. Didn't recognize the number. Excitedly I pressed to read it: KA U R A STPD LES.

Hmm, I'm being bullied by text. I suppose there is a downside to technology.

SATURDAY SEPTEMBER 18TH

Texted Liz. She agreed to meet me in town for a wander round the shops. Had a good time but then disaster struck.

We were walking across the bridge over the Clyde when a group of neds in trackies and baseball caps asked us for the time. I was stupidly taking my mobile out of my pocket to check when one of them lunged at it. I held on fast and bit his hand. Meanwhile Liz started hitting him with her umbrella. The other neds just stood around laughing. 'Haw, Billy, the lassies are gonnae gi'e ye a doin', man, so they ur.'

The ned managed to push Liz away and quickly grabbed for the phone again. 'Gonnae jist geez it. Ahm no gonnae go till Ah get it.'

That will be right. Liz came back to batter him some more – he didn't budge at first and kept trying to yank the phone from me, but I hung onto it with both hands. Under a renewed fierce battering from Liz, which broke her brolly, he suddenly let go. The move was so sudden that my arm swung up and back, then – oh God, no – the phone slipped out of my hand, over the railings, and into the water below.

The ned ran off shouting, 'Serves ye right – an yer mobile wiz crap anyhow, by the way.'

Tosser.

Am totally gutted as I've only had the phone for a day. Thought about diving into the water to get it but I'm not a very good diver, or swimmer, and anyway the phone probably wouldn't work now.

Hmm ... then again, maybe it would. Liz dropped hers in the bath last November and though it didn't work at first, when it dried out it was fine. Well, not totally fine: her predictive text doesn't work, the camera was ruined and she has to hold it upside down and shake it to speak, plus the only ring tone she can access is a naff Postman Pat theme tune, but still.

Was again considering diving in and Liz was trying to talk me out of it when luckily we spotted two policemen walking by. I ran over to them and quickly explained my problem. Decided not to mention my mugger as I wanted them to focus on getting my mobile back rather than tracking down the criminal, especially as it would just mean another asbo for him to boast about to his pals.

The policeman seemed puzzled by my complaint. 'So,

love, that's a shame but we're no' sure what you want us to do about it.'

Honestly, wasn't it totally obvious? What an idiot. But I just said politely, 'Please, Officer, could you get it out of the river for me?' The policemen looked startled so I quickly added, 'Well, not you personally of course, but, erm, the river police division, or, you know, um, frogmen officers.'

'Oh, aye, right. Frogmen, of course.' He nodded to the other officer then spoke into his radio. 'Sarge? Aye, there's a young lady here that's lost her mobile. Fell into the Clyde just a few minutes ago. We need a couple of frog-men right away.' Here he looked over the bridge into the river. 'Nah, cancel that. Maybe a dozen or so in case it's been swept downstream. And send the rest of the lads out to secure the area ... What's that you said? We're a bit short of officers just now because of the bank robbery in progress, the rooftop protest in Barlinnie, where they're holding the prison governor and staff hostage, plus another major terrorist alert at Glasgow airport? ... Look, forget all that, this takes top priority. I want every inch of the Clyde dragged to locate this lassie's phone. She had nearly twenty quid's worth of top-ups in it an' all.'

Of course, he hadn't even had his radio on properly. Hilarious. And the police wonder why they're losing the teenage community's respect.

SUNDAY SEPTEMBER 19TH

When Mum found out about my mobile, she went on and on at me for being an eejit who'd 'lose your head if it wasn't sodding well bolted on'. But luckily Aunt Kate and Great-aunt Winnie came over in the afternoon so Mum was too busy talking to them to slag me off much any more.

They'd come over mainly to have a nosy at Angela's new boyfriend, who she's invited over for dinner at our house even though she's only been going out with him two weeks. Apparently he's already dead keen to meet our family so he must be a real nerd. The good news is that Mum has bought Marks and Spencer's lasagnes, which are my favourite, so maybe that will make up for having to put up with another of the boring, stupid boyfriends my sister seems to attract.

Angela had begged Mum not to have loads of people over 'spectating', but Mum has said Aunt Kate and Great-aunt Winnie can meet him because they're family but they won't stay for dinner. I was relieved about that. Didn't want to share the lasagnes with too many people.

I was at my bedroom window keeping an eye out for someone who looked like he could be Angela's boyfriend, and I'd spotted several nerdy-looking possibilities who all passed by, when this really tall, fit guy got out of an expensive sports car and moved purposefully towards our door, carrying a bunch of flowers and a huge box of chocolates.

Bloody hell. This looked interesting.

I rushed downstairs and opened the door. He seemed startled. Maybe I should have waited until he'd knocked. But he just said in a nice American accent, 'Hi, you must be Kelly Ann. I'm David. Great to meet you.'

I took the chocolates from him, then ushered him into the living room.

Mum, Aunt Kate and even Great-aunt Winnie were as gobsmacked as me when they saw him and just gawped. However, they quickly recovered and soon everyone was chatting away easily.

As well as being very good looking, he seemed really nice too. He talked knowledgeably to Dad about sport, always respectfully deferring to Dad's opinion. And he answered all Mum's, Aunt Kate's and Great-aunt Winnie's nosy questions with a smile, calling them 'ma'am' and saying how honoured he was to meet so many of Angela's wonderful family. It was maybe a bit smarmy but they loved it. He even paid attention to me, asking me what music I liked and offering to teach me guitar as he's been playing since he was a kid and is quite good.

How had Angela managed to get this one? He seemed perfect.

But then suddenly he turned to Dad and said, 'Have you found Jesus yet, sir?'

Dad tried to laugh it off. 'Didn't even know he was missing, son.'

But David ignored the joke. 'He is missing in the hearts of too many poor sinners who need saving.'

And then he droned on for ages about how he'd found Jesus two years ago and how it had totally transformed his life. Might have known it was too much to hope that my sister had at last found a boyfriend who wasn't a total embarrassment.

Soon even Great-aunt Winnie – who's dead religious and goes to church every Sunday – was yawning like a hippo so she and Aunt Kate made some excuse and hurried out. But we would have to put up with him at least until after dinner.

I offered to help Mum in the kitchen just to get away. So did Dad, which is a first. The lasagne smelled delicious, and there was Häagen-Dazs chocolate ice cream for dessert, so maybe the evening wasn't going to be a total disaster.

By the time we sat down to eat I was starving as it was at least an hour later than normal. Couldn't wait to get started but then David said, 'Shall I say grace?'

Next thing I knew he'd taken hold of both Angela's hand and mine, bowed his head, and begun the longest prayer ever. He thanked God, not just for the food but absolutely everything: the table we ate it on, our family home to shelter us while we ate it, Mum and Dad's jobs for providing the money for it and our healthy bodies that would eat and digest it. Wouldn't have been surprised if he'd thanked God for the toilet we'd use afterwards but finally he stopped and I was allowed to eat my lasagne, which had gone cold. Mum's hadn't though – she'd finished hers while he was waffling on and was now smoking her after-dinner fag.

At long last he left. As he said goodbye, I had the oddest thought. Yeah, it was true. Wished Angela was still with Graham.

SATURDAY 25TH SEPTEMBER

Liz has dumped her boyfriend. 'He was so boring, Kelly Ann. I mean, no major traumas in childhood, no phobias, not even the slightest sign of obsessive compulsive behaviour. Nothing. Totally well balanced and adjusted.'

SUNDAY 26TH SEPTEMBER

Stephanie has dumped her Zombie. Apparently he gave her flowers pretending he'd bought them but had actually stolen them from the cemetery. She found a card still attached which said, *For our beloved gran. We miss you. RIP.*

MONDAY 27TH SEPTEMBER

I know I should probably feel sorry that my friends have split up with their boyfriends but it's not as though they're really cut up about it exactly. And I can't help being pleased that at last I would no longer be spending every Saturday night on my own. I was already planning what we'd all do next weekend but Stephanie appeared to have other ideas.

She showed Liz and me a picture of a boy called Harry. 'What do you think?'

We peered at him. Tall and slim with brown hair and a nice smile. He looked OK but not exactly Stephanie's type.

Liz said, 'What does he do? Not another gravedigger, is he?'

'No, he's still at school. Anyway, he's not for me. I'm thinking he might make a nice boyfriend for Kelly Ann.' Stephanie looked at me. 'Do you like him?'

'A boyfriend for me?'

'Yeah, why not? You can't stay a VL for ever. I told you I was going to set you up.'

'You did not!'

Stephanie shrugged. 'Must have forgotten. Anyway' – she pointed to the picture again – 'what do you think?'

'I don't know. I mean, I've never met him. You can't just get me a boyfriend like you're ordering stuff from a catalogue.'

'A boyfriend catalogue. What a great idea.' Stephanie laughed. 'Especially if you can send them back if you're not satisfied. Hmm, yeah, there'd probably be an awful lot of returns.

'Anyway,' she continued, 'Harry isn't from a catalogue. He's the son of one of Mum's friends. So, do you like him?'

I stared at the photo. Yeah, he wasn't too bad looking. Quite hot in fact. But what was he really like? And would he fancy someone like me? I'd need to find out more before I made an idiot of myself like I did with William.

'I don't know anything about him,' I said.

Stephanie sighed. 'He's just a boy. They're all much the same, aren't they? What do you want to know?'

'Well, erm, what school does he go to for a start?'

'It's a private school but he's not a snob.'

'Private school? The same one as Leo?'

'Who's Leo?' Stephanie said.

Liz groaned. 'Don't ask.'

TUESDAY 28TH SEPTEMBER

It's been decided that Stephanie will try to get Harry and me together. Decided by Liz and Stephanie, that is. I wasn't keen at first. Well, more scared really. The annoying thing is, now that I really want a boyfriend, the very thought of even talking to a boy I fancy makes me nervous, never mind actually going out with one.

But Stephanie has said she's going to prepare me before I meet Harry so I'll look absolutely fabulous and be super confident. First I'm to be given a total makeover. Then I'll have to be taught how to talk to boys. Liz had told her about the William disaster.

Am quite excited about it now. Wouldn't it be weird if, for once, *I* was the one with the boyfriend? Weird and, yeah, definitely exciting.

SATURDAY OCTOBER 2ND

Our school was playing St Ann's in the semi-final of the Glasgow schools competition. Liz didn't want to go but Stephanie decided to check out the talent on the Catholic team. Don't think she meant their football skills. For the second half we were standing beside the Catholic team coach, who wasn't a PE teacher but a priest who spoke with an Irish accent. Near the end of the game, since his team were winning one–nil, he took off a striker and sent on a reserve defender. Before going on, the boy crossed himself like Catholics do sometimes, and started muttering a prayer. I assumed the priest would be pleased by this, but no. He hissed at his player, 'Cut the crap and get on the pitch, you eejit. Do you want us playing a man down?'

Charming.

The Catholic team won. Having said that, Osman, who is our best midfielder, was off with a sprained ankle and his replacement, the new guy that Gary didn't like, was useless. Although I suppose he might have been having an off day.

Mr Ferguson took the defeat pretty well. He came over to the priest, shook his hand and said, 'God seemed to be on your side this afternoon, Father.'

The priest smiled back but said, 'You could say that, Hugh. Or then again you could say that we were the better team; more talented, better organized and with a first-class coach.'

Mr Ferguson laughed. 'Fair enough, Father. Are you up for a pint?'

'Is the Pope a Catholic? And you'll be paying, I take it, to acknowledge your well-deserved defeat against an overwhelmingly superior opposition.'

'Aye, that will be right.'

After the match Chris decided to walk home with us rather than go on the minibus with Mr Ferguson and the rest of the team. We talked about the game for a while even though Stephanie was sighing with exaggerated boredom.

Chris conceded that the other team were 'better on the day' and so deserved their victory. I knew he was right but his reasonable attitude kind of annoyed me.

We left him to get changed at his house and Stephanie came back with me.

As soon as he'd gone in she said, 'He's keen.'

'Yeah. Chris loves football. He's pretty good too.'

'No, I meant on *you*. Keen on you.'

'What? Don't be stupid. He's my friend – I've known him for ages. He's, well, more like a brother really.'

Stephanie raised a sceptical eyebrow. 'You think?'

'Definitely.' God, maybe she doesn't know as much about boys as I'd thought. How could she possibly imagine Chris fancied me?

She shrugged. 'OK, so you're still up for meeting Harry then? We'll start tomorrow.'

'I'm going to meet him tomorrow!' I said, suddenly panicked. Oh God, this was too soon. What if he didn't fancy me? Or worse, what if he pretended he fancied me for a laugh then told all his friends about it. I'd be so humiliated. This was a stupid idea.

'I'm not ready,' I said. 'It's too soon.'

'You can say that again. No way are you ready.'

'But why—?'

'Tomorrow you're coming over to my house for a complete makeover. Hair, face, body – the lot.' She paused to examine me and frowned. 'And clothes. What *are* you wearing? Didn't our shopping trip teach you anything?' She shook her head and sighed. 'Brown combats with a khaki T-shirt. This isn't the army. You're trying to get noticed, not camouflaged. God, we've got such a lot of work to do.'

Stephanie had given me another bigger photograph of Harry to keep, so when I got home I took it out and studied his face again. Yeah, he was really OK looking – or 'not too shabby', as Stephanie put it. I wondered what it would be like to snog him. Or any boy really.

Tried kissing the photo but it felt stupid and left a wet bit in the middle, so I put it on a radiator to dry then went downstairs and switched on the TV.

Flicked through the channels and found a programme with Indie music, then danced about for a while until Smashed came on. They were playing a ballad and the camera was focusing on a close-up of the lead singer, Jason. God, he was gorgeous. Much, much better than Harry. I went right up to the screen so I was nearly touching it. Nearly touching Jason, his lips just a centimetre from mine. Well, why not?

I tilted my head to the side, closed my eyes, and screamed. Sodding static.

SUNDAY OCTOBER 3RD

Decided to Google Jason this morning. Not that I was being stupid and obsessive like Debbie was with the guitarist, Matt. Actually I should say 'used to be' as she's now totally gone off him and is 'in love' with some actor in *Doctor Who*. No, I just wanted to find out stuff like what Jason's musical influences were, if he'd plans for a new album and whether he'd a girlfriend or not. Because, of course, a girlfriend can be an influence musically.

Jason doesn't have a girlfriend.

Went over to Stephanie's for the makeover and brought my heels with me like she'd asked. Was nearly late as I'd spent ages finding out about Jason. It's amazing how much information there was on him. Almost feel like I know him now.

Liz was already there. She'd come to 'supervise and advise'. And to eat the smoked salmon sandwiches followed by chocolate profiteroles, which Stephanie's mum had laid on for our lunch.

After lunch Stephanie told me to strip off and put on a white towelling dressing gown. I refused to take off my underwear, which annoyed her.

'A beautician,' she said, 'is like a gynaecologist. Used to seeing and dealing with every part of a woman's body.'

'Not mine.'

She tied my hair back with a white band, then slapped thick, gungy green face pack over what seemed like most of my upper body. Next she looked at my legs and shook her head. 'Ugh. That has to go.'

'My legs? What's wrong with them? I like them.'

'No, you idiot. The total forest growing on them. Gross.'

This was unfair. I've never had hairy legs like some girls do, so I don't need to shave them – or so I thought. But Stephanie insisted that legs had to be as bald as boiled eggs. And shaving was out of the question. I wasn't a boy.

When Stephanie ripped the first wax strip off my leg I screamed in agony and leaped up. There was no way I was letting her do that again – even if, as she pointed out, it would look as though someone had started to mow my shin then got fed up. But Stephanie and Liz were determined, and in the end Liz held me down on the floor by sitting on my chest, and Stephanie continued waxing while I writhed and screamed.

My screams brought Stephanie's mum into the room. Thank God. I was going to be rescued. But she just looked at the three of us on the floor and smiled.

'You girls having fun?' she said, and left.

Hope I never have to fight for my country, get captured and then tortured to reveal important secrets. I would tell everything if the pain was anything like having my legs waxed.

Absolutely refused to have the bikini wax and threatened to report them for indecent assault if they tried to make me. Anyway, as I said, 'It's October. Why would I wear a bikini on a date?'

The rest of the afternoon was much more fun. Stephanie let me try on loads of clothes from her huge walk-in wardrobe and insisted I keep a strappy red Ted Baker dress which she said I looked amazing in and was a bit tight for her.

Then she got out a make-up box the size of a suitcase and did my face lots of different ways, finally going for what she called a 'sultry' look, with slate-blue and purple eye shadow, red lips and just a touch of frosted blusher. It was amazing how old I looked after Stephanie had finished. Fantastic.

Stephanie was pleased with her work, saying she knew all along I had potential.

'Only thing now, Kelly Ann, is your hair. It's a disaster. Who's your hairdresser? He should be arrested.'

Hmm. Didn't like to say it was Aunt Kate, who wasn't a real hairdresser but I thought did my hair OK. Better than Mum anyway, who once cut my fringe so short I looked like Frankenstein.

Stephanie gave me the contact details for Albert, the hairdresser she uses, saying he was the best and to mention her name.

I wore the red dress and heels to go home. Even though I was a bit cold, despite my warm black jacket, I just didn't want to take the dress off just yet. It made me feel so good somehow. Feminine and, yeah, kind of sexy.

Couldn't help noticing the way boys were looking at me. Even some older boys. One of them smiled at me. Not a sleazy smile, more a kind of 'you look nice' smile.

It was strange getting attention from people who didn't even know me just because of how I looked. But nice strange. Exciting. Like suddenly discovering you've got some kind of magical power you never knew you possessed. Yeah, maybe being more grown up and girly wasn't as boring as I used to think.

Not the waxing though. Too much pain.

WEDNESDAY OCTOBER 6TH

Have decided to try Tampax again as I think it's more grown up and lets me wear what I want no matter what time of the month it is. Stephanie hasn't used anything else for years and Liz has now moved on to them as well.

I confided to them that I couldn't get the hang of it before. Stephanie told me to try Vaseline while Liz advised me to use a hand mirror for guidance. Have decided to do both.

Borrowed a Tampax from Angela's underwear drawer. Noticed the condoms had gone. Instead, there was a prayer book and a leaflet on Christian relationships.

It's weird really. Don't like David much but have to admit he's much better looking than Graham ever was. You'd think if Angela was going to do it with anyone, it would be David, but obviously not. Maybe it's the religion thing. Most of her dates seem to consist of going to prayer meetings. OK, I know they play guitars there, but still, it can't be much fun. Mind you, Angela isn't exactly normal either. Maybe she's right into stuff like that.

Couldn't find any Vaseline in Angela's make-up bag but there was some lip salve that I thought would do just as well. The small compact mirror didn't look nearly big enough though, so borrowed Dad's shaving mirror, which he keeps in his bedside drawer so it doesn't get misted up in the bathroom.

Right. All done.

After nearly twenty minutes I gave up. Don't ask, but all I'll say is this: when you can't do something with two hands it's even harder with one slippery one.

Returned lip salve and mirror but unfortunately was spotted by Angela and Dad in the process.

Angela said, 'What were you doing with my lip salve?'

Dad said, 'What were you doing with my shaving mirror?'

I said, 'Trust me, you *so* don't want to know.'

Decided to give up on tampons. Like waxing, they're a part of growing up that will have to wait.

FRIDAY OCTOBER 8TH

In-service day today, so I didn't have to go to school, and as Mum and Dad were at work I'd been looking forward to a lazy, peaceful day at home. However, forgot that Friday is also Angela's day off college. Unfortunately.

And she was in a foul mood all morning. First she barged into my room brandishing a tube of toothpaste that looked as though it had been strangled.

'Look at this!' she screamed. 'You've been squeezing the tube in the middle again and leaving the top off.'

I shrugged. 'I always squeeze the tube in the middle and leave the top off. But not that one. That's yours. The super whitening one you bought specially when you started going out with David. Remember?'

'Oh. Right. Well, um, don't do it again.'

Then she left, banging the door behind her.

Bloody hell. I'm used to the stupid bad moods, but Angela mangling her toothpaste tube? There must be something up with her.

I tried to avoid her as much as possible but she stomped around after me complaining about everything I did, from using the last tea bag to leaving toast crumbs in the toaster tray.

At least she was going out with David this afternoon so I'd get rid of her eventually. I went off to the living room and switched on the TV to drown out her moans but she came marching in after me grumbling about the teaspoon I'd left on the kitchen counter. I ignored her and tried to concentrate on the programme, but when the couple on TV started snogging Angela screamed, 'Turn that off! It's stupid and . . . and . . . disgusting!' Then she grabbed the control and switched it off.

'Bloody hell, they're not shagging. Just snogging. And they're not even using their tongues. What's up with you? You gone mental or something?'

'I don't know. I don't know!' she said. Then she started sobbing.

'What's the matter?'

'I don't want to talk about it.'

'Fine.'

But then of course she did. Every single detail.

'It's David. He won't do anything with me. Not even snog properly, never mind anything else. Says he's keeping himself for marriage. And he won't get married for anther five years at least, until he's finished university and got a proper job.'

'God, that's weird.'

'It was so different with Graham. He was always so passionate. Couldn't keep his hands off me.'

Ugh. Too much information. I changed the subject quickly.

'Why don't you just dump him?'

'I did. Sort of. Said maybe we weren't, you know, quite right for each other, but he wouldn't listen. Just said we were perfect together and we should pray to God for guidance to strengthen our relationship. That's what we're doing today. Going to a prayer meeting.'

'To pray about your relationship?'

'Yeah.'

'What a weirdo.'

'I can't face it, Kelly Ann,' Angela said desperately.

'So don't go. Tell him he's dumped.'

'I can't. He's such a good person. Generous, kind, and he, you know, respects me – maybe a bit too much. I'd feel really mean.' She paused for a moment, thinking, and then continued, 'He's coming round for me at four. You couldn't just tell him I'm ill or something? Or, erm, had to go out because of some emergency?'

'I'd better not tell him you're ill. He'd only bring the

prayer group round your bed to pray for your recovery.' I switched the TV back on. 'I'll tell him you're out but I really think you should dump him.'

'Thanks, Kelly Ann.'

He arrived nearly a half-hour early. Angela had been sitting gazing moodily out the window when she saw his car pull in. She ducked down, hissing, 'He's here!' Then she raced upstairs.

I answered the door.

'Hi, Kelly Ann, is Angela ready?' he said, with a pleasant smile I'd come to hate.

'Sorry, she's not in. I don't know where she is and I've no idea when she'll be back. She's left her mobile here so there's no point in calling her. Bye.'

I started to close the door but he put his hand on it to stop me.

'Now, Kelly Ann, don't you know it's a sin to lie? I saw your sister at the window.'

Bollocks.

'She's not here,' I repeated, since I couldn't be bothered to think of another lie.

'Now don't worry about your sister, Kelly Ann. I know she's had doubts about things recently but she'll feel much better after our prayer meeting. Our group is going to ask God to bless our relationship and grant us guidance and strength. I have great faith in the power of prayer.'

God, what a tosser. How did Angela put up with this? Totally determined to get rid of him now, I said, 'Actually we've just come back from church. I went with her to help her pray for guidance.'

'You did?' he said, surprised and suspicious.

'Yeah. We prayed really hard for ages and ages, then God answered us.'

'He did?' he said, even more sceptical now.

'Yeah. God said you two should split.'

'Don't be ridiculous. You're making this up. That's impossible.'

'Oh really? I thought *you* were the one who believed in the power of prayer. God definitely said it. Clear as anything. In fact, he said Angela should dump you right away.'

I tried to close the door but he blocked it and called past me, 'Angela, come on down. The prayer group's waiting.'

Angela didn't answer. He scowled and was about to barge in past me when, thank God, I spotted Mum walking towards our house, smoking a fag as usual.

'Mum!' I shouted.

David pasted a smile on his face again and waited for her to come up to us.

'What's going on here?' she said.

'Good afternoon, ma'am. Nice to see you as—'

'Angela doesn't want to see him any more, Mum,' I butted in quickly, 'but he won't leave her alone.'

Mum eyeballed him. 'Sod off.'

'There's seems to be some misunderstanding – I—'

Mum dropped her cigarette on the doorstep and, still eyeballing him, crushed it with her foot. And it was nearly a whole one. God, she must be really mad. She said, 'I thought I told you to sod off.'

Idiot still didn't take the hint. 'I can assure you, ma'am, your daughter Angela is just going through a temporary period of doubt which with God's grace will—'

Mum put her bag on the ground then took off her coat and handed it to me, saying, 'Here, look after this – it's my good coat so I don't want blood on it.' She turned to David, who at last had shut up and was looking at Mum with the expression of someone who'd just spotted an unexploded bomb. Finally he got the message.

Mum said, 'Get your pompous arse off my doorstep and stay away from my girls or you'll be meeting that Maker of yours a lot sooner than you'd planned.'

He opened his mouth to say something, but thought better of it, and without another word scuttled off.

Mum watched him contemptuously. 'Seems he isn't in any hurry to sample that afterlife he's always on about. I think that's the last we'll see of him.'

Thank God for that.

SATURDAY OCTOBER 9TH

Albert the hairdresser charged sixty pounds just for a consultation so there was no way I could use him. Stephanie is great but I wish she'd understand that not everyone has rich parents like her.

Managed to persuade Mum to give me thirty pounds for a proper cut though, as it's my birthday next week, and went to the hairdresser's after school. On the windows was an advertisement. MODELS WANTED. FREE HAIRCUTS.

Fantastic. If they took me I could use the thirty pounds to spend on clothes and make-up. And a pizza maybe. I was starving.

It was a trainee who was to cut my hair. She didn't look much older than me, but I was told she'd be closely supervised and if there were any problems one of the more experienced staff would sort things out.

Was relieved about that as the trainee, Tracey, didn't even wash my hair properly. The water was too hot, she got shampoo in my eyes and nearly broke my neck by shoving my head too far back into the sink when I complained.

Before she started cutting my hair, a proper hairdresser gave her some instructions and watched as she started to snip away at the ends, but then the place got very busy and she was called away, leaving me alone with Tracey.

Wasn't too worried though – I knew if Tracey made an

arse of it, the proper hairdresser would fix it later. Meanwhile she snipped away. At first she asked stupid questions as she worked. Was I doing anything special tonight? And where had I gone on holiday? Like, as if she really cared. But she soon ran out of things to say and carried on in silence while I watched in the mirror.

'Um, isn't the right side a bit shorter than the left?' I said.

She looked at my reflection. 'Hmm, yeah, maybe just a bit but I haven't finished anyway. I was just about to even it up.'

Yeah, right.

'And the fringe is squinty,' I said.

'Like I said. I haven't finished.'

She started snipping at the left side, but this time she made *that* too short so she had to take 'just a little bit more off the right'.

But then the right was shorter so it was 'just a smidgen off the left'.

I looked on in horror. Bit by bit my hair was getting shorter and shorter.

Finally I screamed, 'No! It's too short!'

This brought the proper hairdresser running over. Thank God for that. But how could she sort out hair that was too short? Extensions maybe? Though I couldn't see how you could attach anything to the stubble the trainee had left.

She looked at my hair and frowned. Then, after a

few moments' silence, she said, 'It's fabulous.'

'What? But it's too—'

'Absolutely gorgeous.' She beckoned to two other hairdressers, who were busy with clients. 'Come and see what Tracey's done.'

They crowded round me.

'Isn't it fantastic?' one said.

'Yeah, really suits her,' the other agreed. 'Look how it frames her eyes. Emphasizes her cheekbones.'

'Yeah, it's kind of, like, so gamine,' the first one went on. 'And, erm, sort of elfin. It's all the rage this autumn. Celebs are queuing up for this cut.'

Began to feel so much better. Looked at my reflection again. It had been a shock at first, but so many experienced hairdressers couldn't be wrong. This style was all the rage and I really suited it. Bet Stephanie will be pleased with me.

Before I left, I gave the trainee a five-pound tip. After all, she'd done a fantastic job and I was still saving twenty-five pounds on the cut.

Decided to wander into St Enoch's Square and see if I could find a nice skirt or top. Wished I'd gone to the toilet at the hairdresser's, as I was desperate now and I'd have to pay twenty p just to pee. It was a total rip-off but I didn't have a choice, and anyway I'd still saved a lot of money today.

Was just about to go into the loos when I heard a man behind me shout out, 'Oi, you!'

Turned round to see an annoyed-looking security man glaring at me. 'Where do you think you're going?'

I shrugged and started to make my way in again. It was none of his business after all.

But he shouted at me again: 'Get your arse out of there. That's the women's toilets, ya scadgy wee perve.'

Oh God. My hair really *was* too short!

SUNDAY OCTOBER 10TH

Stephanie and Liz are horrified and agree with me that there is absolutely no way I can go to school for at least two weeks so my hair can grow out. My planned meeting with Harry is also postponed.

Mum and Dad are furious at paying thirty quid for me to be 'scalped' and I had a lot of trouble stopping them from going to the shop to complain (didn't tell them about the trainee obviously or they might have thought it was partly my fault). Couldn't persuade them to let me stay off school though – I'd get my arse back there or else – so I'll just have to dog school without them knowing.

MONDAY OCTOBER 11TH

Mum and Dad were at work today and Angela off to college so it was easy to stay home without anyone knowing. Am avoiding mirrors as I really hate my hair. Despite my doubts about God's existence I prayed to him for my hair to grow quickly. Can't do any harm – unless He gets annoyed at people like me just using Him.

To take my mind off my hair problem and pass the time, spent most of the day watching MTV. Saw my favourite band Smashed to Pieces doing a concert in London.

Jason looked fantastic with his sun-bleached hair, eyes so blue they're almost navy and a slim muscular body to die for. He peeled off his shirt during the concert – because he'd just got too hot, not a totally crass show-off thing – so you could see his smooth tanned chest and washboard abs. Mmmm. Stephanie says all these guys wax their chest hairs and use different shades of spray tan to make exaggerated fake abs, but I don't think Jason is shallow and vain like that. The concert was in aid of the environment, for God's sake. That's how serious and responsible he is. No, Jason is just naturally fantastic-looking.

Remembered Liz had a DVD of him – well, him and the rest of the band. Must ask her for a loan of it.

TUESDAY OCTOBER 12TH

Since I'd the house to myself again I watched the DVD over and over all day. Mmmm.

I turned it off just before Mum got back and pretended to do homework while moaning about how much stuff teachers expected us to do out of school time this term. Felt a bit guilty as Mum let me off my usual jobs of setting the table for dinner and stacking the dishwasher afterwards as I was 'so busy'. But really, I hadn't asked her to, had I?

After dinner Mum and Dad went to the pub because there was a quiz on (any excuse) and Angela said she didn't want to watch anything on TV, so I settled down to watch my DVD again. God, Jason really was just so *hot*.

Had just got to the bit where he takes his shirt off when Angela came in and said, 'Kelly Ann, could I have word with you?'

'I haven't borrowed your mascara again, you must have lost it,' I said, without taking my eyes off the screen.

'It's not that,' Angela said. 'I already found it in your blazer pocket two days ago. I just wanted to ask your advice about something.'

I looked up at her now. 'You wanted to ask my advice?'

'Well, yes. It's not something I want to discuss with Mum or Dad and you are my sister after all. It's . . . it's about Graham.'

I paused the DVD. 'Graham?'

'Yes, he's been texting me. For quite a while now actually. He says he misses me and wants to talk things over.'

Oh God. Please no. OK, I know he isn't as bad as

David but that isn't saying much. No way did I want Angela's boring ex back now.

'What did you say?' I asked anxiously.

'Nothing yet. The thing is, I'm not sure I could ever forgive him, Kelly Ann. He's hurt me too much.'

'Course you couldn't,' I said, relieved. 'Just remember the stinking toilet. That should put you off.'

'You're right, Kelly Ann. I could never go back to anyone so insensitive.'

'Totally. Just ignore the tosser.'

'Yes. That's just what he is. And a selfish pig too.'

'And a complete bore.'

'Well, I didn't find him boring . . . But yes, maybe he was a bit, now you mention it. You're right, Kelly Ann: he was nothing but an insensitive, selfish, boring tosser.'

'Totally.'

'I'll text him that I never want to see him again, then I'll go and have a nice relaxing bath.'

'Good idea.'

What a relief. Angela obviously realizes at last what a sad nerd Graham really is. There's absolutely no chance she'd ever get together with him again now.

I pressed the play button and settled back to watch Jason again. Mmmm.

Was only halfway through when the doorbell rang. Angela was upstairs still having her bath so I had to answer it. Bollocks. Who could it be at this time?

Was gobsmacked and annoyed to find Graham on the

doorstep, all dressed in beige as usual. He looked surprised too.

'Christ, what happened to your hair?' he said.

I scowled at him. 'Fell out with horror when I heard you were texting my sister again. What do you want?'

'Is Angela here? I need to talk to her.'

'She's in the bath. A bath she can enjoy without wearing a gas mask now that you're not around.'

He flushed but I wasn't sure whether it was from shame or annoyance. 'I'll wait until she's finished. Can I come inside?'

Bloody nerve. 'No way. Angela doesn't want anything to do with you and neither do I. Now shove off, boring beige boy, nobody wants to listen to your pathetic excuses.'

God, I'd enjoyed that. And it didn't matter how much I insulted him because I'd never see him again.

I was about to slam the door on him when Angela called from the top of the stairs, 'It's OK, Kelly Ann. I'll deal with this.'

She had only just got out of the bath and was wrapped in a large pink towel, but she told Graham she would give him five minutes and let him in. He loped upstairs and they disappeared into her room.

At first I thought she was just going to let him beg for a bit, then slag him off, but when an hour passed and he still hadn't come down, I began to suspect they'd made up. Sure enough, when at last they came down, Angela and he were holding hands.

She said to me, smiling shyly, 'Graham has apologized and I've forgiven him. We're going to try again.'

Graham smiled dopily back at her. Oh God, pass the sick bag.

'Oh, right, that's, um, great,' I lied.

'Isn't it!' Angela said happily, then skipped upstairs to get changed and put on her make-up, leaving me and Graham to 'chat'.

Oh God.

WEDNESDAY OCTOBER 13TH

Mum wasn't at work today so I was forced to put on my uniform and pretend to go to school. Instead I went into town and changed into normal clothes in the toilets. Wore a skirt instead of jeans, and a hoodie to hide my hair, so I didn't risk being mistaken for a boy.

It got boring after a while just wandering around and I was wishing I could be at home watching Jason when, oh my God, I spotted Mrs Valentine, our French teacher, just outside Debenhams. And she saw me. Looked right at me. I'm dead.

I stood, frozen, and just stared at her with my mouth open like a filter feeder, but to my surprise she didn't march straight over and demand in an outraged voice why I wasn't at school. Instead she scuttled inside the store and disappeared.

But she'd seen me. I knew she had. Aha! So that was it. I smiled. Mrs Valentine was dogging school too. I was safe.

Went into W H Smith and searched for magazines with pictures and stories about Jason. Bought five, even though one of them only had two lines on him and cost two pounds fifty. It's cheaper to Google him.

Found a place to sit in St Enoch shopping centre. Had almost finished reading my magazines when an old gypsy woman who had set up a stall near me said, 'Like me to read your fortune, love?'

Looked at the board in front of the stall – PALMS READ £15 – and replied, 'No thanks.'

'I'll do it for a fiver. Business is slow just now.'

Have never had my fortune read. Thought it might be cool to know about exciting stuff that could happen. It would use up the rest of my hair money but I supposed I was bound to get some more for my birthday tomorrow.

'You've got a lucky face,' the woman continued. 'I can see good things happening for you. Great good fortune.'

Hmm, thought it was hands not faces she read. Still, great good fortune. Sounded pretty exciting.

The fortune-teller was amazing. I mean, so accurate. She told me I'd been on a trip across the water in the summer. *And I had*. How could she have known about that? She also said I had good friends, but nasty people who didn't like me too. But maybe most spookily accurate of all, she told me I'd recently had a bad experience but it would be solved in time. *My haircut.*

When she went on to predict my future it sounded so fantastic. I was going to be very fortunate. I would find True Love very early in life and, get this, meet someone famous soon who would have a big impact on my life. The famous person's initial was P or C, or possibly S or J.

Jason!

THURSDAY OCTOBER 14TH

My birthday! Can't wait for tonight, when Liz and Stephanie are sleeping over, but it's a bit lonely staying home on my own.

Googled Jason again. Found out some amazing things about him. Like, for instance, although he has apartments in London and California he was actually born right here in Glasgow. Even went to school here until his parents moved to England when he was fifteen.

And being born in Glasgow isn't the only thing we've got in common. The weird thing is, he's just so much like me.

Unlike the rest of the band he doesn't drink, smoke or do drugs.

Neither do I.

And he really cares about poor people, stopping wars and, most of all, the environment.

Just like me.

He hasn't met that 'special person' yet but is happy to wait for the right girl.

Me too. Although of course I'm waiting for a right boy. The thing is, I think I might have found him.

OK, I know that must sound mental but I'm definitely not just a stupid obsessed fan like Debbie. I don't care about Jason's shoe size (10½), birth weight (3.5 kilos), or rising sign (Aries, same as me!). And I'd never laser his face on my knickers (Jason and I would both find that totally vulgar). I'm interested in him as a real person.

Found his fan site where people can email him. I've never done anything like this before but I really wanted to contact him.

To: Jason
From: Kelly Ann
Subject: Hiya

Hi Jason

Saw your London concert. Thought you were fantastic. And all for charity too. I really respect that.

My name is Kelly Ann. I'm eighteen and study the environment at college. Like you, I think it's just *so* important.

I know you probably think this email is from another

shallow fan who's got a crush on you just because you're famous but nothing could be further from the truth. I'm interested in the *real* you. I think we've got so much in common and would love to hear from you to discuss stuff like the Environment and World Poverty.

Of course, I've got a fun side too and love telling jokes and so on, but not horrible jokes about poor people or farting, which is gross.

Hope to hear from you soon.
Bye for now.

Kelly Ann

PS I haven't met that 'special person' yet either so I'm single too.

Have checked my email about fifty times but still no reply. Even checked my junk mail just in case, but there was only the usual stuff offering to sell me fake Rolex watches or Viagra or penis enlargement.

Maybe he's out. Or maybe his computer isn't working.

Got a reply. But not from Jason, just some stupid admin person who is probably blocking people's messages.

To: Fan
From: Club Manager
Subject: Great Buys

Dear Fan

Thanks for emailing Jason. Your messages are important to him. Did you know that for just £4.99 you can get a signed photograph of Jason? Or, for only £9.99, why not order our super value photo and I LOVE JASON T-shirt. But real fans will probably only be satisfied with a life-size poster of Jason, plus the I LOVE JASON T-shirt with matching hat and socks set. Yes, be in touch with Jason from head to toe. And the good news is you can purchase the lot for just £39.99. Go on, order now while stocks last.

Remember your support means so much to Jason. He loves you all.

Decided to send another email to Jason, this time making it clear that it was a personal communication and not to be intercepted by nosy web administrators.

To: Jason
From: Kelly Ann
Subject: PRIVATE AND CONFIDENTIAL

Hi Jason

FOR JASON'S EYES ONLY!!!

It's Kelly Ann here. Don't know if you got my last message as I think some incompetent office person mistook it for fan mail. Maybe you need to have words with some of the people who work on your site.

Anyway, I've copied it again below. Looking forward to hearing from you soon.

Kelly Ann xx

Wasn't sure about the xx bit, but probably all creative, arty people put this in emails. It's not as though I'm sending him my knickers like some disgusting crazed fans do.

Have checked my email over seventy times and still nothing. Was in the middle of composing another note when the phone rang. Stupidly I picked I up. Still thinking about my note to Jason, I said, 'Hiya.'

Mum said, 'I've just had a call from the school, Kelly Ann. Apparently you've been ill.'

Oh God.

FRIDAY OCTOBER 15TH

Yesterday was the worst birthday of my entire life. Of course, Liz and Stephanie weren't allowed to come over and I didn't get my birthday money. I was allowed to keep my cards. Big deal. And have my cake, but as Mum screeched at me the whole time I was trying to eat it, the thing might as well have been made from papier-mâché for all the enjoyment I got out of it.

Mum and I have to go to the school office to meet Mr Smith today. Don't care what happens, I'm not going to classes looking like this.

Yeah! I've been suspended for a week for truanting. Mum thinks it's mental but I don't care. Another week for my hair to grow.

And another week to watch Jason. All day, every day. Liz, Stephanie and Chris have clubbed together for my birthday and bought me the complete set of Smashed DVDs since Jason joined the group, like I'd asked. They are allowed to bring them round tomorrow although they can't stay for long since I'm grounded. Can't wait.

FRIDAY OCTOBER 22ND

My grounding was lifted today but when Liz called and asked if I wanted to go the pictures tonight, I pretended it wasn't. The thing is, Smashed are on TV live at eight and Jason is being interviewed afterwards. There's no way I could miss that but I don't think Liz would understand.

Don't think anyone could really understand how I feel about Jason now. He's just perfect. Every little bit of him. Even his ears are gorgeous, and I don't usually like boys' ears. He's got beautiful golden skin, but in close up I can just make out that he has a couple of very faint acne scars on his right cheek. But guess what. They just make him look even sexier. No other boy could possibly compare with him.

Now I understand all that stuff about love and passion that Conner used to go on about before her husband dumped her. No wonder Romeo and Juliet topped themselves. How could I ever have thought that a PlayStation game or a Creme Egg would have helped take their mind off things? But back then I was a naive, stupid kid. Now I've grown up and I know what it's like to want someone so much you could burst.

And I want Jason that much. No one else will do. Only problem is, I'm not sure when, if ever, I'll get to see him for real.

MONDAY OCTOBER 25TH

At last I look nearly normal. OK, a few spots, but who cares when you've been practically bald! I've had my pocket money docked, probably for ever, but I've got hair. It's short, but not so bad that I'd definitely be taken for a boy, especially if I wear lots of make-up, which Stephanie has told me I have to do every day now until it gets longer.

She reminded me about Harry but I told her I'm not interested any more. She's suggested other boys but I've turned those down too. No one matches up to Jason.

Liz and Stephanie have both tried to 'talk sense' to me.

'He's about as realistic as Leo,' Liz said.

'Look, you idiot,' Stephanie said, 'if it's that fortune-teller you're thinking about, forget it. You're never going to meet Jason, far less find True Love with him.'

'But she was so just accurate,' I said. 'She knew everything about me.'

Stephanie rolled her eyes and sighed. 'Most people go across the water in summer. We're on an island, for God's sake. And a bloody cold, wet one.'

Liz agreed. 'Everyone has friends, enemies and bad experiences. Accurate my arse.'

Liz and Stephanie just don't get it. Fortune-teller or not, what I feel for Jason isn't just fancying. I know so much about him: his likes and dislikes, his hopes, ambitions and dreams. And we're so much alike. We could have been made for each other. No, what I feel for Jason is much deeper than fancying. It's the real thing. I won't ever want anyone else.

FRIDAY OCTOBER 29TH

Our head teacher called an assembly to tell us that in two weeks' time the school is going to be honoured by a visit from a very famous person. The reason we've been singled out is our wonderful work on the organic garden and contribution to environmental issues. The name of the VIP is being withheld for now, even from non-senior staff, for security reasons. We'll learn more in due course.

Ha ha, Liz and Stephanie. *Now* do you believe me?

MONDAY NOVEMBER 1 ST

Liz and Stephanie don't believe me. Liz says it will probably be some boring business person or local councillor, like all the other so-called VIP visitors we get.

Stephanie says there's no way people like our head teacher would even know the name of a boy band, never mind get them to come on a visit.

Liz agrees. She says the only boy band the head of this school would know is The Beatles, and they'd be too cutting-edge modern for him.

Mrs Conner told us the mystery VIP has said he wants to meet and talk to as many pupils as possible and not just staff. Most of these pupils will be selected by senior staff, but there'll also be a writing competition. The pupil who writes the best essay on the importance of the environment will be among the first to meet and talk with the VIP.

Mrs Conner said 'he'. So it definitely might be Jason.

Liz and Stephanie are probably right but I'm taking no chances. Am going to start working on the essay right away.

Decided to email Jason first. He hasn't answered my other emails, but maybe pop stars like him get too busy at times to check their mail and so have to catch up with it all at once. Also, if he knows he might be meeting me soon, he's bound to reply.

To: Jason
From: Kelly Ann
Subject: Meet up?

Hi Jason

I thlnk when I last emailed I may have said something about my being eighteen and at college. What I meant, of course, is that *when* I'm eighteen I'll be going to college. Actually I'm sixteen but very mature for my age – I look much older than I really am.

I hear you might be visiting my school. I know it's meant to be secret for a while longer to cut the security risk. It must get very annoying for you being mobbed by stupid immature fans. Hope to chat to you soon.

Kelly Ann xxx

TUESDAY NOVEMBER 2ND

They are showing a live recording of a Smashed concert in Liverpool starting at eight p.m. Rushed home from school to get ready in time. Showered, blow-dried hair perfectly straight, exfoliated and moisturized skin. Put on the red Ted Baker dress and high heels, then applied make-up like Stephanie showed me. Applied foundation and concealer first. Then blue and purple eyeshadow, carefully blended, followed by three coats of mascara – very important to let these dry in between. Lastly lip-liner, lipstick (two coats – blot with tissue paper in between) and gloss. God, almost forgot frosted blusher highlights.

Put on earrings and silver chain 'borrowed' from Angela, who was out, and rushed into the living room at 7.59.

Dad was watching football. I grabbed the remote and changed channels. 'Sorry, Dad. I've got to see this.'

He looked at me. 'Are you going to a party or something? Your mother didn't mention it.'

'No, I'm going to watch TV.'

'Why are you all dressed up then?'

'Jason's coming on. He's a singer in Smashed to Pieces. He's, um, very nice.'

Dad stared at me strangely for a moment, then he said in the kind of slow, careful tone of voice people use when they're trying to explain things to toddlers or calm a dangerous maniac. 'It's a TV, Kelly Ann. And the thing is, you see, although *you* can see the people on it, *they* can't see you.'

Very funny. Dad just doesn't understand. How could I watch Jason perform live (sort of) if I'm not looking my best?

Fortunately Mum and Dad went off to the pub so I was able to watch Jason in peace.

After the show, couldn't resist emailing him even if the stupid web manager blocks it again.

To: Jason
From: Kelly Ann
Subject: Ur Amazin'

Hi Jason

Fabulous concert. You were amazing. See you soon?

Love

Kelly Ann xxxxx

Was enjoying just lying on the sofa dreaming about Jason when Chris called. Gary, Ian and he were just about to buy curry. Did I want some? And could they come round to my house to eat it? It was nearer than anyone else's so it meant the curry wouldn't get cold.

Just realized I hadn't had any dinner because I'd been too busy getting ready for Jason. I was starving now so agreed right away.

When I opened the door to them, they all just stood on the step and gawped at me. Then Gary said, 'Bloody hell, Kelly Ann. You look, well, different. Um, quite nice in fact. Yeah, really not bad.'

'Yeah, Gary, I'm a girl in case you haven't noticed before. You coming in or not?'

They came in and we divided the curry takeaway up in the kitchen but took it into the living room to eat so we could watch TV.

Gary settled on the sofa beside me, then said, 'So, you went to all this trouble dressing up for us, Kelly Ann? That's nice. Shows you care.'

'In your dreams, Gary.' God, some guys were so up themselves. Not like Jason, who's gorgeous, talented and famous but modest too.

'Well, I like it anyway,' Gary said. He shovelled half a dozen onion bhajis into his mouth, then picked up a garlic prawn samosa and waved it at me before continuing, 'Never seen you wear a dress before. Suits you.' He looked over at Chris. 'Doesn't it?'

Chris was sitting opposite and, I now noticed, staring at me like he'd never seen me before. When he didn't reply, Gary repeated, 'She looks great in the dress, doesn't she? Pretty hot.'

'Yeah,' Chris said eventually. 'You look, well, amazing, Kelly Ann. Just amazing.'

Then he flushed and looked away. Guess he was embarrassed at being made to comment on how I looked when he's used to thinking of me as just a good friend like Gary and Ian.

The rest of the evening he hardly glanced in my direction and was really quiet. I was beginning to worry he'd fallen out with me for some reason, so when I went into the kitchen to get some Irn Bru as the curry was making us thirsty, I asked Chris to help me.

'You OK?' I asked.

'Yeah, course.'

'Only you've hardly talked to me at all tonight.'

'Suppose. It's just that . . . I don't know . . . you look so, well, different, I guess.'

'The dress, you mean?' I put on a silly high-pitched Pinocchio voice. '*I want to be a real girl.*'

'Not just the dress.'

'Oh yeah, the make-up. Stephanie taught me that. It's great, isn't it? Makes me look older.'

'No, not the make-up. You don't need it. You've got a really nice face. You're, well . . . beautiful.' He flushed. 'I think so anyway.'

Jeez, that was something coming from Chris – he almost never lies or exaggerates about things. And exciting too. Liz and Stephanie have warned me that famous singers like Jason always have hundreds of girls chasing them, so even if I ever did manage to meet him, the competition would be fierce. Maybe if what Chris says is true, he might notice me after all.

WEDNESDAY NOVEMBER 3RD

Seventeen spots, all on my forehead. Maybe it's all the make-up I used yesterday, but then sometimes I just get spots for no reason anyway. So much for having a beautiful face and making Jason notice me. Looking like this, I wouldn't even come up to Terry Docherty's standard. Something Must Be Done. I've moaned about it to everyone who would listen but no one seems to care. Dad just said, 'What spots?' Thought he was being sarcastic at first, but, no, he really never noticed. Just shows how much attention he pays me.

Mum said, 'Away and give me peace – can't you see I'm watching *EastEnders*?'

Hmm, a plot about a mother who ignores her daughter, forcing her to run off with a dodgy older man.

Liz offered me counselling to come to terms with my spots. She says I should embrace my spots as part of my personality; accept them and be proud of them as part of who I am. Yeah, right. All right for Liz to talk – she doesn't have any. Anyway, I don't want who I am to be Pizza-face.

Only Aunt Kate, who came over to help Mum measure

curtains for her bedroom, bothered enough to actually answer. She said she used to be plagued by spots when she was my age but then she discovered toothpaste.

Couldn't see what brushing my teeth had to do with spots and said so. No one gets spots on their teeth after all.

'No, Kelly Ann. You rub the toothpaste onto your spots. Last thing at night is best so it can stay on while you're sleeping. Oh, and wear a turban too. That'll keep your hair away from your face so you don't get toothpaste on it. And keeping your hair away helps stop your skin from getting greasy too. Spots love grease. You'll have to do this for a couple of weeks, mind, but it'll work a treat. Did for me.'

Hmm. Have dotted the toothpaste on every spot. Now for the turban, which obviously is a bit of a problem as I haven't been turban-shopping recently. Who wears turbans now anyway except for Sikhs? Still, Aunt Kate used to have one at one time a long time ago, so maybe Mum had a turban somewhere that she doesn't wear any more. Decided to ask.

Wish I hadn't bothered. At first I thought I was in luck when Mum said, 'Turban? Yeah, just a minute and I'll go and check my turban drawer. What colour would you like?'

Had answered, 'Pink please,' before I realized she was being sarcastic. Hilarious. Mum nearly wet herself laughing anyway. 'Turban my arse. And don't go asking your father either. He's no' the bloody maharaja.'

Supposed I would have to do without the turban but then I thought of Liz's knickers. Well, I didn't actually think of Liz's knickers, of course, so much as what she used them for, apart from the usual. If they could keep her hair out of her face pack, they could keep mine out of my toothpaste. Perfect.

Rummaged in my drawers to see if I could find an old greying pair of knickers I don't wear any more. Hmm, all my knickers are old and greying but I *do* wear them. Have to until Christmas anyway, which is the only time Mum buys me underwear. If I ever get knocked down, I hope it's not too long after Christmas, or I will be totally embarrassed at the hospital.

Fortunately, spotted a pair of pink knickers with yellow and red Winnie-the-Pooh bears on them which my Great-aunt Winnie bought me for my thirteenth birthday and which I've never worn for obvious reasons. Well, not quite true: I wore them once when I'd run out of clean knickers, but unfortunately under white shorts so people could see the pattern, which earned me the nickname 'Bear Bum' or sometimes 'Pooh Pants'. Hilarious.

I hadn't thrown them out though, as Great-aunt Winnie always checks whether you've binned her useless presents by asking to see you using or wearing them, and even though she was unlikely to inspect my knickers I'd decided I'd better not count on it. However, now I was glad I'd kept them as they would be perfect as a turban.

Put the knickers on my head, and yes, they were nice and tight, keeping my hair back perfectly. Must say I looked a bit stupid with blobs of toothpaste on my face and naff knickers on my head, but so what? No one would ever see me and everyone knows you have to be ugly to be beautiful or something like that.

THURSDAY NOVEMBER 4TH

Think the toothpaste is working, sort of. I've still got seventeen spots. Well, eighteen if you count the new one on the end of my nose, but they are definitely fainter. Maybe, like Aunt Kate says, it's just a matter of persevering with it. I'm absolutely going to keep this up even if I do have to buy a new tube of toothpaste after Mum moaned at me that there was none left this morning.

Was gutted at first to hear that I came second in the writing competition and pleaded with Mrs Conner to let me meet the VIP anyway.

'You *will* be meeting him, Kelly Ann, as you were the only entrant.'

Thought about this. 'So, erm, how come I came second then?'

Mrs Conner shrugged. 'Your work wasn't of sufficient standard to merit a first place.'

Bloody hell. I suppose I should be insulted but I didn't care. Soon, I might just get to see Jason for real.

FRIDAY NOVEMBER 5TH

Our head teacher came over the tannoy today to announce that the VIP is a royal but, for security reasons, didn't tell us which one. Everyone is hoping it's one of the young ones but I don't care. It's not Jason.

Mr Menzies is going mental marching about the school and nosing into classes. He even visited the girls' toilets today but sent Miss McElwee in first to throw us all out. I mean, really, it's a total invasion of our privacy.

The problem is that the VIP is planning to take a tour of our whole school so our head teacher is freaking out about the state of the place.

Mrs Conner is furious because Mr Menzies used her English higher class to wash floors and polish banisters during double English. Mrs Conner is a republican who utterly disagrees with the 'very concept of monarchy in a modern society'. She is threatening to stage a protest when the royal person turns up.

None of her higher pupils objected to being used as domestic slaves, however, as they were meant to be reading a Walter Scott novel and most people would rather scrub toilets with their tongues than read Walter Scott.

MONDAY NOVEMBER 8TH

We've just been told the royal is Prince Charles and not one of the young ones. Everyone is pretty disappointed except our head teacher, who acts as though we're getting a visit from God Almighty or something. Honestly, he's such a snob.

Apparently the Prince, as well as congratulating us on our environment award, is also going to formally open our 'new' science and technology building.

Actually it's not really new – it was built two years ago by some company called PPP; however, none of the teachers use it because it's freezing in winter (heating doesn't work), roasting in summer (all the glass means it's like a greenhouse) and the roof has caved in twice. They are supposed to have fixed things now, but nobody trusts it, so it's basically a large ugly glass box beside the school which the jannie uses to grow tomatoes in. We can't get rid of it, even though it's useless and, according to our modern studies teacher, we're only renting it. And for ten times the cost it would take to buy. It's nuts.

On the way home from school Liz was on at me about Jason again. She said, 'Now are you going to admit the fortune-teller was talking rubbish?'

'Totally not. She said I'd meet someone famous with the initials PC. And he's definitely famous.'

'She's right,' Stephanie said. 'He isn't Jason but he is famous.'

'Oh yeah, and how is he going to have a big effect on your life then?' Liz giggled. 'Maybe he's going to invite you back to the palace, then send you off to school at Eton.'

I laughed. 'Eton's just for boys and you have to wear naff clothes. No thanks. Palace might be OK though.'

Steered the subject away from Jason, but I hadn't given up hope. Somehow I know deep down that Jason and I are fated to meet one day. After all, the fortune-teller also told me that I would find True Love early. And I think I'm beginning to love Jason more than anyone I've ever known.

TUESDAY NOVEMBER 9TH

Oh my God. Don't believe it. Smashed are doing a concert in Glasgow on December 11th. It's fate. I really *am* going to meet him. Only problem is, tickets are forty pounds each.

Liz says she can't come as it's too dear, and anyway Zach is in rehab again and it's rumoured the band are kicking him out so he probably wouldn't be there, but Stephanie says she'll come with me. Now all I have to do is get my parents to fork out the money.

* * *

At first Dad said it was too expensive but after I'd pleaded with him for several hours he gave in.

'OK, love, if it really means that much to you, I'll do it.'

I threw my arms around him. 'Thanks, Dad.'

'Ah, well, eighty pounds is a bit steep to listen to four eejits singing crap songs and cavorting around on stage like drunken chimpanzees, but if it makes you happy—'

'It's only forty pounds, Dad. Stephanie will pay for herself.'

'Aye, well, obviously I'll have to come with you. I'm not having you and Stephanie on your own at night with all those dodgy characters around.'

'NO!' I screamed. 'You can't come with me. I'd be a laughing stock.'

But Dad wouldn't give in. And I refused to go with him. Hate my dad. How can I ever grow up if he treats me like a five-year-old?

WEDNESDAY NOVEMBER 10TH

Mum, thank God, has sided with me. 'For Christ's sake, she's fifteen, not five. And there's no way you're going to a boy band concert like some dirty old pervert among all those young lassies. Now get on that phone after your dinner and book her a ticket.'

'Thanks, Mum.'

* * *

Dad called but all the tickets are gone. The guy said they sold out in the first hour. Am gutted. But Jason will be in Glasgow in December. And no matter what, I am totally determined to find him.

THURSDAY NOVEMBER 11TH

Mrs Conner is definitely organizing an anti-monarchy protest on the day of Prince Charles's visit. Our head teacher is fuming but there's nothing he can do as Mrs Conner is insisting that the right to peaceful protest in a democracy is sacrosanct.

People have been making placards during English periods and the head objected to this 'frivolous waste of teaching time'. But Mrs Conner pointed out that the purpose of English was to communicate, and what could be more important than communicating one's dis-approval of the constitutional status quo and the need for reform. In any case it was far more educational than scrubbing floors and polishing banisters.

Don't know why anyone bothers to argue with Mrs Conner. I mean, they've got as much chance of winning an argument with her as I have of winning a wet T-shirt contest.

Liz agrees with Mrs Conner and will be joining the protest. Her placard says DOWN WITH MONARCHY. Gary is joining for a laugh. His placard is shaped like a guillotine and says, OFF WITH THEIR HEADS in red letters with blobs dripping off the end of each word like blood. He was made to change it to PENSION THEM OFF but told he could keep the guillotine shape.

Mrs Conner's said, THE CONCEPT OF MONARCHY IS ARCHAIC IN A MATURE DEMOCRACY AND MUST NOT BE TOLERATED. WE SHOULD ASPIRE TO BE EMPOWERED CITIZENS, NOT SUBJECTS. I thought it was kind of long for a placard myself – the writing was so small you could hardly read it, but whatever.

The only support from other staff has come from our modern studies teacher and Mr Stewart, the physics teacher, who always wears a kilt and sporran to work. He believes in monarchy but says the Queen isn't the rightful heir to the throne. He says he's traced the line from Mary Queen of Scots to the present day and the real Queen is a chiropodist in Govan called Fiona. His placard reads: IMPOSTERS OUT!

Emailed Jason. Surely if the interfering web manager sees the kind of people I associate with, he'll realize I'm not an ordinary fan and make sure Jason gets this.

To: Jason
From: Kelly Ann
Subject: Prince Charles

Hi Jason

How are things? Hope you're having a great time in LA this weekend.

Anyway, just to let you know I'll be meeting up with Charles next week. Of course I mean Prince Charles (heir to the throne). We'll probably chat a bit about the environment 'cos, like you, we're both kinda keen on it. Just wondered if there's anything you'd like me to bring up while we're on the subject?

Gotta go now.

Bye!

Love Kelly Ann xxxxxxx

FRIDAY NOVEMBER 12TH

Am starting to feel a bit nervous about meeting Prince Charles. He really is a Very Important Person after all. OK, I know Mrs Conner doesn't think so, but I've never met anyone so famous. I mean, he's been on TV loads of times and his mum's face is on stamps and money. You can't get much more famous than that.

At least Stephanie and Chris will be with me. Stephanie was picked because of her posh voice and Chris because Mr Menzies asked Stephanie to recommend a boy in our year and she chose him. Mr Menzies seems to think Stephanie is totally responsible just because her parents have got money. Just shows how wrong a person can be.

Chris and Stephanie aren't that keen on being part of the welcome group but they don't seem at all worried.

Unlike Mr Menzies, who's really freaking out about Prince Charles's visit. He's had all the corridor floors not just brushed and mopped but polished as well. They're now so shiny Terry Docherty says you can see girls' knickers reflected in them (which you *so* cannot, but some idiot girls are walking around with their knees squeezed together anyway), and Miss McElwee slipped and hurt her hip. Mr Menzies wasn't very sympathetic, even though she had to go to hospital for an X-Ray. Just asked her if she'd still be able to do the cucumber sandwiches and vol au vents for the Prince's visit.

Mr Menzies has also had all the windows washed, walls repainted and fake grass put on the football pitch, which he said was too muddy. But the most stupid thing was the toilets.

Went in at break today and they were lovely – sparkling clean, jasmine scented and, best of all, every cubicle had fat rolls of three-ply ultra-soft toilet paper. However, before I could use our new luxury facilities we were ordered out and the janitor locked the doors. He told us we wouldn't be able to use them again until after the Prince's visit in case we messed them up.

Tried to argue with him. I mean, Prince Charles wasn't likely to want to use or inspect the girls' toilets, but he wouldn't budge. Said he'd got his orders from the head teacher and that was that.

Of course he also locked the boys' toilets but had to reopen them when the boys threatened to pee in the glossy corridors if he didn't. They weren't allowed to use the cubicles though.

By home time I was bursting and wasn't sure I would make it to my house. Liz suggested I go behind some bushes in the park – she would keep a lookout for me. But I was too scared someone would see me, especially as it was winter and most of the bushes didn't have leaves.

'Did you know,' Liz said, 'that a pregnant woman is allowed to pee anywhere she likes in the UK? Even in a policeman's helmet? It's the law.'

'Well, um, right, Liz, thanks, but I think it might be quicker for me to just hurry home to my own toilet than get myself pregnant and ask for a policeman's helmet.'

'Good point,' Liz said and laughed.

Which made me laugh too. Unfortunately.

SUNDAY NOVEMBER 14TH

Am really nervous about meeting the Prince. What if I say or do something wrong? Our head teacher will go mental. Hardly slept last night thinking about it.

Called Chris, who said not to worry, I'd be fine, and in any case there would be so many people we would have hardly any time to say anything.

That's true at least. As well as the three of us, there's a fifth-year swot who plays the violin and goes to spelling tournaments, the head girl and boy, and two other sixth years. Anyway, the Prince will probably spend most of the time talking to our head teacher and Mr Smith.

Still, there's bound to be photographs – maybe even for the papers – so I need to look good. Don't want Jason to find some awful picture of me with spots, greasy hair and crumpled clothes.

Have ironed my skirt and polished my shoes like Angela would and laid everything out for tomorrow. Have also asked Mum to wake me early so I've plenty of time to get ready. Can't wait for tomorrow to be over.

MONDAY NOVEMBER 15TH

Mum woke me at seven but I was tired as I'd taken ages to get to sleep last night; I decided to just go back to sleep for half an hour.

Oh God – ten past nine already! I'm late. I've missed registration, obviously, but if I get a move on I might possibly make the meeting with Prince Charles. Just as well I got my stuff ready last night.

Scrambled into my clothes, snatched up my bag and ran out. Damn. Forgot shoes and had to run back in. Found a polo mint in my blazer pocket and crunched it. Not much of a breakfast but at least it would stop my breath smelling as I hadn't had time to do my teeth.

Jogged all the way. Knocked over a toddler which was attached to its mum with reins so they both went down. Felt bad but there was no time to waste. Outside the post office I also barged into a pensioner who was a lot sprier than he looked and managed to whack me with his walking stick as I ran off.

Finally got to the school gates, where a small crowd of protestors (including Liz and Mrs Conner) were gathered with their placards. Also saw that – oh my God – it was *him* on the steps leading to the main school entrance. Prince Charles was already there, chatting to Mr Menzies, whose head was tilted to the side, nodding like he'd broken his neck and couldn't control it.

Liz spotted me and shrieked, 'Kelly Ann. No! Go back home!'

I ignored her and ran towards the steps and right up to the welcome group. The head teacher didn't see me at first, though the others, including Chris, stared at me open-mouthed and eyes wide like they'd just seen a yeti or something.

Honestly. Couldn't they be a bit more discreet? I was only a minute late after all. Chances were the Prince wouldn't realize if they'd just stop gawping at me.

Mr Menzies hadn't noticed as he was totally involved in grovelling to the Prince, his balding head bobbing up and down, body bent so low he looked like he planned to kiss Prince Charles's feet any moment.

I sidled along behind them and stood at the end of the queue beside Chris, who annoyed me by shoving me away and sort of pointing with his eyes for me to leave. Everyone else seemed to be doing the same, especially Stephanie.

No way. I was going to stay here and talk to Prince Charles like I was supposed to. Anyway, it would look really rude if I just went off now, like I'd got bored waiting or something.

Mr Menzies was saying, 'Yes, sir. Thank you, sir. I couldn't agree more, sir.'

Then the Prince turned to Mr Smith, who was next in line. I'd thought Mr Menzies hadn't noticed me coming late but he must have realized now, because when he saw me his humble smile vanished and he looked so furious I thought he was going to have a heart attack. His whole face went a purply red and the veins on his bald head stood out like climbing ropes and started pulsing. Oh God, I would be in trouble after this. Wish I hadn't been late, but it was only a few minutes after all.

Anyway, if the Prince noticed, he didn't let on, just continued to move down the line, smiling and talking to people. Obviously he had the good manners to overlook small stuff like this. Unlike our head, who was showing up his commoner background.

The Prince made his way down the line until he came to Chris. 'So, young man, you intend to do medicine. Excellent. Marvellous. Tell me, what are your views on homeopathy?'

'Um, well, it has its place, sir.'

'Indeed, yes. Wonderful.'

Couldn't help smiling at that as Chris has always said it's superstitious crap.

Then it was my turn. At first I nearly clammed up completely. Well, I've never talked to anyone famous or with such a posh voice before. But Prince Charles was great. Really dead nice and not nearly as stuck up as I'd expected. From a royal person anyway. He asked how I was doing at school (not all that great actually, but he admitted he was pretty duff at some subjects too), what my hobbies were (not polo) and other stuff, so I was soon gabbing away, feeling totally at ease about the whole thing. Kind of hoped if the Prince liked me then the head would forget to be annoyed later. Finally Prince Charles asked if I was looking forward to using the new science and technology centre.

Was going to say, *Yeah, totally*, but he'd been so nice I didn't think it would be right to lie to him, so instead I said, 'Not really. You see, no one is allowed in there as it's not safe. We can't knock it down though as it cost a lot of money so it will just have to stay. A pity, 'cos it's an ugly-looking thing, isn't it?'

'Hmm, well, I mustn't say really. Got into rather a spot of bother before, speaking my mind about such things.'

'Oh, you shouldn't worry about all that stuff people say about you. I mean, I know some people say you talk to vegetables and are totally bonkers, but I think you're all right really. Just a bit odd maybe and kind of old-fashioned. Anyway, I think it's good for old people to be old-fashioned and, you know, sort of traditional. There's nothing worse than someone even older than your dad trying to act cool. Cringe.'

'Quite, yes. I, um, see your point. One does value tradition. Sometimes the old-fashioned ways are best, don't you think? Using toothpaste to get rid of spots for example. Marvellously effective remedy, so I'm told. But your, um, snood? I didn't think young people today wore those any more – though I suppose all fashions come round again eventually.'

I frowned. Snood? What was he on about? He was right about the toothpaste though. It's been great for my— Oh. My. God.

The Prince moved away, followed by the head teacher and Mr Smith, both of whom managed to throw me a murderous glare as they passed, but I hardly registered it. Instead, I twisted round and stared at my reflection in the sparkling clean office glass. Then Stephanie came over and handed me a make-up mirror.

Yes. White splodges of toothpaste dotted about my now scarlet face made me look like a tomato infected with a fungal disease – but worse, much, much worse, were the Winnie-the-Pooh pants on my head. I took them off and stuffed them in my blazer pocket but it was too late now. Way too late. I'd worn my knickers on my head when talking to the Prince of Wales, heir to the throne. I *had* to be in trouble. Big trouble.

TUESDAY NOVEMBER 1 6TH

Yeah, I was right. The head told my parents and me to meet him in his office today. Mum couldn't make it as she was too busy at work so it was just Dad and me.

Mr Menzies said I had brought the whole school into disrepute and that I was a disgrace. He was only thankful that the press photographer had been late, so this outrageous event had at least not been publicized in the media, but that was no thanks to me. What I had done was unforgivable.

Dad tried to reason with him, saying that it was just a kid's mistake and no offence was meant, but the head ranted on some more about how I'd shamed myself, my fellow pupils, the entire staff and even my country, which I thought was a bit OTT. Then he said it would be better for all concerned if my parents set about finding another educational establishment, otherwise I might be formally expelled.

Oh my God. Hoped Dad would start pleading with the

head to let me stay, but instead he got totally up himself. 'Aye, well, you can keep your sodding school. I never thought it was good enough for my Kelly Ann anyway. I wouldn't let my daughter spend another minute here if you got down on your knees and begged. C'mon, Kelly Ann. I think we're about finished here.'

Oh my God.

WEDNESDAY NOVEMBER 17TH

Mum went mental at Dad last night, but the damage had been done. I'm suspended until I find another school. I don't want another school. Not that I'm all that mad keen on the one I had but at least all my friends are there.

Dad rang my now ex head teacher to say he'd maybe been a bit hasty in the heat of the moment yesterday but it was hopeless. I'm out. For ever.

THURSDAY NOVEMBER 18TH

Mr Smith has turned out to be helpful for once, maybe because he thinks our head has been a bit harsh, but he can't say that of course. But anyway, he says I've already missed too much school with absences and suspensions, especially as I would be sitting my standard grade exams next year. He offered to help us cut through the red tape and has rung round schools to see if anyone can take me, but the only school near us that has a place, or admits to having a place anyway, is Blackhart Academy, which has an awful reputation.

Told Mum, 'I can't go there. They'll steal my dinner money to buy methadone and carve out my tongue with a broken beer bottle if I tell anyone.'

Mum said, 'You'll be fine. If not, blame that eejit of a father of yours.' But for once she didn't sound very sure of herself and kept glancing at me anxiously all evening. She wasn't even able to concentrate on *EastEnders* and switched it off. Things must be bad. Now I was really worried.

FRIDAY NOVEMBER 19TH

Dad took the morning off work to go with me to (maybe) my new school and meet the head teacher. On the drive there he tried to calm me down.

'You'll be fine, love. I'm sure the reputation of the place has been exaggerated. In fact, I've heard things have improved a lot since the new head took over. Mind you, he's the third one this . . .'

Dad's voice trailed off as we approached the school. There was barbed wire around the walls and a notice on the gates saying BEWARE OF THE DOGS. We went in anyway and Dad parked the car. Immediately a hooded ned appeared and offered to 'look after' our car for a fiver. Dad told him to away and boil his head, which I thought was a mistake, but he wouldn't listen to me.

The school office buzzed us in, then, after passing through a metal detector like you do at airports, we were allowed into the head teacher's office.

The head seemed quite normal, except for a twitch under his left eye and the way he looked over his shoulder at the wire-meshed windows behind him.

Dad said, 'I was a wee bit worried about your sign outside. You know – the one that says BEWARE OF THE DOGS.'

'Ah yes. Nothing to worry about. We used to keep guard dogs to patrol the school grounds at night as we'd had some bother with break-ins. Had all our computers burgled once and our funds for disadvantaged teenagers taken. But we don't use the dogs any more.'

'Right, good,' Dad said. 'Things improving round here then? Crime going down?'

'Erm, well, not necessarily. No. On the last break-in they stole the guard dogs.'

'Oh.'

Dad didn't say much after that. The head prattled on for a while, then suggested that the head girl give me a tour of the school while he and Dad had a private chat.

The head girl was called Destiny Charmaine McCluskey. She had most of her face pierced and set off the metal detector when we went through, but nobody bothered. She also had joined-up chunky gold rings on four of the fingers on each hand, which looked a lot like – and probably were – knuckledusters.

Destiny seemed quite friendly to me though, showing me where all the CCTV cameras were placed and advising me on which ones were not working if I ever needed to have a snog or a smoke in private.

She stopped at one of the broken ones and lit up a fag, generously offering me one. I said, 'No thanks.' But, worried in case she thought I was a snob, added, 'I'm try-ing to give up.'

She shrugged. 'Me too.' Then took a deep drag.

A skinny ned in dirty grey trackies and hoodie passed close by, nodded 'Hi' to Destiny, then hurried off.

She called after him, 'Oi, ya scadgy wee bam, come back here and geez the purse over. Can ye no' see Ahm looking efter her.'

Bloody hell, he was good. I hadn't noticed him nicking my purse out of my pocket.

He handed it back and Destiny gave him a swipe with her ring-knuckled hand, so that his lip started to bleed.

Oh well. Maybe I'd be all right here if Destiny was looking after me.

'You wouldn't happen to have a couple of quid on ye by any chance?' she asked. 'The thing is, Ahm running oot o' fags and Ahm a bit short this mornin'.'

Hmm. Then again, maybe I wouldn't be OK here. I handed her the contents of my purse and we continued our tour.

Afterwards I met Dad at the exit. We made our way to the car without saying a word. I was surprised to see that it was still there and in one piece with no broken windows or scratched paint. Only the hub caps were missing. The boy who'd offered to 'look after' our car was also still there and was perfectly polite and helpful to us. He promised to 'find out' who had nicked the hub caps and return them to us for a tenner. Dad paid up.

MONDAY NOVEMBER 22ND

It's been decided that I'll not be going to Blackhart Academy. Instead Mum gobsmacked me by saying I'd be going to the Catholic school, St Ann's.

'I can't go to a Catholic school. I'm not a Catholic.'

'Aye, well, you are now. That's what I've told them. And that's what you'll be. We're going for an interview tomorrow. Keep your mouth shut and leave the talking to me. Unless you want to go to Blackhart Academy and come back in a flaming body bag.'

Good point.

Called Liz and Stephanie, who came over to discuss the move. They agreed it would be much better than Blackhart. Anything would.

Stephanie said, 'Let me know if there are any hot Catholic boys there. But make sure they're OK about using condoms first. Some Catholics are weird about stuff like that.'

'Yeah, right, Stephanie. Fine. So, like, I'm really going to go up to some boy and say, *Hi there, I'm new here, but you look OK. So, I was just wondering, how do you feel about using condoms?*'

Stephanie sounded puzzled. 'Why not?'

Liz told me it's rumoured that Jason went to the exact same Catholic school for a couple of years.

Oh my God. Just imagine. If I go there, I might end up sitting on a seat that Jason once sat on. Seems so intimate somehow. Yeah, I'll go.

TUESDAY NOVEMBER 23RD

The head teacher seemed nice. Much friendlier than my last one and not nearly as snobby. The priest, Father O'Reilly, was also there. I stayed quiet, like Mum had told me, while she talked about why I wanted to join St Ann's.

Father O'Reilly said, 'So, Kelly Ann, according to your mother, you've both been lapsed Catholics for . . . let's see now, nigh on ten years, but have seen the error of your ways and want to rejoin the Holy Mother Church, and that's why you left your previous school to come here.'

'Yes, sir.'

'Father.'

'Um, Father.'

'And you've lost your baptismal certificate but will send us one in due course – however, this may take a wee while, given your mother can't remember which parish issued it.'

'Um, yes.'

'So your wanting to join St Ann's would have nothing to do with your having flashed your knickers at the heir to the throne then decided that the ethos of Blackhart Academy is a bit too exciting for your taste. Word gets round, you know.'

I flushed. 'No, Father.'

'Well' – he turned to look at the head teacher – 'I see no reason why she can't start right away then.'

The head nodded his agreement and Father O'Reilly turned to me again.

'Right then, we'll see if we can make a good Catholic out of you. Haven't managed that with any of the rest of our pupils but, well, you never know. Miracles do happen.' He laughed at his own joke, then continued, 'Mind you, you don't have to be Catholic to join the school. We have quite a number of non-Catholic pupils here.'

Now he tells us. But what could I say?

'Oh, right. Thanks, sir – Father.'

The head teacher added that Father O'Reilly was likely to be around the school more than usual over the next few weeks as he was monitoring the delivery of RE and also collecting funds for the church roof.

He looked at the priest. 'So, Father, you'll help keep an eye on our new pupil and deal with any concerns she may have in adapting to a Catholic education?'

'Certainly, I'd be glad to.'

Mum left me to it then. I was given a timetable and Father O'Reilly escorted me to my first class.

There were loads of holy statues in the school, mostly of Jesus' mum Mary, but some of Jesus too. Seemed odd to see them in maths and geography classes, instead of just in a church, but I didn't mind until I went into the school dinner hall, where there was a gigantic cross with a life-size figure of Jesus nailed to it.

I mean, really. How was I supposed to enjoy my lunch with the image of a person being horribly executed stuck in front of me? Why do Catholics do stuff like that? They wouldn't show people being hung, or guillotined, or strapped to an electric chair, would they? Why show someone being crucified?

Unfortunately I mentioned all this to Helen and Theresa, who were supposed to be looking after me for the first week. They told me I was weird and left me alone. Yeah, right, so *I'm* the weird one. They've got a nerve. They're the ones who can pig out on chips with macaroni cheese while watching someone being cruci-fied.

Was beginning to feel uncomfortable sitting there all by myself when a group of boys sat down next to me.

Great, I have no problem talking to boys. I kept my eyes off the huge cross and joined in their conversation about football. Unfortunately they were talking about an old firm match last week where Rangers won one–nil and I stupidly disagreed with them when they said that the goal was offside.

'No,' I said, 'it was definitely OK.'

'Rubbish. The Rangers striker was offside. Anyone could see it. Referee was blind.'

'Wasn't blind,' I said. 'Didn't you see the replay? Ref made the right decision. Definitely. Rangers won fair and square.'

There was a long silence as the boys looked at me; then one of them said, 'You're that new girl from the Protestant school, aren't you? Bet you're a bloody Rangers supporter as well. Why don't you just shove off?'

Oh God, my first day was not going well.

WEDNESDAY NOVEMBER 24TH

Took sandwiches to school today but still had to eat them in the dinner hall as it was freezing outside and they don't have a social area. I sat with my back to the crucifixion and tried not to think about it. Succeeded in that but then started to feel uncomfortable as no one sat at my table. I might as well have had a notice stuck to me saying, SAD PERSON WITH NO FRIENDS. DON'T COME NEAR HER

After lunch I wandered about on my own, the shame of my friendless state obvious to everyone. Tried smiling at some people but they didn't smile back – just ignored me or scowled back in a 'what are you smiling at, you idiot?' way, so I felt like a retarded person smiling at nothing.

Wanted to shout, 'Look, I'm not weird. I've got loads of friends – well, some anyway. People do like me. Normal people. Quite normal people anyway.' But that would have made me look stupid and I'd be even more unpopular if that were possible.

Since I'd nothing better to do, I found out from a passing teacher where my next class was, then just went and waited outside the door, even though the bell hadn't gone. It was a personal and social development class taken by a guidance teacher called Mrs McKind. She came along early too, I suppose to prepare things for the class. She had a nice, kind-looking face like her name, but I hated the pitying look she gave me as she said, 'You're the new girl, aren't you? Haven't you made any friends yet?'

But it got much worse when the lesson started as she went on at the whole class for being 'uncharitable' in excluding me. She even said, 'Now I hope you are all feeling thoroughly ashamed of yourselves and will make sure Kelly Ann has someone to play with next lunch time.'

Play with! I mean, for God's sake. But, whatever, I was socially doomed anyway. Mrs McKind had just guaranteed my status as the saddest, most pathetic person in the whole school. For ever.

THURSDAY NOVEMBER 25TH

Decided to eat my sandwiches in the toilets today so no one would see that I was too unpopular for anyone to sit beside. Went to the quieter ones, which were tucked out the way behind the science block. There was another girl in the cubicle next to me and, oh, thank God, she talked to me.

'No one wants to sit beside you either?' she said.

'No.'

'Me neither. People say I'm too boring.'

'Yeah, well, what do they know?' I said. 'I'm sure you're really interesting if they bothered to get to know you properly.'

I decided to do exactly that.

Her name was Bernadette Donnelly. Asked her if she liked Jason from Smashed and told her how gutted I was that I was going to miss the concert, but she told me she wasn't really interested in bands. She also didn't like sport and never watched TV or listened to music. She wasn't keen on boys, movies or games. This made finding something to talk about a bit difficult but in the end we had quite a long conversation about her lunch.

Bernadette always has her lunch in the same cubicle, the second from the end. She has tuna and mayonnaise sandwiches every day except Fridays, when she has ham and tomato. She prefers ham and tomato to tuna mayonnaise so Friday is a treat. One time, by mistake, her mum made her ham and tomato on a Thursday. It was such a surprise. How her mum and she had laughed and laughed about it when she got home. And guess what? Her mum made her ham and tomato sandwiches on Friday again anyway. So she'd had ham and tomato sandwiches twice that week. Wasn't that amazing? But not as amazing as her birthday lunch, when she always had roast beef sandwiches and two fairy cakes.

Yeah, amazing. Seems like I'd done the impossible and found someone in the world even more boring than my sister.

Liz, Stephanie and Chris rang me tonight to ask how I was getting on. They'd done this every day since I started, and like every other time, I just said I was doing fine.

Don't know why I'm lying to my best friends like this. I suppose I feel a bit embarrassed about being such a loser. Also, if I admitted to them how awful things were, it would make it more real somehow.

I get the feeling Chris doesn't believe me as he keeps asking questions about my day and ends every call by saying, 'You sure you're really OK, Kelly Ann?'

However, Liz and Stephanie don't seem to have guessed there is anything wrong and I just listen to them babble on about school. How boring double maths had been and how Conner is refusing to do the *Cinderella* pantomime this year because the story is sexist, trivializes extended stepfamily problems and glorifies monarchy.

Tonight Liz also told me that our head teacher read out a letter from Prince Charles saying how much he had enjoyed his visit, particularly meeting the wonderful young people with interesting ideas and refreshing candour.

'The head is really pleased now, Kelly Ann. Bloody snob. And it seems that Prince Charles was impressed with the pupils after all. Especially you. If only he'd said this sooner you wouldn't have had to leave school.'

Yeah, if only. But it was too late now. Finished the call quickly before I started to cry.

FRIDAY 26TH NOVEMBER

RE is even worse here than in my last school – all they talk about is Catholic stuff. We also have a really awful teacher, Sister Mary Benedicta, who is so old she makes Miss McElwee look like a teenager and so bad-tempered that Mr Smith now seems as jovial as Santa Claus in comparison. And we have five periods with this fossilized penguin person every week.

It doesn't help that she's taken a dislike to me. Just because I had the nerve to correct her when she got my name wrong. Not that she paid any attention to my correction and insists on calling me Mary Ann.

Today she was banging on about hell. 'Don't listen to these people who tell you hell is a myth. Hell is real. As real as I'm standing before you. It's where God sends all those evil souls who die in mortal sin to be tormented for all eternity.'

And dying in mortal sin seemed scarily easy actually. According to her anyway. Miss Mass on Sunday, then get knocked down by a bus, and that was you. Thought this was a bit harsh and said so, which earned me a punishment exercise for insolence. Then she just went on about what happened to sinners.

Father O'Reilly came in and interrupted her, thank God, to make a collection for the church roof – and, I suppose, to check on her teaching, although he didn't seem that interested in the second bit. She filled him in anyway.

'I was just telling the class, Father, not to listen to this new-fangled nonsense about hell being a metaphor. As Catholics, we know that hell is a real place of eternal suffering and torment.'

'Listen to the good sister now,' Father O'Reilly said. 'It's just as she says. Hell is real all right. A terrible place of perpetual pain and unimaginable agony.'

Bloody hell. Everyone started to look a bit worried, except Sister Mary Benedicta, who smiled approvingly.

But then the priest went on, 'Not that our good and merciful Lord would ever actually send anyone there, mind, but it's the principle of the thing. Now, c'mon, I want you all to put your hands in your pockets and give generously, for the Lord can't stand misers.'

Tiptoed quietly into the toilets at the beginning of lunch and settled in the cubicle furthest from the one Bernadette used. Tucked my feet up for good measure so she wouldn't realize I was there.

No such luck.

'You think I'm boring too, Kelly Ann, don't you?' she called through the cubicle door.

Oh God.

So relieved to get home tonight. A whole weekend before I have to go to school again. I really hate it there; mostly because I have no friends, but also because I hate Sister Mary Benedicta and we have RE every day. She's mental and really scary too. All that stuff about the afterlife. Wonder if there really is anything in it.

I think Mum knows there's something wrong with me – she's always asking what's up with my face – but there's no point in talking to her about it. I mean, what can she do?

She was nice to me tonight though and sent Dad out to get a KFC for dinner, which is one of my favourites.

But even at dinner I couldn't stop thinking about school. Mum looked over at me. 'Something wrong with chicken? I thought you liked these. What's with the torn face?'

'No, they're great. I was just thinking about stuff.' I picked up a drumstick. 'Mum, do you think there's a life after death?'

Mum shrugged. 'Don't know. I'm beginning to wonder if there's a sodding life before death in this house.'

'What do you think, Dad?' I asked. 'Is there an afterlife?'

'No, love. It's all rubbish. Like your grandfather used to say, "When yir deid, yir deid, jist like a dug."'

Hmm. I took another bite of my drumstick and thought about this. 'But some people think animals have souls. So maybe dogs have an afterlife as well.'

Dad laughed. 'Well, Kelly Ann, if that's what you think, maybe you should leave that drumstick alone. The chicken mightn't be too pleased with you when you meet it in the afterlife.'

Looked at my delicious KFC drumstick. Have just decided that animals don't have souls after all.

RE again. This time she was on about condoms. Yuck. Someone like her even mentioning condoms is disgusting. She's mental too, going on about how they're sinful even for married people, and how if we all followed Catholic teaching and practised chastity, then no one would need condoms anyway.

Father O'Reilly came in halfway through the lesson and again she turned to him to back her up.

'Isn't that right, Father? Abstinence from sin and the avoidance of temptation is the Perfect Way to conduct ourselves as good Catholics.'

'It is indeed, Sister Mary Benedicta. Of course, the good Lord knows we're none of us perfect and temptation is hard to resist.'

'I beg your pardon, Father?'

'Oh, not for you, Sister, of course not.' He stared at her face, which was heavy and solid like a warthog's and just as glum looking. 'The good Lord has been merciful and made sure that you would never suffer temptation of the flesh.' He turned to the class. 'But for others not similarly blessed like the good sister here, well, it's a matter of the lesser of two evils.'

'You're not condoning the use of contraceptives, Father!' Sister Mary Benedicta said.

'Of course not, Sister. I'm merely echoing the teachings of the great saint, Ignatius Giuseppe Marcellus of

Iquabeth. You'll be familiar with him naturally, Sister, and what he said on these matters?'

'Oh, well, yes of course, Father, but perhaps you'll just remind me—'

'Certainly, Sister. As the sainted martyr Ignatius Giuseppe Marcellus was wont to say to all those privileged to listen to his holy words of wisdom: *If you can't be good be careful*. Or words to that effect anyway.

'Now, boys and girls' – he rattled his collection box – 'as the blessed saint also used to admonish the children of his parishioners, if you can afford to buy those new PlayStation and Xbox games, you can afford to dig deep into your pocket and give from your hearts. And I don't want to see any coppers, mind.'

TUESDAY NOVEMBER 30TH

RE again. Decided to do what I normally do at RE classes and tune the whole thing out, so I was dreaming about being back at my old school, where I had friends and didn't have to eat in the toilet, when the penguin got at me.

'Mary Ann, have you been listening to me?'

'What? Me? Um, yeah. Course, miss – I mean Sister.'

'Then you'll be able to tell us why the Holy Trinity is like a shamrock.'

'Erm, yeah. Right. What was the question again?'

The old bat repeated her question while I thought frantically. Hmm, Trinity. Had to have something to do with three like a tricycle. Right. 'A shamrock's got three leaves, Sister.'

'Yes. Go on.'

'And it's, um, green?'

Some people in the class started to giggle. The nun scowled at them.

'Are you mocking me, child? Or is it the Good Lord himself whom you're mocking? The Father, Son and Holy Spirit.'

'I wouldn't take the p— erm, make fun of you, Sister. I was just, er, thinking aloud. What I meant to say is, it's, er, Irish.'

More laughter.

'Right, that's it. This is blasphemous. I'm sending you to Father O'Reilly.'

But Father O'Reilly wasn't in so I had to wait until after lunch time to see him. When I went into his room I saw he was just finishing off some work on a spreadsheet, which kind of surprised me. I thought priests would be doing stuff like reading the Bible or praying maybe. Not working on a computer.

He saved the file, then told me to sit down in the chair opposite him.

'So, Kelly Ann, Sister Mary Benedicta tells me that you're having some trouble with certain aspects of

Catholic doctrine. Seems you're a tad confused about the Holy Trinity, and who can blame you? It's puzzled theologians for centuries. Mind you, none of them have suggested that God the Father, the Son or the Holy Spirit is a green Irishman yet. Still, is there any other part of Catholic doctrine you're unsure of? Don't be afraid to speak your mind now. I'd be interested to hear what you've got say.'

I was relieved that he wasn't going to go mental at me like the nun had. He was smiling and seemed genuinely interested in my views, so I said, 'Well, yeah, there are a few things actually. Like the God thing.'

'The God thing?'

'Yeah, like, you know how people say there really must be a God because life and the universe couldn't just sort of spring out of nothing? So God must have created everything?'

'Yes.'

'Well, you've still got the same problem really, haven't you, because, well, who made God then?'

'An interesting question.'

'Yeah, and then there's the heaven and hell thing. Well, it's a bit mental really, isn't it? Hope so anyway, as I've never been to Mass. And I'm not even really sure about the life-after-death stuff . . .'

I paused, thinking maybe I'd said too much. A holy person like a priest might think I was being really cheeky and get mad at me.

Father O'Reilly was staring at me but he didn't have an annoyed expression. In fact, if anything, he looked as though he was trying to stop laughing, so hopefully I wasn't in trouble.

He said, 'So go on now, Kelly Ann. You were talking about the, er, life-after-death stuff?'

'Yeah, well, maybe there isn't anything afterwards, you know – kinda like it was before you're born.'

'I see,' Father Reilly said. 'It would appear you are struggling with a number of issues of Catholic doctrine that are, shall we say, not too trivial. Perhaps Sister Mary Benedicta isn't quite the right guide for you at this particular period of your, er, spiritual journey, shall we say.'

'Don't think this *school* is right, Father. And I'm a Rangers supporter too. I just don't fit in. Can't I go back to my old school? I don't think the head's so mad at me any more.'

He paused, considering what I'd said, and I waited, desperately hoping he'd say yes. But he didn't.

'I don't believe you could make another placing request so soon. Not unless you were expelled of course. No, you've just got off to a bad start, Kelly Ann. Things will settle down fine soon. You have to be patient. Give it time.'

Instead of telephoning, Chris came over tonight to see how I was getting on. At first I just said, 'Yeah, OK, fine,' but face to face there was no way I could convince him I was OK and soon I was blubbing out the truth to him.

'I hate it there, Chris. Nobody likes me. I . . . I've got no friends. I just don't fit in.'

At first he tried to soothe me like the priest had. 'You just got off to a bad start, Kelly Ann. Give it time. I'm sure people will realize you're OK eventually – you'll make loads of friends.'

'I won't. Nobody wants to get to know me except Bernadette, who's the saddest person in the whole school and just makes it even worse.'

Chris argued with me for a while, but then gobsmacked me by saying, 'OK, look, Kelly Ann, if that's the way you feel about it, then I'll come and join you. That way you'll have at least one friend there. You won't have to eat in the toilet any more.'

Oh God, it would have been so fantastic to have Chris with me. 'But how could you do that?'

'I'll ask my parents to arrange it. Make a placing request.'

'They wouldn't do that. You get on fine at our school.'

'They will. If not, I'll get myself expelled, then they'll have to.'

I looked at Chris's determined expression. He meant it. And he'd do it. There wasn't anyone as stubborn as Chris once he'd made up his mind.

Found myself getting a bit tearful again. Chris was the best friend anyone could have. But I couldn't let him change schools just for me. However, he'd given me an idea.

Thought back to what the priest had said this morning. That the region were unlikely to agree to another transfer so soon *unless I was expelled*.

Yeah, that was it. All I had to do was get myself expelled. Should be easy enough – and, yeah, might even be fun.

WEDNESDAY DECEMBER 1 ST

RE first thing. I've been removed from Sister Mary
Benedicta's class and put into another RE class. The
teacher seemed quite nice and normal; she's really a
maths teacher but all the Catholic teachers have to take an
RE class. She just told us to get on with any homework we
might have or chat quietly amongst ourselves while she
did some marking. Seems this is what she does every RE
period.

It's a pity she was nice because I needed to cause
trouble to get expelled. Oh well.

I shouted out. 'Religion's rubbish!'

She said, 'We're all entitled to our opinion, Kelly Ann.
Haven't you got any homework to finish off?'

'Total crap.'

'How about a book to read? Why don't you go off to
the library and see if there's anything you like there?'

Tried a few more times after that but still couldn't get

her annoyed. Decided I'd have to pick on a teacher who wasn't so nice and laid back.

Art next. We were meant to be painting a bowl of fruit. Instead, I graffiti'd ART SUCKS on my desk in jagged blood-red letters.

Art teacher said my work was amazing. 'Raw, powerful, totally original'. I had 'passion' and 'soul'.

Bloody hell, it was going to be a lot more difficult to get expelled from this school than I thought.

English. Took out a packet of fags I'd nicked from Mum's stash in the morning and lit up. God, it was *so* disgusting. How could anyone actually like these things? Even though I didn't inhale and just puffed the smoke out, I nearly choked. Teacher said, 'Put that out at once.'

This was more like it. Instead, I flicked some ash on the floor, then swung back on my chair and put my feet on my desk. Looking her straight in the eye, I took a Bacardi bottle (an empty one of Mum's that I'd filled with water this morning) from my bag and swigged it.

'Right, that's it. Go to the head teacher's office immediately and wait there while I write out a referral about your outrageous behaviour.'

Yeah. At last.

Waited half an hour before Mrs McKind, the guidance teacher, came and ushered me into the head's office.

He and Mrs McKind couldn't have been nicer. Young people like me with addictions would receive understanding, counselling and support. I needn't worry that I'd be condemned or abandoned, far less expelled. They were an enlightened school at the forefront of the substance abuse programmes (SAPs) initiative. Meanwhile I was to go see Father O'Reilly for spiritual guidance to overcome my problems.

Father O'Reilly wasn't visiting the school until the afternoon, and then he needed to discuss things with the head teacher first, so it was nearly home time when he finally talked to me in the RE base.

He said, 'Now tell me, Kelly Ann, do you really have a problem with the demon drink and are you addicted to the vile tobacco weed?'

I looked at my toes. 'No, Father.'

'So correct me if I'm wrong here, but this was a ploy to get yourself expelled. Right?'

I nodded.

'Well now, you'll be pleased to hear that after our discussion yesterday, I've been in touch with Mr Menzies and talked to our own head and we've agreed to a kind of prisoner exchange.'

'Sorry?'

'We'll take back Mick McKenzie, one of our poor disadvantaged thieving, lying – well, never you mind – ex pupils, in exchange for your good self. We'll have another go at putting the fear of God in him. And I plan to do more than give the disadvantaged wee bug – er, soul more than three Hail Marys and an Our Father for his sins.'

'Oh my God, I can go back to my old school? Really? Thanks, Father.'

'Och, you're welcome, Kelly Ann. You've given me a good laugh, so you have. But we'll have to OK it with your parents. Your mother having been so keen to make a good Catholic out of you and all.'

'Father, if every priest were like you I'd definitely want to be a Catholic.'

Father O'Reilly smiled at me. 'Ah, but you have to like the song as well as the singer, Kelly Ann.'

Not sure what he meant by that but asked him, 'Do you believe in any of it, Father? Religion and stuff?'

He was silent for quite a long time. I suppose he was surprised by my question – which, when I thought about it, was a really stupid thing to ask a priest.

But then he said, 'Ah now, Kelly Ann, that's a deep theological question you're asking, especially so near home time, but I'll tell you one thing.' He paused and fixed me with a serious gaze. 'I believe Celtic will wallop the bejesus out of Rangers next Saturday.'

I'm leaving today and, though I can't wait to get back to my old school, have discovered that I'm now suddenly very popular. Seems everyone was well impressed by my rebel behaviour and wants to hang out with me. Maybe I would have got on OK here after all.

Loads of people wanted to spend lunch time with me today but I decided to go and see Bernadette in the toilets. This time, after knocking, I went inside her cubicle instead of sitting in the one beside her.

'I'll really miss you, Kelly Ann.'

'Yeah, well, I'll miss you too, sort of,' I lied. 'Here.' I handed her a roast beef sandwich I'd prepared this morning and two fairy cakes I'd baked from a mix last night. 'I know it's not your birthday but I thought you'd like these.'

Her eyes teared up. 'Oh, thank you, Kelly Ann. That's so nice of you. You're the best friend I've ever had.'

'Oh God, please don't say that, Bernadette.'

'It's true.' She sniffed. 'I've got something for you too.' She took an envelope from her bag and handed it to me.

I opened it. For a moment I couldn't speak. It was two tickets for the Smashed concert.

'Where . . . where . . . I mean, how did you get these? Are they real?'

'Oh, I'm always getting tickets to Jason's concerts but I never use them. Not really interested in music.'

'How come? I mean, these are, like, totally impossible to get hold of.'

'He's my cousin. You won't tell anyone, will you?'

'Your cousin? Yeah, right.' Maybe all the lonely lunch times in the toilet had turned her a bit bonkers.

'Knew you wouldn't believe me.' She took a photograph from her blazer pocket and handed it to me. I stared at it. And stared at it. It was a photograph of her and Jason. Both of them looked younger – she was maybe ten – but it was definitely Jason and he had his arm around her shoulders. Oh my God.

'His real name's Sean,' she said, 'but he's told even family to call him Jason now. He chose Jason because he was a Greek hero but I don't think it goes with Donnelly, do you? He should maybe have changed that too.'

'But, but . . . I mean, bloody hell, if he's your cousin, why didn't you tell everyone? Most people would. It's, like, so totally cool. You'd be the most popular girl in the school.'

She shrugged. 'Don't know. I'm scared people would expect me to be more interesting and exciting if they knew we were related. And, well, I don't want people pretending to be my friend just so they can get to meet him.'

'Meet Jason!'

'Yeah. I could tell Jason you'd like to see him after the show if you want. You want me to?'

Would I? Oh my God. Threw my arms round

Bernadette and hugged her. Unfortunately this was witnessed by a crowd of third-year girls who'd just come in. Hmm, yeah, maybe it's lucky I'm leaving tomorrow.

MONDAY DECEMBER 6TH

Was so happy to see my own school this morning I nearly kissed the gates but contented myself instead with grinning at Mr Smith, who was waiting to issue detentions to latecomers. He gave me a punishment exercise for 'dumb insolence' but I didn't care.

Later double maths was just as boring as I remembered it; then, in English, Mrs Conner droned on for an hour about feminist writers. Loved it all.

And even Shelly ... Well, no, I wasn't happy to see Shelly again, but still, I was 'home' with all my old friends and didn't need to eat lunch in the toilets. Bliss.

Mrs Conner has decided, at the very last minute, to do the school pantomime this year, after having initially vetoed the idea. But there isn't much time now and it will be all hands to the pump to get us ready. Also, we'll just be performing to fellow pupils and not parents or anything.

She said we could use most of the same costumes and sets from the year before last. She'd decide on casting tomorrow.

Hope I'm not the back end of a cow again.

Don't believe it! Mrs Conner has given me the star part as Cinderella. She must actually think I have real acting potential. Wait till I tell Jason about this. Maybe both of us will be famous one day. Hope our glittering careers don't come between us.

Shelly was furious. She confronted Mrs Conner. 'Kelly Ann as Cinderella is ridiculous. The heroine has to be the nicest-looking girl and, let's face it, she just *so* isn't.'

Mrs Conner gave her a cold look. 'I suppose you imagine that role belongs to you, but Beauty, they say, is in the eye of the beholder. That is to say, subjective. The size of one's feet, however, are not, and each of yours could fill a small canoe. Quite inappropriate for Cinderella.'

Everyone except Shelly and her friends started to laugh. Shelly flushed scarlet. 'Well, I'm not going to be an Ugly Sister – don't care what you say.'

'Of course not, Shelly,' Mrs Conner said calmly. 'Such a part would be quite unsuitable for you.'

Shelly seemed a bit happier with that and the angry red colour of her face began to fade until Mrs Conner continued, 'The Ugly Sisters are speaking parts and your acting ability is quite inadequate to the task. Instead, you will be the pumpkin. A much more appropriate role.'

Mrs Conner's gaze swept the class. 'Now then, does

anyone else have a problem with my casting decisions?'

Nobody did.

WEDNESDAY DECEMBER 8TH

We got to try on our costumes for the play after school today. My Cinderella rags costume is really nice. A black top and short flared skirt with a cool jagged hem. Much nicer than the naff pink ballroom dress with puffed sleeves and ballooning skirt.

Still, I didn't complain, especially when I saw Shelly's outfit – orange tights and a huge cardboard pumpkin the size of a small room with holes for her head and legs. Hee hee.

THURSDAY DECEMBER 9TH

Has just occurred to me that Jason is probably a Catholic if he's Bernadette 's cousin and once went to St Ann's. Am concerned that this might cause a problem for our future relationship as I've heard the Catholic Church can get awkward about stuff like this.

I mean, just suppose when I meet Jason after the concert he likes me so much that we become really good friends. He'll call and email me when he's on tour abroad and give me and my friends free tickets to all his gigs in the UK. Gradually, over time, his feelings will deepen until he realizes that he actually loves me and we get engaged. We plan a huge celebrity wedding then, *wham*, just as we're about to take our vows the priest says: 'And just where is your baptismal certificate, Kelly Ann? Sorry, but if you're not a Catholic, that's it I'm afraid.'

Thought about contacting the Pope and asking him but reckoned he might be too busy praying, running the Vatican and looking after billions of Catholics to answer me before the concert.

Decided the bishop would do instead. Looked up his number and called but it was answered by an administrator person who said the bishop was saying Mass and did I want to leave a message?

Saying Mass on a Thursday? He was probably just trying to put me off. Told him I needed to speak personally to the bishop and it was urgent, so could he ask him to just come to the phone right away? It should only take a minute.

But the administrator person got really annoyed with me. He refused to interrupt the bishop and told me quite snootily that I would need to call back and wouldn't be able to speak personally with the bishop until I'd told him what it was about.

Put the phone down. There was no way I was discussing personal business with some nosy secretary person.

Found an American Catholic website called askabishop.com, where you could email questions to bishops who weren't too stuck up to deal with normal people.

To: Bishop
From: Kelly Ann
Subject: Marriage

Dear Bishop(s)

I am very much in love with a Catholic boy but am not one myself (Catholic). I hope that you are not the narrow-minded bigots some people say you are and that it would be OK for us to get married. Please let me know ASAP.

Thanks

Kelly Ann

Got an answer:

Dear Kelly Ann

Thank you very much for your enquiry. I just wondered whether
1.   you are both over sixteen
2.   this boy actually wants to marry you.

The Catholic Church, for moral and legal reasons, cannot of course condone underage or forced marriage. If you could reply to these questions we would be happy to provide you with further information regarding inter-faith marriage.

So annoying. Why do they need to ask nosy questions instead of just responding to my polite enquiry? Hmm. Obviously they are all narrow-minded bigots intent on spoiling young people's happiness. I'm sure Jason won't let them interfere with our relationship.

FRIDAY DECEMBER 10TH

Will see Jason tomorrow. In the flesh. It's really going to happen. Oh my God!

SATURDAY DECEMBER 11TH

We went to the concert early because I was too excited to sit at home any more and Stephanie likes to watch the guys who haul things about on stage before the band comes on.

A security person took our tickets, noted the number and said, 'Right, you're the ones that are meeting Jason back stage after the show. Wait till I come for you and for

God's sake don't go telling anyone about it. You'll get lynched.'

Bernadette had got us fantastic seats right at the front. At first the place was nearly empty but gradually the hall filled to bursting point.

The supporting band came on first. They were OK, I suppose, but everyone just wanted to see Smashed and couldn't be bothered with them. Especially me. When they finished I applauded loudly though. Partly because I felt sorry for them and partly relief that I'd see Jason soon.

However, another ten minutes crawled by and still Smashed hadn't come on. Everyone started to chant, 'We want Smashed. We want Smashed.'

At last the lights dimmed then came up again and, oh my God, there *they* were. I was sitting, like, only about five metres from Jason. And he looked even more gorgeous in real life.

Everyone stood up, then started screaming and cheering. I shouted, 'Jason, I'm over here,' but I don't think he heard me because of the noise.

When they launched into the first song, people quietened down, just waving their arms and dancing along to the beat. The band did a few fast songs, then Jason came right to the front of the stage and did a solo love song.

I swear our eyes met and his gaze held mine for the entire number as he sang, *'Baby, baby, baby, I love you'*. It was as though we were the only two people there, right until the end, when I got knocked to the ground and trampled on as people behind me surged to the front and had to be pushed back by security men.

Never mind. None of those desperate idiots would get to meet Jason one to one. Only me.

After the show the security man who'd checked our tickets came up to us and hissed, 'Right, you two, come with me and keep your mouths shut.'

So it was really going to happen. I was going to see Jason. Talk to him. Oh my God.

He took us through a side door into a corridor at the back of the stage, then stopped at another door and knocked, giving his name and code which I didn't catch.

The door opened and *he* came out. Stood right in front of me. Near enough to touch.

Jason said, 'Hi, Kelly Ann. Great to meet you.'

He said my name. He said Kelly Ann. That's me. I gazed at his gorgeous face and felt my knees tremble, then my throat closed up so that I could hardly breathe. I opened my lips to speak but my tongue had dried up and was sticking to the roof of my mouth.

I said, 'Nnnnng.'

Jason said, 'So how are you doing?'

I said, 'Nnnnng mmm nnnng.'

Oh God, what was happening to me? I must have sounded like a constipated orang-utan.

Jason said, 'Hope you liked the show. Cool T-shirt. Did you get it from my fan club site?'

I closed my mouth, which had been hanging open, and pressed my lips to together. This time I would form proper words like a normal person. *I would*. Tried again.

I said, '   '

Nothing. Not a sound. I'd lost the power of speech. Maybe I'd never talk again.

'I'll sign it for you if you like.'

I said, '   '

Stephanie said, 'Oh, for God's sake,' and handed him a pen.

He started to sign the sleeve of my T-shirt. Actually touched it, so I could feel the heat of his fingers through the thin material.

He said, 'Well, it's been great talking to you anyway.'

Then I fainted. Totally passed out.

Stephanie told me later that Jason picked me up and carried me to the medical room, where he put me on the bed. He stayed with me while a paramedic examined me; then his manager came and told him his car was waiting, and the paramedic said that I was round. Then he asked, 'Sure she's OK?'

Stephanie said I wasn't but the paramedic said I was fine now, and he'd better be off or I might just pass out again when I saw him. Then Jason left.

Jason had picked me up. Actually held me. And I don't

remember it. The most important moment of my entire life and I was unconscious. Don't believe it.

SUNDAY DECEMBER 12TH

Bernadette called to ask how I was. She'd been talking to Jason on the phone and he'd asked if I was OK.

Jason asked if I was OK. So he must really care.

Thinking quickly, I said, 'Oh yeah, I'm fine. It was just, you know, the heat that got to me. The hall was *so* stuffy. Look, if you give me his number I'll call him myself and tell him.'

'Sorry, Kelly Ann, I don't know his mobile number. But he's coming over to our house later for an hour or so before flying back to London. I'll let him know you're fine.'

Oh my God. Another chance to see Jason – this time I vowed I wouldn't make an idiot of myself. But Bernadette was really reluctant to let me visit her house, so I had to beg and plead with her for ages, at the same time frantically getting myself ready for him. Finally she gave in. She didn't have an exact time for his visit, and I didn't want to risk missing a moment with him, so as soon as I was ready I got Dad to drive me over. I'd wait for Jason there.

Hadn't asked Bernadette for directions but fortunately Dad knew the area well so he found the street no problem and dropped me off outside her house.

Bernadette 's house looked ordinary from the outside but I nearly freaked when I went in. The hall was painted black and lit with candles, and there was a large red pentacle drawn on the floor.

The living room was more normal, but her mum, who was sitting watching TV, was definitely not. She was dressed in a long white robe decorated with strings of beads and shells. On her head she wore a wreath of twisted leaves which I found out later were 'magical' herbs.

Bernadette 's mum is apparently a white witch. I was not to worry about the hall decorations, which were for protection against evil forces and not a place to practise the Dark Arts. Actually, she was very nice and friendly, but totally bonkers of course. No wonder poor Bernadette tried so hard to be ordinary and boring.

Once I'd got used to Bernadette's odd mum I started to panic about meeting Jason. What if I just keeled over again? How could Jason ever get to know me and, when I'm old enough, ask me out if I was constantly un-conscious when we were together?

It didn't help that he was late: my stomach was twisted into knots by the time the doorbell rang. Bernadette's mum went to answer it but I stayed on the couch trying to breathe normally. If I stayed sitting down, I couldn't faint, could I?

Didn't recognize Jason straight away as he'd on dark glasses and a baseball hat – I suppose to disguise himself from fans or the media. Didn't recognize the girl with him either to begin with, as she was wearing a hat and sun specs too.

Jason took off his hat and glasses, then, looking at me, said, 'Hi, how are you? You feeling OK now?' He turned to the girl, who was a stunning blonde and seemed vaguely familiar. 'That's the kid I was telling you about. Bernadette's friend, who passed out.'

His girlfriend is called Grace. She's a successful actress who's appeared in quite a lot of Australian soaps. Despite this she wasn't stuck up at all and chatted to Bernadette and me like we were equals. A really friendly, lovely person in fact. Have never hated anyone so much in my life.

MONDAY DECEMBER 13TH

Stephanie and Liz were really sympathetic when I told them.

Liz said, 'Gorgeous looking, famous *and* nice. You'd think she'd have the decency to be a horrible person you could hate without feeling guilty. Bitch.'

Stephanie flicked through a magazine to find a picture of Grace wearing a bikini which clearly showed a bit of cellulite on her thighs but it didn't help much. The truth is, Jason had called me a 'kid' and that's all I'd ever be to him. The idea of him ever being my boyfriend, even in a few years' time, was about as real as Leo had been.

I know Liz and Stephanie were trying to cheer me up but they don't really understand how I feel. I don't feel guilty or angry. I feel totally humiliated and stupid. Which is much, much worse.

Both of them offered to come round and keep me company tonight. Stephanie said she'd give me a makeover but with definitely no waxing involved. Liz suggested a DVD with pizza and promised not to psychoanalyse me. But I turned them down. Knew I'd be about as much fun tonight as a wet duvet at a sleepover.

Instead I came home and moped. Even my family noticed there was something up with me. Mum asked, 'What's up with your face?'

'Nothing.'

'Hmm, so how come you look like a hen that's trying to lay a pineapple then?'

Charming.

Dad said, 'Leave the girl alone, Moira. Can't you see she's upset? You could try a bit of diplomacy, you know.' He turned to me and said with a kindly smile, 'Cheer up, love, it might never happen.'

That was it. 'That's the whole sodding point,' I screamed. 'It *isn't* going to happen. Nothing is going to happen. Ever. In my whole life. I'll just go on and on, living in this house day after day, with nothing ever happening until I rot and die of old age and am buried, an old maid in a white coffin.'

I ran out, banging the door behind me. Once in my room I threw myself on my bed and sobbed with frustration. After a few minutes Angela tapped softly on my door and whispered, 'Kelly Ann?'

Thought of ignoring her but eventually decided to let her in. It was nice of her, I suppose, to be concerned about me. OK, Angela and I didn't have much in common but she was my sister after all. We shared a genetic bond, a house and bloody awful parents. Maybe talking to her about my devastated life would help.

I opened the door but she didn't come in. Instead, she said, 'Kelly Ann, did you borrow my pink lip gloss again? It's Graham's favourite and we're going out tonight.'

Hmm, or then again, maybe it wouldn't.

I denied the lip-gloss theft, but after she threatened to ransack my room I took it from its hiding place (in my right trainer underneath the bed) and handed it over. She left without even saying thank you.

I put on some music to cheer myself up, but either they were really sad songs about lost loves which depressed me, or really happy songs about people totally loved up which depressed me even more.

It was nearly eight o'clock when someone tapped on my door again. Probably Angela looking for her dusky plum eye shadow. Bollocks. I thought she'd already gone. I took the eye shadow from its hiding place in my pencil case and opened the door, saying, 'Here, take it. I hope it chokes you.'

Chris said, 'No thanks, Kelly Ann. It's not really my colour.'

Was never so glad to see anyone. I knew Chris wouldn't mind if I was lousy company. If I didn't feel like talking, he'd just sit and mess about with the computer or PlayStation until I felt like saying something or joining in. He was the only person who could really deal with me in this kind of mood.

He came in, sat on the floor beside my bed and said, 'Liz and Stephanie called me. Said you needed cheering up. Want to play Monopoly? I'll even let you cheat tonight.'

Didn't approve of this interference by my friends of course, and will have words with them tomorrow, but actually I was glad Chris had come as I was getting fed up being miserable on my own.

Got the board out. I love PlayStation games but Monopoly is still my favourite. Most people won't play with me any more as I get seriously competitive about it and won't quit until I've bankrupted everyone, even if it does take twelve hours and people's wrists have seized up from dice rolling (which I so didn't believe). So, yeah, I decided it just might take my mind off things tonight.

We spent ages playing Monopoly, which I eventually won without cheating too much, then just messed about on my computer until nearly midnight, when Dad came in and said, 'I'd better drive you home now, son. Any later and your parents will be waiting by the phone expecting a ransom demand.'

Dad gave us 'five more minutes' to finish off what we'd been doing. Actually this was nothing now but I didn't want Chris to leave right away. I hadn't spent so much time with him in a while and it was great to know we were as close as ever. Maybe even closer somehow.

Before he left I said, 'Promise me you'll never change, Chris.'

'I can't promise that, Kelly Ann. Everyone changes.'

'Suppose. What I mean is, we'll always be friends, won't we? You'll still want to see me, no matter what happens? Still have time for me?'

He stared at me silently for a moment, then said slowly, 'I'll always have time for you, Kelly Ann.'

'Even if you get another girlfriend,' I persisted. 'Promise me.'

'I promise.' He paused then continued, 'And if she's the right girl, I expect I'll see you as much as ever. Maybe more.'

God, I hoped the next one was OK and not some jealous, stupid liar like Emily. Maybe she'd even be someone I could like and get on with. Someone more like me. Yeah, that would be great.

Went Christmas shopping with Mum straight after school and passed the place where the fortune-teller had been but her stall wasn't there any more.

She'd been eerily right about my meeting famous people, and it having an effect on my life, although the effect had been pretty traumatic both times. Remembered that she also said I'd find True Love early in life but there's been no sign of that so far. In fact, I'm practically the only girl in my year who's never had a boyfriend. Not even a single date.

Wished I could talk to her again and ask her why that bit of her prediction hadn't come true. Just the bad stuff.

Mum went into La Senza and told me to stay outside so I guessed she was buying me some underwear for Christmas. Spotted a store security person and decided to ask if he knew where the fortune-teller was now.

'Most likely prison, love. She got done for benefit fraud. Been claiming unemployment for years while she's been raking it in as a clairvoyant. Didn't foresee the Fraud Squad coming though, eh? Some fortune-teller. Bloody con artist.'

He was probably right. I'd been stupid to believe her.

That's it. Mum's been right about me all along. I'm going to stop being stupid and start growing up. From now on I'll be mature and sensible at all times.

Put itching powder in Shelly's orange tights at dress rehearsal today. Had a great time watching her desperately trying to scratch her legs while wearing a huge pumpkin costume. He he.

It was the only fun thing to happen in this play though. Mrs Conner has 'modernized' the script so that Cinderella's stepmother employs a therapist to resolve conflicts arising from extended family issues. Cinderella attends assertiveness training, which helps her refuse to do more than her fair share of the housework and insist on an invitation to the ball and decent clothing without the aid of any fairy godmother.

At the end of the story she refuses the Prince's offer of marriage because she wants to pursue her career and anyway disapproves of monarchy.

Totally boring, but no one argued with Mrs Conner except Shelly.

'If there's no fairy godmother, how come we need a pumpkin then?'

'Iconic symbolism,' Mrs Conner said smoothly.

This shut Shelly up as she didn't know what it meant. Me neither. But I do know not to argue with Conner.

Was talking to Chris about the holidays today. He told me they were going to an aunt's in Manchester over Christmas but would be home for the New Year. He also said that both his mum and dad were working night shifts on New Year's Eve, so there wouldn't be a party at his house and he wasn't sure what he was doing then. I said he could come to our house – I was sure it would be OK with my parents – so he said, yeah, he'd like that.

Am really pleased about this as usually it's just family and nobody my age comes. Don't adults know how totally boring and stupid they are when they get drunk? If they're not dancing around like chimps on ecstasy they're repeating the same awful joke and laughing themselves sick. Thank God for Chris.

FRIDAY DECEMBER 17TH

Called Bernadette and asked if she'd like to meet up on Sunday. Didn't really want to as she's incredibly boring company, but she'd been so nice to me I felt I had to. Also felt sorry for her having no friends and an embarrassing mum. I now know what both those things feel like.

Was gobsmacked but really pleased when she told me she was too busy because, guess what, she'd got a boyfriend.

She prattled on for ages about him. He sounds just as boring as she is. Bernadette says his parents are nudists who walk around the house all day totally starkers. She and Thomas have bonded over having embarrassing parents.

'But I think Thomas's parents are worse, don't you?' Bernadette said happily.

Oh God, yes. Much, much worse.

Bernadette dating and all loved up. It's hard to believe. Maybe it's true what Mum says: 'There's someone for everyone.'

Not for me though.

SATURDAY DECEMBER 18TH

Went to watch our school in a friendly match against St Ann's. Hardly anyone turned up to watch as it was so cold – even players' girlfriends and parents mostly stayed away.

We didn't play very well, and lost again, but by the end of the match I wasn't really caring as I'd practically stopped paying any attention to the game at all. Instead, all I could think about was how good *he* looked in his football strip; so much fitter and more confident than any other player. Why had I never noticed this before?

Of course, I knew he was a good-looking guy – lots of girls fancied him, but not *me*. I wasn't starting to fancy him, was I?

Oh God, I hoped not. It would just lead to trouble and me making a total idiot of myself again. I was *not* going to let that happen.

MONDAY DECEMBER 20TH

He turned round to me and asked to borrow my rubber. I fumbled in my pencil case and found it. Kind of wished it wasn't in the shape of frog – I haven't replaced all my stupid kid's stuff yet – but handed it to him anyway. Our fingertips brushed together and he smiled and said, 'Thanks.'

I looked at his familiar but gorgeous face and felt blood rush to my cheeks and my tummy tighten. Oh God, there was no denying it. I definitely, totally fancied him.

Turned my face – which was now all blotchy, red and sweaty – away from him. It was hopeless. Like most boys, he'll probably only want to date blondes, so I've no chance. Why, oh why did this have to happen?

TUESDAY DECEMBER 21 ST

But it has. I can't fight it any more. Don't want to. I could spend all day just looking at him and thinking about him. But should I tell him? Just march up and say, 'Hey, I know I've never said anything about this before but actually I really fancy you. Maybe more than fancy you'?

No, the old stupid Kelly Ann would have done that. The new mature, grown-up version is going to be sophisticated. Subtle. Yeah, this time I was determined to get it right. I would wait for the right time and place. Be patient.

Anyway, unlike Jason he wasn't an unobtainable celebrity living in London. I could see him almost every day. He was in the same classes as me for maths and English after all, and, thank God, we get five periods of each a week. Who'd have thought I'd ever look forward to maths? Or imagined in my wildest dreams I'd be sorry we had holidays coming up.

Thought about asking Liz and Stephanie for advice but decided against it. It was time to really grow up and make my own decisions. Wondered what they'd say if they knew who my secret love is.

WEDNESDAY DECEMBER 22ND

The pantomime was awful at first. Even though people were allowed out of classes in the afternoon to see us perform, it was mostly only first years who decided to come. Ten minutes in, when Mrs Conner told them that they couldn't chat or mess around while it was going on, they all begged to be allowed to go back to their classes but she wouldn't let them.

However, everyone cheered up when Terry Docherty (dressed in a large mouse costume) 'accidentally' barged into Shelly, who fell over but couldn't get up again.

Nearly wet myself watching her rolling over and over in her huge pumpkin costume with her orange legs sticking up in the air. Hilarious.

Yeah, turned out to be fun pantomime after all.

SATURDAY DECEMBER 25TH

Mum got me trainers, three new PlayStation games and a bicycle pump instead of the suede high heels and make-up I'd asked for. Wish she'd listen. I mean, does she want me to grow up or not? She did put a Wonderbra, some Clearasil and a Creme Egg in my stocking though, so at least she got that right.

Angela got her usual sad stuff – bath foam, pleated wool skirts and white cotton blouses plus a new clothes brush and her very own iron and ironing board. This last was a surprise present and she threw her arms round Mum and Dad to thank them. No, honestly, one of us *must* be adopted. I just can*not* be genetically related to my sister.

Angela's boyfriend got her a pale blue angora scarf. Imagination and originality are not his strong points.

Christmas dinner was fantastic and I stuffed myself as usual. Angela is allowed to have wine at the meal now. Mum and Dad said I could have a glass too but I wasn't sure I'd like it. I asked if I could try a sip of Angela's and, thinking she wouldn't mind, picked up her glass.

Before I could take even one mouthful she'd grabbed it back from me, saying she wasn't going to drink from anything I'd dribbled saliva on. Then she complained about me smearing her glass with my greasy fingers. If I had to touch someone else's glass I should hold it by the stem.

Bloody hell, felt like a leper. And all this from a person who does it with her boyfriend. Wonder if she makes him have a bath in Dettol first.

SUNDAY DECEMBER 26TH

Caught Angela rummaging through my room today. Bloody nerve. Said she was looking for her silver heart-shaped locket with the picture of Graham and her on the inside and suggested that I'd 'stolen' it.

Yeah, like I'd really want to hang a picture of my sister and her sad boyfriend round my neck. It's true I *had* borrowed the chain part for one day – however, I'd definitely intended to give it and the locket back right after, but just forgot. However, now that she'd practically ransacked my room and accused me of being a thief she'd have to wait much, much longer before they were returned.

Then I saw she had my diary in her hand. When I confronted her with this she just said, 'Huh, like I'm really interested in your silly life. As if. You didn't really expect to be Jason's girlfriend, did you? I mean, you're just a schoolgirl and he's a famous—' She stopped and blushed. 'I wasn't snooping. It just kind of fell open at that page and I sort of glanced at it . . . just for a second. Honestly.'

She put the diary down and scuttled out. Yeah, could be a very long time before she gets her naff locket back. Meanwhile I have decided to write the rest of this diary in code.

Mlkdjsfhafjfind dodfodop=mdskajd idds djdkosagke-jjoia fjmfwipmfdoodd, p**1 ajdfafeoeo fapekfd. Amda djadoejf, aj eodo. Asddere ereel e[=e.

MONDAY DECEMBER 27TH

Think I must have chosen a code that's a bit too complicated as I've no idea what I wrote yesterday. Have decided instead to store this journal in a new safe place where no one would ever possibly find it. But just to make sure it will never reveal the identity of my secret love if they do, I will call him 'G' – which isn't even his real initial, so no one will ever guess. Unless of course I choose to reveal it, and I don't intend to do that anytime soon.

TUESDAY DECEMBER 28TH

Liz and Stephanie came over. Decided to tell them about my secret love, especially as I wanted to use the holidays to look perfect for G and would need Stephanie's help.

Liz said, 'Don't believe it. Why him, for God's sake? Of all the boys to pick!'

Stephanie shrugged. 'He's not bad looking, but Liz is right, Kelly Ann. There are plenty of other boys.'

'There may be plenty of other boys,' I said, 'but no one compares to G. I think he's The One.'

'You mean the one you're going to shag? God, you do move fast once you get going,' Stephanie said in an admiring tone.

'Of course not,' I said, shocked. 'But if I *did* do it with him, it wouldn't be shagging. It would be the physical expression of our deepest feelings.'

Stephanie yawned.

Liz said, 'So, has he asked you for a date?'

'No,' I said. 'He doesn't even know I'm interested yet. Do you think I should tell him?'

'No, I think you should forget the whole thing. It will only end in disaster.'

'I can't, Liz. He's the only one I want. The only boy I'll ever want.'

'The only one!' Stephanie said, horrified. 'Don't be stupid. That's like, well, like going into Blockbuster every week and only ever taking out the same DVD. Boring.'

'Yeah,' Liz agreed. 'Like being offered a box of Roses chocolates and saying "I'll just have the orange cream, thanks. Don't care for any of the others."'

'But G isn't a DVD or a chocolate,' I protested. 'I've got real feelings for him.'

Liz wasn't impressed. 'I've got real feelings for orange creams but it doesn't stop me—'

'I'd do anything to get G to be my boyfriend,' I interrupted. 'I don't want anyone else.'

'Anything?' Stephanie asked.

'Yeah.'

'Including a leg wax?'

'Um, well, yeah. If you think—'

'Bikini wax?' Stephanie said.

'Maybe. But I don't think he'd really want me to—'

'Using hot wax strips?' Stephanie persisted, staring at me for any sign of weakness.

I hesitated. For a long time. Then, 'OK.'

'She's serious,' Stephanie pronounced.

WEDNESDAY DECEMBER 29TH

Stephanie has gone to Austria on a skiing trip with her mum so I won't have to prove my total commitment just yet, thank God. However, she's left instructions for a special beauty routine to be followed every single day without fail.

Every morning I've to exfoliate my entire body thoroughly, then cleanse, tone and moisturize my face, neck and décolletage area (though I'm not exactly sure what that is). After this, I've got to apply an intensive hydrating masque to my hair, wrap my whole head in cellophane (though not my nose and mouth of course) and leave it on for a minimum of two hours, before rinsing the lot off with clarifying volcanic spa water and adding a touch of pure shine restructuring serum to the ends. All I have to do next is a quick French manicure and pedicure, then I'm ready to do my make-up.

Once I'd mastered my morning beauty routine Stephanie would give me a night-time regimen.

Unfortunately I slept in until twelve thirty today so was too late for my morning beauty routine. Will have to start tomorrow.

THURSDAY DECEMBER 30TH

Woke at eleven thirty today so only had time for exfoliating bit. Didn't have the exfoliating product Stephanie recommended – expensive stuff with marine mineral extracts of Atlantic phyto-plankton – but scrubbed every square inch of my skin with pumice stone and an exfoliater made from sugar, which I'd heard can work almost as well.

I'm sure it probably did my skin good even if I was a bit red and sore afterwards and Mum said I looked like a boiled, skinned rabbit. But just so long as I am beautiful when G finally sees me I don't care.

However, I did feel bit sticky afterwards – maybe it's salt and not sugar you're supposed to use. Think I'll create my own beauty regime next year instead of relying on Stephanie.

FRIDAY DECEMBER 31 ST

New Year's Eve. It was nearly midnight and all the adults were totally plastered. Mum and Dad had fallen out three times already but had made up again; they were now supposedly doing a Highland fling, though it looked more like they were trying to swat flies while jogging on ice.

The only consolation was that the rest of the grown-ups were equally bad and all the curtains were shut so no one could see them.

Chris and I moved into the hall and sat down on the stairs. Although we could still hear drunken singing and guffawing coming from the living room, we could now talk in relative peace.

We chatted for a while about how embarrassing drunk adults were, then talked about last year and what might happen in the coming one.

'Conner says she's going to have to finish the *Romeo and Juliet* we started last year but from a different viewpoint,' I said. 'Wonder what she means.'

Chris said, 'She'll probably give us assignments like

Romeo was a useless tosser and Juliet should have dumped him. Discuss.'

I laughed. 'Maybe. Seriously though, do you think people our age can find real True Love like they did?'

Chris thought for a moment then said, 'Yeah, I do. In fact I'm sure it happens.'

'But how would you know it was real love and not just a crush?'

'I'd just know. Definitely.'

I smiled happily. 'Me too.'

'Kelly Ann,' Chris said, 'there's something I need to tell you. Something I've been thinking about for a long time now. I—'

But whatever he was going to say would have to wait because Mum was calling us into the living room. It was nearly time for The Bells. I grabbed an Irn Bru and Dad gave Chris a beer. I volunteered to get Angela a glass of wine from the kitchen as she was busy picking blue fluff off her skirt.

Handed her the glass, holding the stem carefully so as to avoid leaving greasy fingermarks like she'd told me before. She took it from me without seeming to notice my thoughtfulness as she was still engrossed in her never-ending task.

We counted: *'Ten, nine, eight, seven, six, five, four, three, two, one. Happy New Year!'*

Chris and I moved over to a corner of the room to avoid the orgy of slobbery kisses and drunken hugs adults seem to think essential at this time. We sat on the floor and I looked over at Angela, who was struggling to unstick her fingers from the wine glass I'd smeared with superglue earlier.

Well, OK, maybe I wouldn't be totally grown up this year. Not all the time anyway.

Chris glanced at Angela too, then smiled at me. 'Happy New Year, Kelly Ann.'

We clinked glasses and I smiled back. 'Happy New Year, Chris.'

And, oh God, I hoped it would be. Maybe this would be the happiest, most important new year of my life. The year when, like Juliet, I would find True Love (but not top myself of course); the year when I would finally be totally sorted and grown up. This could be the most amazing year of my entire life.

Hmmm . . . or then again, maybe this was the year I would make a total idiot of myself and remain the only virgin lips in the senior school except for Patricia McPherson.

I looked at Chris's smiling face anxiously. Liz and Stephanie had warned me against confiding my secret to Chris tonight. But if he couldn't understand me, who would? It was time he knew too.

'Chris,' I said, 'I've got something I want to tell you . . .'

SATURDAY JANUARY 1ST

If I were blonde, the flat chest and spots wouldn't matter so much. Honestly, you could have two heads and if one of them is blonde some bloke is going to fancy you, but with mouse-brown hair you have to try a lot harder.

It's so depressing. Even my parents have noticed there's something the matter with me. My dad keeps telling me to cheer up, it might never happen. Ha ha. My mum sometimes looks up from the TV long enough to ask what's up with my face.

Have tried to explain how I feel to them. How if they won't let me bleach my hair then the least they could do is pay for breast implants but the response was typical. My dad said not to be so daft, I was fine as I was. My mum just laughed and told me I would know all about it when I was approaching forty and my nipples fell to my knees. That's what happened to her because she'd been a good mother and breast-fed my sister and me and what thanks does she get for it? And she said if she ever met that eejit of a nurse who'd advised her on baby care again she'd tell her where to stick her 'Breast Is Best' pamphlet.

But she bought me a Wonderbra and a bottle of Clearasil spot buster for Christmas anyway.

The bra didn't work. As my mum said, no amount of rigging is going to make a cleavage out of two fried eggs.

My dad said: 'Why do you always have to call a spade a bloody shovel, Moira? You'll give the girl a complex and she's fine as she is.'

The spots are worse than ever too. My mum says if I were more like my big sister Angela and didn't eat so much chocolate my skin would clear up, but my Aunt Kate says it's my hormones and my dad says they should all leave me alone and that I'm fine as I am.

It's obvious my family are no help at all. They don't understand what it's like being practically the only girl in the fourth year who hasn't had a boyfriend yet. Only Patricia McPherson is in the same boat as me and she's so ugly even my dad couldn't say she's fine as she is. If she gets a boyfriend before me I'll die of humiliation.

Besides, I'm in love with G. There, I've said it. If you read this, Mum (I know what you're like), it isn't even his real initial so you'll never guess. G is the most gorgeous guy in the whole school and absolutely everyone fancies him like mad. Well, all the females anyway. Well, all the females except Liz and Stephanie who say he's a tosser and so up himself it's not true, but they just say that to annoy me. Liz and Stephanie are my best friends but they can be a total pain sometimes.

Anyway, I need to become beautiful so that G will fall madly in love with me back and tell everyone I'm his girl-friend and maybe even ask me out. On a date.

Since I'm not blonde or busty I'll just have to concentrate

on making every part of my body as perfect as possible, so here are my New Year beauty resolutions:

1. To cleanse, tone and moisturize my skin every morning and evening without fail. Even when I'm late for school and I can't find my gym stuff and I have to get a copy of my maths homework from Liz before first period. Absolutely no excuses.

2. Never *ever* to squeeze another spot, no matter how much I may want to, even if it is right on the end of my nose or chin.

3. To leave my hair conditioner in for at least three minutes every time I wash my hair and always to buy hair products from a proper chemist and never *ever* make my own from 'cheap, natural ingredients you can find in your own kitchen'. If I'm tempted I only have to remember the vinegar rinse that made me smell like a fish and chip shop. Or worse, the shampoo made from Dad's beer that had me grounded for a week and threatened with Alateen.

4. To always have perfectly manicured nails and never again go to school with chipped varnish. Even when I'm running late, have forgotten my packed lunch, and need to copy my French home-work from Stephanie before first period.

5. To eat healthy foods like broccoli and bananas and never again to snack on chocolate and crisps when

I am bored. Instead I'll write my beauty progress in my diary every single day without fail.

SATURDAY JANUARY 8TH . . .

Kelly Ann's adventures in dating continue in:

My Desperate Love Diary

MY desperate LOVE DIARY

By Liz Rettig

Kelly Ann is fifteen and desperately in love
with G – the biggest idiot in school.
Her best friends Liz and Stephanie can see
how awful G is – and also that Kelly Ann's
quietly gorgeous friend Chris is madly in
love with her. But Kelly Ann stumbles along
blindly, unable to see what's right in
front of her eyes.

Navigating her way through teenage
embarrassments, sick-filled parties and
terrible poetry, Kelly Ann is a hilariously
endearing character to root for!

'Heartfelt but at the same time fantastically
funny, this is a holiday must-read.'
Mizz

MY now or NEVER DIARY

By Liz Rettig

Kelly Ann has only just come to her senses
and realised that G, the boy she's fancied all
year, is a total nerd and Chris, the boy next
door who's been in love with *her* all year, is
actually the man for her. But does that
mean she'll live happily ever after with Chris,
discovering the joys of sex and smugly
advising her friends in the ways of true love?
Of course not.

With the help of her faithful friends Liz and
Steph, Kelly Ann manages to muck it all up in
her own hilarious style.

A riot of teenage fumblings, terrible teachers
and skincare made from porridge.

JUMPING TO CONFUSIONS

By Liz Rettig

I'm Cat – and I'm the fat, plain one in my family.
When I say fat, I don't mean 'have-to-be-prised-
out-of-a-hoola-hoop' fat, but when your mum
and sister are practically size zero, it's hard not to
feel like the elephant girl in comparison.

My twin sister Tessa is blonde, gorgeous and
gets any boy she wants. Right now she's got
her eye on Josh, a really fit American guy
who's just moved to Glasgow.
But he doesn't seem that interested in her.
It's weird. I've never known any boy
who didn't fancy Tessa. Well, not straight
ones, anyway . . .

Of course! It all makes sense . . . funny that he
doesn't want to tell anyone about his secret, not
even me, his new best friend . . .

Could Cat be jumping to conclusions about Josh,
in this wonderfully funny tale of
romantic confusion?

SPLIT BY A KISS

By Luisa Playa

I'm two different people. Literally. I'm split.

Jo has never been one of the popular kids . . .
until she moves to the USA. Suddenly the
coolest girls at her new high school adopt her,
and the hottest boy, Jake Matthews, notices her.
But when Jake picks her as his partner in the
kissing game Seven Minutes in Heaven, it's
not half as heavenly as she imagined!

Jo has a choice: should she carry on with Jake
for guaranteed popularity – or should she
tell him where to get off and risk losing
her new friends . . . ?

At this moment, Jo splits. She's Josie the Cool –
girlfriend of Jake, member of the in-crowd.
But she's also Jo the Nerd – rejected by the
It girls, single . . . ordinary. Will her two halves
ever come together again?

'A cute, sweet and funny read. Fans of
Louise Rennison will love it.'
Meg Cabot